Kindling Love

Ashton Stevenson

Kindling Love by Ashton Stevenson

Published by Pen It Publications in the U.S.A.

713-526-3989

www.penitpublications.com

ISBN: 978-1-63984-237-7

Edited by Nicole Mullaney

Cover by Donna Cook

Dedicated to:

My amazing family

Thanks to all the down to earth, rad people who have shined sunshine in my life.

Also by Ashton Stevenson:

Love on the Fireline

ACKNOWLEDGEMENTS

There are so many people without whom this book would not have been possible, so many wonderful human beings that made me who I am today. Thank you, Grandma, for always being there for me. Thank you to my Mom and Dad for sharing their adventurous spirit and supporting me in all my escapades. Thank you, Mom, for always sharing my passion for reading. Thanks, Dad, for always being down for an adventure.

Thank you to the best big brother ever, Patrick. You have always been the Samwise to my Frodo and lead me through this quest called life. Thanks for bonding over our pop culture nerdiness and being able to speak in pure movie quotes with me. Thanks Lindsey, I really love having you in the family, it's nice to have someone as klutzy as me around.

Thank you to my amazing friend, Eden C for all the laughs, support and love throughout the years. You are forever my soul sister. I couldn't ask for a better person to be crazy and weird with. Thanks, Bethani C for always being such a fantastic friend. Beth, you have always been such an inspiration to me, and I really treasure our friendship. Love you and Roman so much, thankful for both of ya'll. Thank you, Brittany E and Lacey H for always being my forever friends and in my sisterhood.

Thank you, Trevor W for bringing absolute sunshine and grooviness into my life. Thanks for vibing with my water loving spirit and for all the thrills. Thanks Haden S for your rad friendship and awesomeness! To all my Camp Lakota staff of 22, thanks for all the laughs, craziness, and bringing me into the family. Keep living it up you beautiful souls!

Thank you to all my family and friends for always shining bright and showering the world with love. You guys bring me so many good vibes and smiles. I am who I am today because of ya'll.

Thank you to every teacher, librarian, and random people I have had in my life who has encouraged my love of reading and writing. Thank you to everyone I have met along my travels and adventures who have loved me exactly for me. Thank you to all my church family and fellow believers for walking beside me. Thank you to everyone who has believed in me and supported me throughout the years. I am so blessed by every adventure pal, road trip buddy, bunkhouse mate, school comrade, teammate, and everyone in my life who made a difference.

Thank you to every fireline brother and crewmate.

Thank you to Lexi Wilch and Katie M for the tips! Thank you, Krystal, for being a great friend, and thanks to you and Kamron for being my cover models. Thanks for always hyping your gal up!

Thank you to Nicole Mullaney for helping my book be the best it can be.

I just can't imagine where my life would be without all the amazing people in it, thank you. Thank you, reader, for taking a chance on my book, hope you enjoyed the adventure.

Lastly, thank you to the Lord for all these amazing people, and every single rad adventure life has taken me on. Here is to many more to come!

CONTENTS

CHAPTER 1

Being the new girl anywhere is hard enough. Being the new person at a Fire Department, in a whole new state, while a fire is burning… that's a whole new ball game. I haven't even been issued proper turnout gear yet, and here I am slinging hose up a massive, steep hill sweating like a pig. Adrenaline coursing, my heart thrumping, and yes, my breath is wheezing hard. Being from Ohio, I am definitely not used to these hills.

"*Walking on Sunshine*" plays over and over in my head. Yes, it's getting annoying, but at least it keeps my mind off the fact I'm hiking a mountain with one hundred pounds of gear and an extra hundred in hose. *Ugg.*

I showed up to the Fire Department for my first day only an hour ago. The tones dropped about five minutes later. They shoved Cam's extra bunker gear into my arms, I climbed in the jump seat, threw my blonde hair into a bun and here we are. Whomever Cam is, must be a little bigger than me. And by that, I mean a foot taller and at least fifty pounds heavier with elephant feet. Not that it's hard to be taller than me when I am a solid five-feet-two and one hundred thirty pounds. Pretty much every sixth grader across the nation is my size.

Boots slogging back and forth, I trudge up the hill with my hundredth load of hose. Every now and then stopping to pull the pant legs back up so I don't trip. Why would someone even build a house this far up a mountain with no access for a fire truck? Not fair. Don't get me wrong, it is a gorgeous setting overlooking the ocean, and I'm sure the house used to be nice. But really, who are you? The beast hiding from the village with a telescope spying on the town?

Finally, we have enough hose up here to charge a second line. It's all hooked up and ready to go. I give the signal to Garrett, one of my new crewmates, and he radios the engine. Water starts filling the hose and it snakes across the ground as if it's alive. Garrett braces, widening his stance and opens the nozzle. Water rushes towards the house as smoke streams out. Angry clouds pour out of the house, tearing to get out into the sky.

Casting another glance at the house, I hike down the mountain yet again to grab some tools. Luckily, everyone made it out safe, and we're starting to get the house under control. I wish I had been doing something more useful than being a pack mule. I mean seriously, packing hose? I want to be doing something exciting! I guess it's better than traffic duty, and yes, I know, every job on a scene is important. But it's my first day here, correction my first morning, and I know that without a line in, those guys couldn't have gotten that fire contained, or their search initiated. Before you can save lives, you must lay out the groundwork.

As I get down to the engine, I glance across the bay. Isn't that just gorgeous? The Pacific spanning out as far as the eye can see. No time for that though. I rummage through the compartments. Ahh, there, hanging up. I grab a set of irons and clutch a pike pole. One last trip up this hill... hopefully.

One of the boots starts to slip off, and I shove my foot back into it. I can tell the sock has already worked its way off and sits balled at the toe. I am so going to have blisters tomorrow. Well, maybe the sock will add some stabilisation. When I was younger, I remember always shoving socks into the toe of my hand me down shoes to make them fit. Using the pike pole as a staff I hike up the mountain feeling much like Gandalf the Grey. Or at least I wish I were that cool.

Looking around, I notice some Mutual aid engines and firefighters have arrived, so there's a conglomeration of people up here. Medics work fast on scene starting to take peoples stats one by one, making sure no one is overexerting themselves.

Currently, Titus is sitting down, helmet, coat and SCBA off, his face covered with dirt, sweat and everything else. It's obvious he is itching to get back in there, but his blood pressure is too high. As he sits there, he absentmindedly scrubs at his SCBA mask, or his 'Self Contained Breathing Apparatus'. Besides fire resistant clothing, our masks are basically one of the most important things we wear.

That's the worst. When you are on a rescue, knowing there are things I could be doing but they bench you for five, ten, fifteen minutes, whatever it takes as long as lives are not at risk. I live for the trauma, the high adrenaline calls. I hate standing by when I could be doing something, anything. So, I feel his pain.

Rounding the corner, I see one of the guys in the bushes. That's odd. Maybe there's a spot fire. Coming from a Wildland background, it wouldn't surprise me. Rushing over, I decide I better help him if needed. Oregon seems wet, but I would hate to let a spot go uncontained and start something bigger. As I approach, his butt sticks out and he squats making me freeze. Oops! Oh, my goodness. What a way to make a first impression Kara. Goodness! At least he's one of the guys from Seal Rock, and I shouldn't have to see him real often. Don't be awkward, don't make it worse.

Scuttling away, I hurry out of eye shot, hoping he didn't see me. My face feels hotter than the fire. Ugg, why do I always make things weird? I reach the top of the hill and catch my breath for a hot second before engaging my SCBA. Feeling like Darth Vader, I pull in a few extra breaths, and strap my helmet back on. Tools in hand, I head over to Garrett, he was the Officer on Duty when I left, though I know we have our Captain, Lieutenant and Chief here now.

"Is there anything I can do to help?" I yell through my mask.

He closes the barrel of the hose, and the water shuts down as he turns to me. "Nope, the structure is contained, we are just working on hot spots now. Want to take over?" He hollers back.

Knowing things are not time sensitive and I won't hinder any progress, I nod and stumble over to him. Heck yeah, I want to take over! I've been dying to do something this entire time. His jaw catches my eye, slick with sweat and soot, but still very appealing to look at. I mean gosh darn, those cheekbones shimmer even through his mask. Garrett looks like one of those sexy, lean firefighters with perfect hair and amazing eyes. A dreamboat, hard core smutty book cover model. I'm not gonna' lie; he's kind of intimidating. I about choked when I saw him for the first time at the station. Brown wavy hair, killer smile, and like 6 feet tall. But that perfect kind of guy isn't really my type. Still, I think he belongs in some sort of Firefighting Magic Mike movie. Focus Kara. Focus on the fire.

With Wildland, we practically never have enough water, so we always need to be careful. I passed the academy as a volunteer just a few years ago, and we only get about three house fires a winter in my little district back home, so my house fire experience is limited.

He passes off the hose to me and my eyes widen as I grasp it. Wow! They have him on a three-inch line! Holy smokes. That's way bigger than I'm used to. The biggest I usually work with as an attack is like-two-and-a-half-inch hose. Think of all that water! As he lets the weight drop in my hands, I brace a little just to not drop it. I think I see him smirk a little behind his mask. Honestly, if I were back in Ohio, I would've used it from the ground, not standing. Yup, I would definitely straddle it using all my body weight to hold it down. But he's the officer, so I guess I'll do it his way.

"Okay, you're going to open that barrel slowly and just spray into that pile right there." He directs.

I nod eagerly. It is my turn!

"Now you're going to want to get a good stance."

I position my feet like I'm going to start throwing some punches. I've got this. Just like Ohio, no different. Although I was sure of myself there, why am I suddenly nervous about everything here? Slowly, with the massive gloves trying to grip the handle, I pull back.

With a big blast, I'm catapulted right to my butt as I hang on to the hose for dear life. The water continues scooching me backwards across the ground. Slowly, I close the hose down and look up to see Garrett dying with laughter. Well, at least I remembered the slowly part. Oh, boy. What a way to make a good first impression. I feel tears brimming in my eyes and rapidly blink them away.

Ugg, he's going to think Ohio doesn't teach us anything in the Academy. Great. I have done this before. Why did I have to mess up? I wanted people to think I'm competent at my job! I am a good firefighter! I swear. Goodness. I should have just knelt to the ground and did it from there like we were taught in Ohio. Why did I think I could do it like Garrett?

He walks over and extends a hand to me. I grasp it and he hauls me right to my feet like I weigh nothing. I clamber up and drag the dumb hose with me. Stupid, large men. I know I'm not as strong as them. I've always had to find alternative ways to do things with this line of work. Yet, I start to brace my feet again. I will prove that I can do this. I've used hoses on a hundred other fires, so why did I just look like a fool?

"Would you like a backup? A lot of times if we have a large diameter hose, we will have a guy right behind us."

Okay, yeah that sounds right. I usually don't have this large of a diameter hose, maybe I should have backup. Besides, he knows way more about how they do things here. Why didn't he offer before? I always like a backup when I'm going in with an attack line, yes please on the backup! So, I just nod, figuring he will just stand behind me, but I see him kneeling with one leg propped at a ninety-degree angle. He pats his knee.

My entire body jerks back in shock. What? Is he saying what I think he's saying? No way. We never learned that in the academy. Maybe I should just do it by myself. Prove that I can. Then again, what if I refuse his help and get knocked down again. They would think I'm an idiot, incompetent. They might kick me off the crew. Or at least make me retest my training. I can do this. I am a firefighter. Maybe this is how they do it out here in Oregon?

"Since you are a smaller person, we often have the backup real close. So, if you want to sit right here on my knee, I will brace you."

I don't have any sort of argument against him, but I'm sure my vitals spike. I'm the type of person who is usually awkward with hugs let alone sitting on a large, cute guy's knee; a hot, sexy guy even. I think this is the closest I've been to a guy, like ever. Am I heavy? Oh gosh, what if he thinks I'm heavy? Are my legs supposed to be on both sides of his leg? Oh, my goodness. Keep your head in the game Kara. Fire, there's a fire. Well not a fire now, but still hot spots. Heat that we need to put out.

I sit back and glance at him, he just nods. I try to keep most of my weight on my feet. Just because he's huge, doesn't mean he can handle all my weight, plus all my gear. Oof. I'm glad I have a mask on because I'm sure blushing like no other. And without the extra oxygen, I might have started hyperventilating.

My legs press against his and if I didn't have all this gear on, I'm sure many different body parts would be in contact with each other right now. Oh goodness. Giving my head a slight shake, I push all those thoughts from my head. I am still on the job. This is the job!

I open the nozzle again and this time with him helping me hold the hose and a hand bracing me to him, at least I don't go anywhere. Slowly, we work the hose over the remnants of the fire as the heat leaves the home.

CHAPTER 2

Honestly, as I unpack, my mind wanders to Garrett. Did that mean anything to him? Was it purely work, or is he just that way with any girl? Honestly, I need to get my mind off him. It constantly keeps wandering back, but he is my officer, a co-worker, and I still don't know anything about him. Besides, like I said, he's not really my type. But I can't get how his arms felt around me out of my head. I never really thought any guy could like me, let alone someone who looks like him. I legit just moved out here, I can't go catching feelings for the first guy I talk to. Plus, think how unprofessional I'm being, well, and how pathetic. Besides, I would never want to be with him anyway. If a guy acts like that with a girl and it really wasn't for the job, then no way, he would be too much of a player for me.

I'm completely terrible. I spent a whole fire and 48-hour shift at the fire department, and so far, I only caught like five names. I just suck at names, no matter how hard I try. Logan is our Captain, huge guy, built like a tank. Lily is the only other girl at the department. She looks like she could kick any of those guys' butts. Built with some hard-core muscles, tall, but with some gorgeous red hair. The Lieutenant is Garrett's cousin, John. He's pretty darn cute too. More my type. What is their family feeding those boys because goodness? They could start a fire themselves by just looking like that.

He has this perfect little crooked nose. Blue eyes shine on his face, and I do all I can do to not just stare into them. Blonde hair frames his face and I have to physically hold my hand back from running my fingers through it. His smile just makes me smile back while my heart flutters. He's tall, but a little more on the nerdy looking side. My heart just skipped a beat when he put his glasses on. Yass, love me those nerds, especially a firefighting nerd. Johnny was really nice all shift, helping teach me where to find things and getting my gear all sorted out. He's such a sweetheart, even opened some doors for me. Like swoon! I can really see us becoming friends. Now there's a perfect guy. The personality, and when he winked at me, my breath caught in my throat. I think I'm in love. Ugg, Kara. I really am pathetic. Friends, co-workers. No guy could like me anyway I think as I slump on my bed.

Unpacking doesn't take long at all. With only a small car to travel across the country, I have a duffle bag, a couple of plants and most importantly a box of books. I know that I will be through these books in less than a month, luckily, Waldport has a great library. It's even less than a block away from the fire department. It is a little sad that this is all I have. However, it's about all I've travelled with for years now. My life's a bit of a gypsy lifestyle, working wildland in the summers and volunteer firefighting back home in the winters.

This is the first permanent job I've been offered away from home ever, so maybe I'll have to actually buy some home stuff at some point. You know like a pot or a skillet and not just eat food from a can every night. That's kind of a scary thought for me though. Like I would be putting down too many roots. Too much commitment you know. That's why I move all the time. Although I did totally buy a few little plants over the winter, and that felt like a huge commitment, so what's a few extra skillets and such going to harm? I'm constantly flipping between loving the adventure life, but missing home and family. I love who I am when I travel, free, yet it's lonely. This is the first time I don't have an end date to look forward to where I can go back to my little cornfields.

Being completely lucky my little house is right on the ocean. My soul instantly sang with joy seeing the blue shimmering water. I'm staying in a little run-down cottage, admittedly half falling apart, but it has the most amazing views. Situated right on the edge of a forest, the ocean lays only fifty yards away. Plus, I couldn't beat the rent prices! I will live in a shack in the woods for this price, so a little sand, leaks and a few bugs won't bother me. I can hear the waves from my living room. Ahh! How satisfying is that?

I finally have time to explore, to enjoy my brand-new state. This is so very exciting. Oregon always seemed like a fantasy. I mean deep rain forests, looming beautiful mountains, it's all just so fantastic. It always felt like a place people in movies lived, not someplace a woman from Forest, Ohio would live. It feels like a fairy tale. Any moment now, I'm waiting to see Hobbits roaming, or Elves emerging from the woods.

Digging through my clothes, I find a pair of gym shorts and a t-shirt. Even though it's raining, I'm determined to go into the ocean. I haven't seen the ocean since I was a kid. There's just something so mesmerising about those rolling waves, the crashing sounds, and the wind whipping around your face. I've always been drawn to water, it feeds my soul, the ocean is just the king of water bodies. As I wander through the little wooded section, with the fog and chill, it makes me think I'm already walking through water.

There it is, I see it! The ocean. Oh, it's just beautiful. A smile instantly slides across my face, my heart is happy. This right here is what I moved out here for. I've spent summers on the Snake River, the Gulley, Lake Erie, and grew up on the Blanchard, but this, this is just the cherry on top, the cream of the crop. How is it that a God that made such amazing natural features, also made me? I just don't get it.

Brrr. It sure is cold here. The rain begins coming down in a light, yet steady downfall, grey coating the world around me, setting an eerie vibe. A nice place for a Stephan King novel. I slip off my Crocs and leave them over by the path's edge. At least the bright yellow color will help me find the path again through the hazy, grey afternoon. I haven't even made it to the water's edge yet, and I'm soaked from the rain. Makes me think I should be in Twilight right now or something. A smile seeps across my face at the thought, I live in a movie world.

Feet squishing across the sand, sinking in the puddles, I find the water's edge. It's frigged as a glacier. Tiny needles prick across my feet from the cold and my lungs squeeze for air. Oh, my sweet goodness! I wander in up to my ankles. A wave rolls in and soaks me to my knees, so I wander into my knees. Standing there, I'm utterly at peace. A breath escapes my mouth as all the stress leaves my body. The tension easing from my shoulders, and it feels like I can breathe for the first time since pulling out of my parents' driveway. The waves splash me, trying to lift my feet off the ground, as my feet sink further and further into the wet sand. The waves continue to roll in and all of a sudden one jolts me, saturating me up to my waist. Ope. Well, this is it. I may as well jump in. I dive under as the next wave catapults at me. Shock runs through my body. I break the surface and a scream escapes me.

"Woohoo!" Wow, what a thrill! I bob with the waves as they lift me up and down. Weightless, floating, both physically and mentally. Calm is all I feel.

Okay, okay, that's about all I can stand. March in Oregon is not the most ideal time for swimming. But it was completely necessary. Running as fast as I can, I reach the sand and sprint to my shoes. Barely slipping them on, I charge through the woods to my little cottage. With not much heat there, it's not quite the relief I was hoping for. I strip off my wet clothes, leaving them in a heap on the floor. Slipping on some fuzzy socks, a hoodie and some sweats, I jump into my bed. At least I had the good sense to make it before my little adventure.

My grandma, such a sweetheart, gave me my great grandmother's wool quilt when I left. It's a very thoughtful, heartfelt gift that's now coming in very handy. I really can't believe that I just moved across the country from my whole family. An absolute move, a permanent job. A contract, I am here for a while whether my heart gets used to it or not. My chest tightens as my heart aches for the sudden realization. Three thousand miles away. My family is everything to me. My grandma, my brother, mom and dad, my best friend, Elizabeth. My little Hardin County. I have been gone a week and I miss it so dearly. I won't have the means to go back home until next March, when I have more money and vacation time. It's starting to hit like a tidal wave. My heart starts to throb.

My anxiety begins spiking a little as my heart races. My breaths come faster as the tears start to flow. I am alone. No one. I have no one out here. Alone, and I truly feel it, gasping as my chest squeezes. I can't breathe! I curl up in my bed, letting the warmth of the blanket try to fix my sadness. Before long, wracking sobs escape me. Alone. My heart physically hurts. I gasp for breath between sobs. Why did I do this? The emptiness I'm feeling is haunting. How could I go from feeling such a high in the ocean to this painful, dark, void?

Okay, Kara, breathe. I take a few deep breaths and practice some box breathing. This, right here, Waldport. This is my new home. Think of the ocean, all the little stores, the library, my little cottage. Really, Waldport is a lovely place to be for a while. Just like a storybook town. I'm the leading lady in this story. The tears start to slow as I remember my job, of feeling so calm in the sea. Of driving up through the Siuslaw National Forest right in my backyard. It will be okay. I have the Lord; I am not completely alone.

Lord, please be with me. Grant me peace, please. Please be with me, Lord. Peace. Hold me, guide me. Please be with me, Lord.

With my silent prayer, the heaviness starts to seep away. It always works out with his will. Heaven knows I always get myself into trouble when I try to do things my own way. I trust him, I really do. He's gotten me out of some rough times and lead me on some awesome adventures. A lot of times I don't like where I am in the beginning, it's because I don't like change. Change makes me feel like I'm not in control anymore. But I've ended up falling in love with some of those changes.

Maybe I should go out and see my new home. No sense in waiting for a nice sunny day. Those don't really exist here, at least not yet. Perhaps in the summer, we will get a few sunny days. The guys at the fire department told me it won't really ever get past sixty degrees either. Honestly, I quite enjoy this type of weather. Sixty degrees and rainy is my idea of a perfect day. I've never had it every day before though, so this will sure be different.

With a big sigh, I shove off the blankets and almost instantly regret it. Shivers wrack through my body, but it's now or never. If I don't get up and do something now, then I know I will end up in bed reading or watching movies on my computer all day. Not that that's a bad thing, I actually do it quite often, but I know it won't lift my mood like I'm hoping. Mitigating my mood before my mind goes to a depression episode. Stay busy, that's what I've learned over the years. I switch to some hiking pants and a rain jacket. I am still sticking with Crocs though because let's be honest, I know I will be walking through some sort of water at some point. Plus, Crocs are like the king of shoes.

Jumping on my bike, I pedal with no big destination in mind. Passing the fire department and the library, I find the bridge. It's a pretty cool bridge with a big arch. Pedalling fast, I make it to the middle and look out across the bay.

Wow. For a grey day, it is still peaceful. Eerie, but peaceful. Closing my eyes, I breathe in the crisp air. Coolness sweeps around me, my body shivers, but a smile slips across my face. Peace fills my heart. Calm.

I pedal past stores, homes, trees, everything that makes Waldport home. Maybe I should stop at the fire department, say hi to the shift on duty today. Decision made, I quickly pedal over there and soon enough I'm leaning my bike against the building and opening the door. Peering into the desk window, I see a familiar face.

"Hey, it's Johnny, right?" I ask to the face, him I remember for sure, but I don't need to let him know that. I mean who can forget those Caribbean blue eyes?

"Ha-ha. Yea, that works. Most people around here call me John, or Lieutenant. Um, you're the new girl, Kara, right?" He questions, struggling to come across my name for a second.

Guess I made quite an impression... not. "Yup, you've got it. But ya'll can call me Kar. If you want. So, you're on shift again?"

A few people at home call me Kar, but why did I say that? Kara is fine, I like Kara better. *Ugg*, cute guys kind of make my brain be an idiot. And I mean really? I thought he was on my shift, and I thought we would stick with the same shift partners unless we switched shifts. Disappointment washes over me. I was really looking forward to working with him. Well, and Logan and Garrett.

"I'm working for Pacific West today," he enlightens me.

Oh, the ambulance company that shares a building with us. Now I feel like an idiot, if I looked at his uniform, it would have been apparent. Stupid me. Oh well. But my heart flutters with happy little dances knowing I will still get to work with him. I mean after he was so nice to me the other day, I know he will be a good officer. That of course is the only reason I'm excited. Obviously.

"Well, cool. I just wanted to come check out who was on shift today, say hi and all that jazz." I blurt out.

My heart skips a beat. I think I have some arrhythmia going on from the fact I still get to be on shift with him. Good thing I am not hooked up to a monitor right now. He stands and holds the door to the bay open for me. Ducking under his arm, I walk through.

I always love seeing the engines. Whether it is here, home in Ohio, or on a wildland base, I feel like a little kid every time I walk into a bay the first few times. Once I work there for a week or so, it wears off, but each engine is slightly set up different and I love that. They're like their own beings.

I'm introduced to a man named Caden and one named Shay. Both seem super nice. Shay's personality instantly makes me feel like we're friends with a constant bubbly aura and a big hug as I greet him. Caden is probably the tallest man I've ever met in my life and could probably reach the top of the engine without the steps. It's nice to get to meet more people. Really, I should get to know everyone at the fire department, you never know when someone might trade a shift, or come down to volunteer on a call.

"Would you like a piece of pizza before you go home?" Johnny offers.

Pizza? Always! I am a total fat kid at heart. Well, maybe not just at heart. "Heck, yea! I will never turn down food." I claim following him to the kitchen. Biting down on my tongue, regret pings through me. Wow, I shouldn't have said that. It so made me sound like a fatty. But I guess if the slipper fits, own it right?

"The pizza place in town often gives us the leftovers. My guess is half your shifts there will be some pizza up for grabs." He proclaims with a laugh.

Great, I am so going to gain weight. But not like I make a ton of money, so I will take anything free. I grab two slices and munch on one while we head towards the front. Double fisting pizza slices, what a move.

"Cool, less money I have to spend on food then ha-ha. Hey, thanks, Johnny. I will be seeing you on Thursday then, right?" I prompt as I have tomorrow off too.

"Honestly, you will get sick of the pizza fast. And yea, for sure. Anything, anytime. What are your plans for tomorrow?" He questions.

"Um, I'm not really sure. I was thinking I might explore around. Any suggestions?"

"Well, sure, I could give ya' suggestions. But I am off tomorrow, if you would like, I could show ya' some of my favorite spots." He winks. My breathing completely stops for a minute as I legit die. That wink, oof.

Hmm. I am usually more of a loner, but it might be nice to see a local's perspective. Besides, most of the time, I am a loner because I have no one to go with. Just because I've been alone for a while now doesn't mean I always enjoy it. And I would so be dumb to turn down hanging out with Johnny. He seems like he would make a seriously awesome friend. Or look at it from a professional perspective. I will be getting more acquainted with my Lieutenant. Right? Totally all for being professional.

"Yea, I would love that, thanks. Where should I meet you?"

"Well, I noticed you rode your bike here, do you want to just meet here? I actually live in Portland, so I will be staying here over the nights this week. And if I'm here, I have to work calls, so I would love to get away for a little bit, have a break you know."

Hmm, okay then. That's kind of cool that he lives in Portland. That is definitely on my list of places to see. But the commute would suck! At least since typically we work forty-eight on and seventy-two off, he only needs to do it there and back about once a week, and if he spreads it out as if he's doing a commute every day, then it's nothing really.

"Yea, that works. So, are you driving? Or would you like me to drive?"

Really, I could drive my car, I just figured I would ride my bike to and from work and for groceries because they're all so close. I'm kind of a penny pincher when it comes to money, but so is the rest of my family. May as well save where you can, right? I'm going to have to get used to the rain either way, so I may as well save on gas money. Plus, I really hate driving. Driving just totally stresses me out. There is so much you can't control, like things running out at me, other drivers, something could break with my car, and thousands more things could go wrong.

"Sure, we can take my truck." He offers with a shrug. Relief washes over me. Awesome! No driving for me!

"Well, thanks very much. Eight AM work?" Cool. I have an adventure buddy for tomorrow. A super rad adventure buddy.

"Na nah, let's make it like ten, okay? I only wake up that early for shift."

A laugh burst out from me. Wow, he wouldn't survive in my family. On weekends while growing up, if we slept past seven, we would get woken up. Sleep is for the weak my father always said. But then again, growing up in Midwest Ohio farmland, no one much sleeps in. It's the nature of the beast.

"Okay, that's fair. See you at ten tomorrow then," I agree. I turn, leaving with a smile on my face and a happy heart.

CHAPTER 3

Johnny's truck is a noisy beast. I had to practically scale a mountain face just to climb into it this morning. Now, rain beats against the window and some sort of loud music plays I don't recognize. I'm not into today's type of music. Unless it's Broadway, Classic Rock, Disney, or contemporary Christian, I probably have no idea. Well, that's not entirely true. Being from the corn fields of the Midwest, my family are all big Country music people, so I can recognize most of it and even sing along if I wanted to, liking it is a whole different story though.

As he winds along Highway 101, I can't help but think this place reminds me a lot of Twilight. Technically Forks is on 101, but it's just like five hours to the north. The dense, green forest, the rain, ocean coast, I'm just waiting for my sparkly vampire.

Looking side eyed at Johnny, I scan him over. Yup, he would definitely be way more of a werewolf. Tanned skin, muscles all over, werewolf for sure. Not that there's anything wrong with that, anyway; I've always been more of a team Jacob person, Bella was so dumb for choosing Edward. I could handle having my own Jacob. My lips press into a mashed straight line as I work hard to hide the fact I'm smiling way too big from my wayward thoughts.

"Okay, our first spot is Cape Perpetua. We're going to wait for the top until the rain clears a little, give it about an hour. First, we'll go hike over to the tide pools." He smiles.

"I love tide pools! We went to some when I was a kid." I inform him. "I was so fascinated that if you put a rock in the anemones, they spit them out. Well, that is until I put a poor little hermit crab in one. I waited and waited; it didn't come back out." I continue, my voice full of remorse.

Now he knows I am a killer. A murderer. He laughs, probably at the fact that I see dead people on my job often yet cry when I kill a hermit crab. There's a stark difference though when I'm the one who killed it, accidentally on purpose. Plus, I might not show it on the outside, but each death does bother me. Maybe a little less and less with each one. You just can't show it with this type of job as you slowly go numb to it all. And I need to believe God called them home for a reason. Or at least, I hope they go home.

His truck plunges up into the forest until we come across the visitor center. From there we start walking down the winding path to the ocean. Come summer, I bet this path is great, it has hedges taller than me, and looking closely I can see it's spotted with all sorts of blackberry and salmon berry bushes. Yum. I wonder if I can pick them here. Perhaps make a pie. OOOO, I bet maybe in some of the higher spots, they have huckleberries too. Those are the absolute best.

We emerge from the vegetation and the ocean glimmers in front of us. I am still in awe. I live on the beach, how cool is that? I feel like a movie star, a beach babe. However, I don't think I'll get my California tan here. We scurry over rocks, him pointing out various pools, filled with anemones, urchins, sea stars, and all sorts of cool creatures. For it being such a dreary day, the colors of the pool organisms still appear stunning.

"Oh, my goodness, look at that one!" I point to a ginormous yellow starfish.

"That's Big Mac. He's famous around here. He showed up about two years ago. Before then, we didn't have a ton of star fish due to a sickness killing them off," Johnny explains. "But they are on the comeback as you can see. But Big Mac doesn't move a lot. So, he's our local celebrity," Johnny proclaims with a grin.

"Aww, Big Mac! That is so cute." I croon. "What a cool little guy. I get that. Heck the closest thing around my house that everyone knows about is the Artesian well. It's our little local famous spot. The Kellogg's plant tons of sunflowers every year, and the water flows all year long, so you can stop any time of year for a drink."

Thinking about home, I realize I'll be missing all the sunflowers this year, no cool drinks of water for me after the bike ride down there. No more apple picking or golf cart rides. His laugh swiftly brings me out of my spiralling mood.

"Yea, that sounds about right for Ohio. I guess I can't laugh though, I just showed you a famous star fish."

With that I laugh. I have only been in Waldport for about a week, but the size of it reminds me of like a slightly bigger Forest. It just seems like a happy little, small town. Instead of farmers, it's fishermen and crabbers. In the end, the old guys still end up at the Moose, and the women probably still gossip around a breakfast table.

We follow the path around the tide pools until we come to some basalt rocks jutting out from the vegetation. That's cool! I'm sure Johnny already knows, but that means this place was a source for volcanic activity who knows how many years ago. Probably under the ocean or something.

"That's Thor's Well," he states, pointing to a hole in the rocks where water constantly flows into and drains out of. It's really kind of rad making a mini circle waterfall over and over. I love Thor and Marvel, but I don't particularly get what a hole in the rock has to do with it.

"That is really awesome!" I exclaim over the wind. It is pretty, even if I don't get the name. Maybe it's named as if Thor struck the earth with his hammer and made a hole? Who knows.

"It is! We have idiots that fall into it every year though trying to get too close. This is technically Yachats Fire territory, but occasionally we will get called to help for Mutual aid."

"Oh..." I mumble, sobering a little. Wheels turn in my head, as I can picture the incidents and how you could go about the rescue. I've forgotten what it feels like constantly thinking about the next victim, always being on alert. Always going through the what ifs.

"Over there is the spouting horn, but it's not active right now, you will have to try and check it out some other time." He pulls me out of my thoughts. We continue walking along the rocky coast, the spray soaking me to the bone. Even though it's freezing, I'm content. There's nothing like being by the sea.

Once, back in his car, we drive up to the Cummins Ridge Trailhead. Winding curves, bumpy roads; there's a good chance, this would normally make me sick. Luckily, with my damp clothes, it cools me enough I don't have to crack the window. I hate being one of those people who get motion sick. It's totally embarrassing. My parents used to keep a 'Puke Bucket' in the van at all times for me. I was the child who even if we drove thirty minutes to a Walmart, I might be throwing up. So many traumatic memories, a shudder courses through me at the thought.

We get there with no incident, thank goodness and start our hike. I love walking through here. Sticking my hand out and letting the ferns, mosses and everything else run across them. It really is beautiful. Too bad the Pacific Crest Trail is all the way in the middle of the state, I would love to get to do that someday. For now, I will stick with this ridge trail. The vegetation grows so thick, you could picture dinosaurs walking through here. That or fairies and goblins, a smirk strikes across my face at my own lame nerdiness.

We hike wordlessly, which is fine by me. If I'm being honest, I don't think Johnny can spare the breath right now. But I didn't say anything. After an hour or so there's finally a glimmer of light shining through the canopy. We break through to see the most amazing view. My eyes widen as my mouth drops open from the gorgeous vista. Out in front of us, the rolling hills of the Siuslaw lay, but there's the stark contrast of the ocean in the background. I can't imagine how gorgeous this must be when there's actual sunlight too.

Soon, we find ourselves walking to the top of Cape Perpetua. When we get to the top I stand in awe, the view absolutely breathtaking. I just can't believe this dense forest goes right up to the ocean. Green runs alongside the blue, the large waves coming in long strips against the treeline. Yup, this is absolutely what I came here for. My soul is happy.

After getting back in the car, my teeth start to chatter. I don't think I will ever be warm again. Can you die from being too cold? Okay don't answer that. Of course, I know I can, it's just, I'm miserable. Sensing how cold I am, Johnny cranks up the heater, and come to find out his truck even has butt warmers! I sag against the seat thinking, aren't butt warmers just the best? As warmth finally starts ebbing into my bones, I take a glance over at him. He's in a freaking t-shirt! Ugg, am I that much of a baby?

"How aren't you cold?" I ask incredulously. I mean seriously, maybe he is like one of those werewolves.

"Eh, I grew up here. It may always be about sixty on the coast, but right now in Portland it's like twenty degrees. So, this feels like spring when I come to work," he explains with a laugh.

"That's fair, I suppose. I don't know, I still wouldn't be in shorts and a t- shirt. I wear hoodies even when it is like eighty in Ohio."

"You've got to be kidding me. Ugg I would be dying," he states.

The rest of the afternoon, he takes me all over. Who knew just within an hour of me there would be so much? We go to the Heceta Head Lighthouse, the Oregon Dunes, and a number of other things. I just can't believe this isn't a vacation. This is my home now. Wow. Home. It's sure a different sort of home, but in a way, it's starting to feel more and more like it. I may not have my family and friends, but the natural beauty of it speaks to my heart.

Besides, I would say some of the guys at the fire department are becoming my friends. Heck Johnny is taking me all over in his own truck. That's more of a friend than I've had in a long while.

Elizabeth is amazing, she just doesn't live close enough that we can meet up more than a few times a year. My two best guy friends in high school constantly had me drive them around and I bought them food all the time. Wincing as I think of me trying to buy friendship. Lame, I admit. But back then, I was a little more desperate for friends. This kind of feels like a huge deal to me. Pathetic.

"Okay, Kara, this is the absolute best burger place in the US, but you have to get the Big Chub," he insists with mock seriousness as we pull in front of a tiny little black box.

It's like a trailer. This reminds me of one of those cute little food carts you see in movies. Where I come from, we don't have any taco trucks, or hotdog on a stick trucks, except maybe fairs.

"Oh, yea? I have to get it?" I repeat rolling my eyes.

Yes, I'm going to order it since he's so highly suggesting it, but I also kind of hate it when people tell me what I should do. I know, I know, it is just a sandwich. But like I am my own independent woman, don't tell me what to do. Besides, I just want to tease him.

"Hi, um, can I please have the big chub?" I ask the lady in the window.

Johnny walks right up behind me. "Make that two with everything on it," he requests, his body half shoving me to the side. He moves to pay.

"I can get my own," I declare. I hate the guilt that follows when someone does something for me. Like I appreciate their niceness, but it also kind of kills me, thinking how I can repay them, what if I can't repay them?

"Nope, it's on me. Thanks for going on adventures today," he states appreciatively.

Before I can protest again, the lady takes his money dooming me. "Well thank you. Next time it's on me, okay?" I suggest.

It's definitely a new experience to have a guy buy my food. Has that ever happened before? I don't really think so. Wow. A guy just bought me food. Oh, my goodness! Cool, but the guilt still hits a little.

The food truck sits only a block off the ocean and if I peek around the building across the street, I can just see the waves. So calming. Seagulls squawk and fly about, hopping around the concrete looking for burger pieces and fries.

"Lieutenant Kaisley, your food is ready!" The lady calls from the stand.

Hmm, I wonder if most people call him Lieutenant. Maybe I should be more professional? Nah, I've already committed to Johnny, and he hasn't said anything about it yet. May as well stick to it.

I figure, we will sit and eat at the table, but he grabs the bag and starts to walk towards the street. I scramble to catch up. What is it with men and their super long strides?

We cross the street, and he rounds the building. Following, I realize we must be headed for the beach! He expertly leads us around the little homes to find a path leading through the grasses. I follow along until we reach the sandy edge. I plop down in the sand stripping my socks and boots, dumping mounds of sand from them already. I hate walking in boots in the sand. I definitely learned that in the dunes today. The stupid sand kept piling over my boots and as we walked up the sand mountain, I slid back a foot for every two steps. It sucked!

Hopping up, I continue following, enjoying the cold sand squishing with every step. He stops at a big washed-up tree. My eyes widen at the one-hundred-foot tree. He sits down with both legs facing the ocean, while I straddle the tree facing him. This way, I'll have someplace to set my sandwich because let's be honest, I am a hella' messy eater.

"Here you go," he offers, handing me the little basket. My jaw drops and my stomach starts dancing at the sight of this gloriousness. This burger is so seepy and bloating it wouldn't have handled being wrapped very well.

"You are never going to be able to eat a normal burger ever again," he claims laughing.

"Well, thank you for ruining normal burgers for me, I so appreciate that," I grumble, my voice laced with sarcasm. To be honest, it's not like I eat many burgers anyway. Well, my family eats them a lot, but they eat deer burgers, and if there's a hot dog or shredded chicken option, I'm definitely going for that.

There is a fork sticking out of the bun, I don't even bother trying to bite the monstrosity, I go straight for the fork, stabbing off a hunk. Hurtling the goopiness in my mouth before it falls off, I end up slopping cheese on my face. Oh, my good golly! That's attractive, Kara. Oh well, who am I trying to impress? He's just a co-worker and he will definitely see me in worse states than cheese on my face.

"This is amazing!" I mumble around a bite of lumpy gloriousness. I mean seriously, who would have thought to put bacon, nacho cheese, French fries, and everything else on a hamburger? Sure, bacon, or lettuce, or normal cheese, but French fries? Amazing. My body wiggles around in a happy little dance from the taste.

After we both finish our monster burgers, we shove our trash in our shoes, stack them on top of the log, and then head out to the water. Stooping down, I wash my hands off in the cool waves. Suddenly, water splashes over me from the side. Looking up, I see Johnny trying to hide a smile. Can't fool me! I retaliate with a kick, spraying water up to his waist.

"You may as well give up; you will never win!" I claim in my meanest voice.

I grew up with a brother and many boy cousins, I know how to hold my own, and I don't back down, ever.

"Ha, girl, you wish!" In a matter of seconds, he rushes over and throws me over his shoulder, charging into the water.

"No! Put me down! You're cheating!" I squeal, laughing.

With a big heave he tosses me into the ocean. I sink down in the waves. Before completely surfacing, I plunge towards him. With the waves help, I crash into his legs, and he topples in next to me. *Splash!* Yes! A whoop escapes me as I jump up in victory.

"Well, I still don't think I would call that a win for ya'. Maybe a tie?" He concedes, sputtering water.

I think about splashing water into his face, but decide it might be a tad childish, and well, maybe I should get to know him better first. Nah, another day. My hand wiggles under the surface of the water, feeling for anything useful.

"Sure, I will take a tie," I claim, fully knowing I'm going to get a little lead in about five seconds. He holds out a hand to shake. My hand full, I sling it into his firm hand, seaweed and all.

"Ugg. So childish," he groans, but he shakes his hand to get all the gunk off nonetheless, so I still feel like maybe I got a little bit of the upper hand.

CHAPTER 4

Work at the fire department is always exciting for me. Not just the calls. Calls can really get your adrenaline flowing, but even just the camaraderie at the station, this is what I've been missing. I love how we oversee certain meals, and our beds must always be made. There are always chores to be done, but everyone steps in to help. Most of all, I love the guys. I mean seriously, I love them all, but being on shift with Garrett, Logan and Johnny makes for some good laughs. I can't believe guys gossip so much! There is always some sort of complaints, rants, or drama coming out of their mouths.! About everything!

I feel like I already know these guys on a very personal level. A very personal level. They share everything. Although, I did see them all in their underwear on my very first day of work, so what better way to get to know someone. I was slightly shocked when they stripped off their pants, right to their undies before jumping in their bunker gear. Wow. I definitely wear my tac pants under the gear, I don't want people seeing me in my undies! Yet, no one even spares a second glance at each other or says anything negative. Guys seem better than girls in this way, I guess. But seriously the gossip is some serious stuff, shade being thrown from every direction.

Tonight, however, all our chores are done, meals eaten, lives saved... for right now, so it's relaxation time. Our kitchen has become a battle zone. The game, Spector Ops. As of right now, I'm going with the strategy of just trying to stay alive and get away from them. But everything I do, they counter! Gosh darn, I feel like an idiot because I can't even meet one objective. It has literally been all I can do to stay alive, and I am so going to lose. I hate feeling dumb, but it's like they know where I am going every single time even though I think I am being sneaky.

Before long, I am down to only one health point. I am so fed up with myself. I used to call myself smart? I should scratch strategy games off the list of things I am good at because I so suck. Really, I am pissed. Pissed at myself because I must not have any tact. I will say hearing Garrett, Logan, and Johnny argue about moves is kind of funny. I think we will be lucky if they are all on speaking terms by the end of the game. But at least they are getting me to smile. Even though I could cry at my own stupidity, I am enjoying it. And just spending this time with them, let alone all the laughs is worth it. Then, the tones drop. We all jump up and head to our bunker gear lined up by our engine.

"No one touches the board till we start again. The war room shall stay intact!" Logan shouts while jumping in his boots. I haul my suspenders up over my shoulders and jump in the seat. Sliding my headphones on, I press the button to dispatch.

"Dispatch, Engine 7901 enroute," I announce. My voice ricochets across the bay, as Logan jumps in and the engine pulls out.

Since I'm in the front passenger seat, or the officers' seat tonight, it's my job to work the sirens. Contrary to normal belief, it's not just one switch and they're on. Yes, there is the normal siren, but the one that winds up, and winds down, that is foot powered. Luckily, everyone knows what it should sound like, yet my anxiety always goes through the roof wondering if I'm running it too long, or if I shut it off too quick, or if we hit a bump and my foot accidently goes down a little too fast, which happens frequently around here. Don't get me wrong, it's an honor to be assigned the officers seat while I'm still a probie here, but there's so much that goes along with it.

However, since Logan is our engineer, he drives. Glancing in the back, Garrett and Johnny, our medics, sit with the med gear so they can grab it if needed. Plus, they're closer to any fire gear we need. While I'm one of the least experienced, a big part of my job is talking to dispatch, keeping us connected, yet the brains and muscle are putting in other work.

Pulling up the dispatch screen, I inform the crew this is just a lift assist, so we will take minimal med bags in and don't have to put on all the fire gear, just the pants and boots we already wear since after office hours, we can wear shorts in the station.

Once we arrive, the guys in the back pop out, as I radio dispatch. "Dispatch, engine 7901 on scene," I state.

"Copy, engine 7901 on scene."

I go join my crew, finding them talking with an older lady sitting on the floor. She appears okay, but she fell and couldn't get back in her chair. My heart squeezes. How awful would it be to have to call the fire department for something like this. My heart goes out to her for sure. I walk over and give her a reassuring smile. Garrett goes around behind her as I stand in front of her.

"Okay ma'am, use my boots as a foot stop and give me your hands," I instruct as I brace my feet to hers. I clasp her hands and Garrett grasps her under her armpits.

"On my count," Garrett begins, "One, two, three." On three, in an instant, she's standing. We help her shuffle the few feet to her chair and she sinks down contently. Poor little lady, she couldn't have been much more than one hundred pounds.

Seeing her though, makes me think of my grandma back home. She's my best friend, the lady who has always been there for me, all my life. Here I am helping this lady, but who's helping my grandma at home? I miss her, I miss all of home. My heart squeezes giving me acute chest pain. I suck in a few short breaths and calm myself. Keep your composure. I will have to call her later though.

Once we leave the scene, I keep waiting for the next big thing, but it doesn't come. Some shifts are exciting, and we have call after call. Other shifts are spent washing engines and picking up the elderly. I am a bit of a white cloud, so a lot of my shifts fall on the latter. However, I don't mind. Even in my few years back in Ohio, I'm thankful for shifts where not much goes on. It's the ones that you think will be exciting are the ones that can haunt you forever.

We pull back in the station and all go through the motions of pulling our pants down to perfectly fit around our boots, laying the suspender straps on top and having our gear hang in its assigned spots on the engine. It's all very organized making my brain super happy. Everything has a home, there's order in my little world, just the way I like it.

No one really feels like getting back to our war, so we prepare for bed. The rules are the same, once we get in the bunks, we remain quiet, trying to only get up for a call. Granted some guys will just stay out in the social quarters all night, but to each their own. Logan and I head to our beds, while Garrett and Johnny stay out to talk. Part of me wants to hang out with them, but I know I will be better off in the long run by getting sleep.

I do still think about the first fire when I sat on Garrett's leg. I mean seriously. I can't believe how stupid I feel. That had to of been a move. But no moves since... Thank goodness! I'm definitely over that and never want to go that route again, especially after witnessing his antics. I've seen him hit on waitresses, talk endlessly about recent one-night stands, and even seen him flirting after a call was over. He's such a ladies' man, a little man-whore.

Now Johnny on the other hand... A sigh escapes me at the slight longing for the perfect man that can never be mine. We had a ton of fun yesterday. But he is my lieutenant, he can't feel anything for me... right? No, don't even question it, he will never like me. Someone like him would never fall for someone like me. Plus, he is kind of my boss. But I'm starting to have a hard-core crush on him. My mind wanders to him way too much for someone that is out of my reach, well, and out of my league. But yesterday on the beach felt like the perfect Hallmark moment. I wish I was the type of girl who could have a Hallmark ending.

Before I know it, morning comes along with no interruptions during the night... well none except Johnny's snoring. That dude slept all the way across the room, and I swear his snoring sounded like a train echoing in circles through a tuba. Ugg.

I have a few spare minutes until I need to be downstairs, so I decide to call my grandma. Luckily, if it's 8 a.m. here, it is 11 there, so at least she will be up, hopefully. My grandma is like a college student. She stays awake until 5 am and stays in bed until noon. The phone rings against my ear.

"Hello?" comes her groggy voice. Okay, guess she wasn't quite up yet.

"Hi, Grandma. How are you?" Just hearing her voice makes me want to cry. Oh, I miss her, and home.

"I'm good. Micah still isn't shitting," she states, informing me about her cat. My eyes roll so hard they could cause an avalanche. I hear way too much about his bowel movements. Poor cat probably just feels like it can't go in peace.

"Oh, that's too bad!" I murmur with exaggerated concern. I put her on speaker phone so I can get ready while I talk. Glancing up, I notice most of the guys are across the room or out of earshot anyway. From there she asks about my job and life and how Oregon is. We talk for about fifteen minutes before the boy conversation comes up.

"So, have any of the guys caught your eye?"

"Uh, Grandma, I've not been here that long yet," I claim knowing it's a complete lie. But I mean what am I supposed to say, that I am falling for my Lieutenant, he's roguishly handsome and older than I am?

"Well, you keep a lookout for that rich husband. But don't go bringing home any Spics from out there!"

I gasp, fumbling to turn off the speaker. Oh my gosh. I see both Garrett's and Logan's eyes shoot over to me, both Hispanic men. Oh, my goodness. Heat floods my face and tears spring to my eyes in absolute embarrassment. I grasp for my phone, my face stuck in gaping shock.

"Grandma! I got to go, work started. I love you!" I garble, rushed out. Oh my gosh.

"Love you, too," she states, and I click off the phone. No more grandma on speaker phone... ever!

I turn to Logan and Garrett with an apology flooding my whole soul. "I am so sorry. She is a racist little old woman. I'm sorry. She doesn't mean anything against you guys." I gush out., They burst out laughing.

Garrett turns to Logan wagging his finger. "Now don't go bringing home a spic, you hear?" He mocks in an old woman's voice. My heartache lessens. I think I've been forgiven. Guilt still washes all over me though. I busy myself with making sure my gear is immaculate.

Still raining all day with no calls, how do we stay busy? Well, Johnny decides to set up a practice search and rescue obstacle course. He scatters it all throughout the bay with confined spaces and entrapments. My head nods in appreciation, like seriously, this is awesome. Could I ask for a better job? I wiggle around with excitement as I get my gear on. Garrett is my partner and will be sweeping the space for victims while I navigate.

"Now, just like real life, I want you to be blind. While we cannot fill the bay with smoke, we can blindfold you guys. Before you put on your helmets, I want you to go on air and put your hood on backwards to cover your mask. Then put your helmet on and we will roll. Your goal, make it through the course and back out with your victim or victims," he orders.

I go through the motions of getting my mask ready. I always have a slight panic attack from the moment I put the mask on to the moment the oxygen starts flowing. Dumb, I know, considering the first step, I can still breath before I put the respirator on, but if I wait too long it gets all foggy and I can't see. My brain begins going into a frenzy, what if I put the respirator on and the air doesn't come? Yes, all I would have to do is take it off, but I worry about those stupid little things. Confinement. I hate confinement. No air, or space. My air comes on just fine though, and I breathe a sigh of relief sounding like Darth Vader. We walk over to the starting point with helmets and hoods in our hands.

"You ready?" I lean over, asking Garrett.

He nods, "Yup." Of course, he is, but I still need to check.

He has the irons in his hands and gets down on his knees. Grabbing the axe from him, I sink down to my knees and brace my shoulder to the wall. This won't be exactly like orienting through a house, because sometimes we will be against the wall and other times, we will be following a hose, typically it's one or the other, but I'm impressed with the course Johnny made. My pack starts screaming and I have to give a little shake. Sure, I feel like an idiot, but if I don't shake, it just keeps yelling. It is a safety mechanism so that if a firefighter goes down, unconscious or trapped, others can find them.

Johnny walks over to Garrett and clashes helmets with him. "Be careful Brother," he states with a laugh. It's just a practice course, but habits are habits. I heard they went through academy together and this is what they do before any sort of fire call. It just makes my heart tighten for them. Both out of the sweetness of it, but also knowing the what ifs.

As Garrett slides his hood over his face, I lock eyes with Johnny one last time. He gives me a wink and I slide the hood over my face before I can grin like a silly girl. I think he winks at me now just knowing that it makes me react.

I slip on my helmet and pull on my gloves focusing on the task. Things are so much simpler when you can see. After beginning my firefighting career as a cadet in Ohio, I will never take my sight for granted. I have blindly gone into too many situations, and I hate it. That feeling, a little on edge, it just makes my whole body hold its breath the entire time. I feel Garrett grasp my ankle letting me know it's time to begin.

Feeling along the wall with my left shoulder, I slide my axe along with me.

Garrett's tools echo in the space as he hits objects looking for victims, I pause. "You good?" I bellow. This is a question we are going to be continuously asking each other the entire time. A constant state of communication. It's just something you get used to as you do searches. Admittedly, it's so much quieter here in the bay than a real situation. Communication always remains key. Rounding corners, going around objects, sweeping along the way, we push on.

I feel a tug on my ankle. "Hold, I feel something," Garrett states. I hear scuffling and tugs.

"Very funny John!" He hollers off into nowhere.

"It was just a leg, no body attached," he informs me with a laugh through his mask.

I let off a short laugh and continue on.

Even though I know it's not real, I want to succeed. It still gets your adrenaline flowing and heart pumping. All of a sudden, the wall disappears, and I start sweeping around. My tool bounces off something to my left and keeping my foot along the last bit of wall, I stretch out. The hose! We transfer over to that and move along counting couplings. Even though it doesn't give us an accurate distance today, in a normal fire if we follow the hose, couplings will give us distance, but that means someone else has already taken it in in an initial search.

The hose winds us around, taking us over stuff and under others. All the while, Garrett and I continuously asking how the other is doing. *Thud!* My helmet smacks right into something. Feeling around, the hose goes through a tunnel of some sorts. No bigger than a foot-by-foot square opening.

In real life, I would want to check it out more, but today we're supposed to follow the hose. Poor Garrett.

Shoving my tool in first, I make myself into a pencil. My SCBA catches on the lip. I pull it off and I have to wiggle it through before me at an angle. Shimmying through, I hear Garrett banging around behind me. As I come up, I'm surprised as something of his hits me from behind. Interesting. I can't imagine how his body had to squish to get through that, but I'm thoroughly impressed.

We only make it a few feet farther before hitting the castle. At least that's what I would call it. It's a big platform with two stories, a fake window, and a small triangular basement tunnel. We use it for a variety of different training exercises. Unfortunately, the hose seems to be running down the tunnel and not up. At least I've seen it before, so I know what it looks like. It shouldn't be too hard.

But then my tool rattles the chains. Sticking my hand out, I feel chains, bungies and chords have been added. Great. Ugg my face scrunches in a grimace knowing what comes next.

"Garrett, we have another confined space ahead. Watch for entrapments." I advise, though I'm fully aware he has a lot more experience than me with confined space rescue. He used to work for the coast guard and had a lot of boat rescues, which always entail confined spaces. Nope! I am not a fan. I don't do any sort of confined spaces. I feel my pulse jump just knowing what I'm about to encounter and thinking about all I don't know.

Ducking and manoeuvring works for all of three seconds before I feel a chain get caught on my SCBA. Backing up a little I decide to go over it. Then something pulls at my helmet, the chin strap catching roughly. Trying to yank my head to the side, it catches even tighter. I try to lift my arms to untangle myself, but they're caught on something too. How can my whole body be stuck? I wouldn't even be able to reach my radio! What do I do? My heart rate starts skipping. Breathing coming faster. I'm stuck. Pulling my head down again, it catches my mask and I hear it! The air whooshing out of my mask. Oh my gosh! I'm going to die. Panicking, I thrash trying to get untangled.

"Garrett! Garrett! I can't get out, my mask is leaking! Mayday!" I cry. I can't even get my arms up to reach my helmet, things are catching it all around. Stuck, I am truly, truly stuck. My breathing comes faster and faster. My head feels dizzy, if the hood didn't make things pitch black, I know black spots would be dancing.

"Kara, you need to calm down." Garrett urges calmly.

Calm. Calm. Yes, this isn't real. I'm not in a burning building right now. There are no fumes that are going to kill me with my mask leaking. I'm not dying. My breathing slows and my heart rate lowers. My mask continues leaking but I manage to wiggle enough to get a hand free. From there, I wiggle backwards, untangling from the traps. Surprised that I didn't back up into Garrett, I feel around for him. My tool hits someone's shoe.

"Ow," grumbles the voice. "Kara, you can take the hood off."

"But we didn't find the victim," I argue. I don't like feeling like a failure. If this were real, someone would have died. I don't want that on my conscience, not even for a dummy.

"Kara, take your hood off," Johnny repeats. Well, I'm not going to argue with my lieutenant, so I quickly strip my head gear and turn off my oxygen. I see Garrett already has his gear off and is holding a rope in his hand. Johnny stands on the other side of the platform holding a rope end as well. What? Could they have been behind that? They are the reason I got stuck? My brain begins whirling.

"Yea, it is what it looks like. You didn't fail. There was no hidden victim, well besides the leg," Johnny explains. "I put that there to be funny. This was to test how you do when you get trapped. Yes, the goal is for that never to happen, but we need to prepare for how to escape." Oh, well shoot. I really screwed that up. I really failed at that then. My heart sinks. Darn it. I stand there thinking it all over, not being able to make eye contact with either of them.

"Now, before you go and think you did terrible, that really was not that bad. I've seen worse, but we need to work on your composure," he describes.

Really, he's right. My composure. Garrett comes over and claps me on the back.

"You did a good job being lead though! Navigation was spot on," he praises me.

Well, at least I did something right. But it still doesn't really make me feel better.

CHAPTER 5

Glancing around my little Ford Escape, I'm shocked to see everyone packed in there. About fifteen minutes before shift ended Logan asked if we would all like to go to Eugene to hang out. Everyone else agreed, and since I have no social life, I may as well. So here we are, me driving, Johnny riding shotgun and Logan and Garrett in the back.

Our first stop, breweries. Now, I don't really drink, and I don't get the appeal of places that make beer, but that's what the men want. As we pull up, I have to drive around the block twice just to find a parking spot that's not parallel parking. Nope, I've driven across the country multiple times, and I still cannot parallel park. I blame it on the fact that I'm a woman. Eh, driving sucks anyway.

Luckily, our spot isn't too far away. As the rain falls the stress leaves my body in a tidal wave. A smile grips my face as a plan forms. Walking through the rain, I jump in a puddle, splashing all three guys clear up to their waists.

"Dude! Watch it!" Exclaims Logan. My heart explodes with joy from my own childishness.

Garrett and Johnny just laugh. Shuffling in the door, we find a table.

"Challenge coins! Go!" Johnny yells as he slams down a large thick circle.

Quickly, I open my billfold and grab mine. It may be different, but it's a challenge coin. Luckily, the other two guys had their wallets in their back pockets, so I'm not last.

"Whoa, look at that! How do you have one already? Isn't this your rookie season?" Johnny inquires, arching his eyebrows in surprise.

"For paid structure, not volunteer, and I've done wildland for a few years." I chuckle.

He thought they were going to get me to pay. Nope, not today. This one is from a wildland fire. He twirls the coin in his hand inspecting it.

"I suppose that counts. Pretty rad coin too. I give the wildland guys props for sure, too much hiking for my liking," he proclaims with a laugh. It is a pretty cool looking coin.

Garrett slaps his coin down before Logan. "OOOO Logan pays!" Garrett shouts.

Hanging out with enough firefighters, wildland or otherwise, I knew I did not want to be last. Whoever's last has to buy the first round, and if you don't have one at all, then you might have to buy the whole night. My first year of wildland before I earned my coin, I certainly had my fair share of buying nights. But hey, the next few years, I got some free sweet teas out of it.

For the next hour, I munch on my food while the guy's drink. Roaring laughter echoes around me as stories are told. These guys are riots, I'm so glad to have a crew again. A brotherhood, knowing someone always has your back, it's just something very special. Family, a belonging. Yes, I was honestly so ready to go home and sleep and watch Lord of the Rings after my shift, but this, this was worth it.

"Hey! We should all get nipple piercings!" Garrett yells.

Or not... "Nope! Count me out!!" I refuse.

At the same time, the guys yell, "Yes! Let's do it!" The guys all fist bump and clap each other on the shoulders.

No way am I doing that. I passed out when my friend got her ears pierced at the mall. I don't do needles. It's one thing if it's a necessary medical patient or trauma victim or something. One where I have at least some adrenaline flowing and I'm in professional mode. A whole 'nother thing as a civilian just happily sipping a sweet tea.

They down the beers and order a round of shots.

"No, thank you," I mumble as one is passed to me.

Garrett shrugs and tosses it back.

"This is going to be so rad!" Garrett shouts.

"We are going to look so bomb all the ladies are going to want us!" Logan exclaims.

"Umm, honestly, I do not see how this will attract the ladies at all," I argue. They either didn't hear me or ignore me.

"Come on, Kara, we need you to drive." Garrett whines.

"Hurry up, Kara," They shout over each other.

I slouch back into the rain after them. Okay, this is all on them. I am so not to blame.

"Could someone tell me where I am supposed to be driving?" I ask. I'm half tempted to start the drive back to Waldport, but hey, they're adult men and this will be hilarious. Someone hands me a phone with it speaking directions at me.

While they jabber and laugh, I drive us safely to the tattoo parlor they have picked out. At least it's spring and before any tourists arrive, so they should be able to get right in. I would hate for them to come to their senses and give up on getting them done.

They barge right in and demand they get their nipples pierced. The guy behind the counter looks like he wants to laugh but holds back. He sets them to filling out paperwork then looks at me.

"Are you getting anything done today darlin?" he prods.

"No thank you." I answer politely.

"Aw come on Kara! Do it for the crew! Do it for your brothers," Garrett pushes.

"Yea Kara, we are a team," Logan chimes in. My arms cross in defiance as I look at Johnny, knowing he's next.

"How about just a piercing anywhere?" He suggests with a wink. Ugg men. But thinking about it, well we are a crew. Maybe… Johnny comes over and hugs me from behind, putting his chin on top of my head. My body stiffens at the sudden closeness, but then sags as I breathe in his cologne.

"Just one." He pleads as he rocks me with the hug.

"Fine!" I sigh. How can I say no to him? I turn seeing his puppy dog eyes light up into a smile. Looking at the tattoo artist I request, "Could I please get my cartilage done in my left ear?"

"Yes! A crew that gets piercings together, stays together!" The guys cheer.

"Sure, no problem." He agrees and the guys all laugh.

Ugg needles. Once paperwork is all done, he leads us back to a room. At least we all get to watch each other, and most importantly, at least they're drunk enough, if I pass out, they might not remember.

Logan sits up first. Squirming in his chair, you can tell, even intoxicated, he's starting to get nervous. You know, I want to feel bad for him, but then again, he's choosing this. Derrick, the tattoo guy, holds a clamp and walks over to him. Logan jumps when the cool metal presses against his right nipple and the clamp closes. Squeezing his eyes shut, Logan's face contorts into a squished mess of lines.

"Ready?" Derrick asks.

"Not in the slightest but do it already," Logan replies through clenched teeth. In a second the needle stabs through.

"Yeaoooooow!" Logan cries while laughing. He's laughing.

"Ooooo, Ooooo!" He makes high pitched noises as Derrick wiggles the needle and gets the ring set. The second one goes smoother and before long, he's beaming with two sparkly nipples. Men.

Johnny steps up next. My eyes skim his shirtless figure over and over. Act like you've seen it before Kara, composure, keep it together. He sits there all stoic, waiting like a rock for it to begin. The clamps go on, the needle through and the ring set. Wow. I am semi impressed. He didn't even blink. He took it like it was nothing.

"Nope, that's it! Just the one for me!" he exclaims. He may not have made a noise, but little tears glisten in his eyes. I burst out laughing with the other guys.

Guess he didn't take it as well as I thought. He's just getting one, and why? So, he doesn't show he's in pain? Big bad men can't show weakness. I can't say I blame him, though, I mean seriously.

Garrett walks up to Johnny, looks him square in the eye, then flicks the ring. Johnny howls and shoves Garrett back but Garrett is laughing too hard to even care. Derrick all the while still holding back his smiles, staying professional. Well, Garrett is still laughing like a hyena, so before I can chicken out, I hop on the table. He marks it and makes sure I like it, then I crush my eyes shut. They're leaking tears already and nothing has even happened.

I feel my whole-body start shaking. I can't help it. I peek an eye open to see Derrick all the way across the room. The boys continue giggling and having a good time, but I see Johnny cast a look at me every so often.

He wanders over. "It's just an ear, you'll be alright," He encourages with a laugh.

I nod, yes, I can do this. My mind remains okay for all of three seconds, until Derrick starts walking over with the needle. Nope! Nope!

"I can't do this!" I blurt out as I make to get up. Johnny's firm hands pull my shoulders back down. He moves to stand in front of me, eyes staring directly into mine. Those eyes, so crisp. Glorious blue. My heart rate lowers, sinking into a comfortable rhythm again, his breathing matching mine. Until Derrick comes around to my side, needle in hand. My whole body automatically starts sweating. I'm not doing this. Johnny's hands remain on the sides of my arms, and I look back into his eyes. Those eyes. Heaven. He takes deep breaths in and out, as I match mine to his. Then I feel it! A gasp escapes me before my teeth grind together with all the force of a typhoon. My eyes instantly have tears flowing down them.

"Well, that wasn't so bad," Derrick prods and hands me a mirror.

"You did good kid," Johnny prompts with a pat to the shoulder and walks away. Kid. What was I thinking? Ugg getting lost in his eyes. I am so dumb.

Garrett happily walks up and sits on the table, grinning like a child. He sits barely moving as the clamps go on. I notice a slight twinge when the needle goes in, but other than that a minute tops and he has two twinkling nipples as well. Okay! I think it's high time to get out of here. Before the room starts spinning. Or worse, they want tattoos.

I can't believe we just did that. Granted an ear is much different. At least all I have to worry about is my hood and helmet, they will have to worry about SCBS straps, coats, suspenders and countless more things. Good luck boys.

CHAPTER 6

My days off go much too fast, and here I am back at the grind. Our day went by smoothly with only one call, a medical call at that. So, relatively low stress for what I do.

We're all going up to get out of our class B uniforms and into shorts and comfy shirts. Thank goodness, I'm so ready to be comfy. I live for the night shift portion. This is when I really love my job, not that I don't love it all the time, but this is the perfect time. Less people coming into the office, more bonding time with the guys, and usually if a call does come in, besides the frequent flyers, it is one of those high adrenaline calls. But really, I love when we drive the engine down to the bay, or play board games, or even just chill watching a movie while we wait. Having people around, people I vibe with, that is truly what makes life okay.

As I'm walking out of the room to go change, I notice Garrett's nipples look extremely red. I walk over and see they're swollen and seeping... Barf!

"Garrett, those don't look so good. Haven't you been cleaning them?" I ask concerned.

"Cleaning them. Nah," He murmurs nonchalantly but I notice him flinch as his shirt drags across them.

"Come on, Mr. Medic, even you should know better than that!" I say as I drag him to the bathroom.

I start the hot water running and grab a cloth, shaking my head in disbelief. Like really, he takes care of people for a living, but lets his own wounds get infected. That is messed up. Self-care first.

"Take your shirt off," I demand, blushing. "Or um, you could just pull it up," I amend. He laughs at me and skins it off. I'm sure my face turns redder than a ripe strawberry. Ugg why am I so awkward?

Wringing out the rag, my fingers tingle from how hot it feels. I know this is about to hurt a lot. I step up to Garrett, my face at chest height and press the compress to the affected area. He draws in a breath quickly but doesn't say anything. After I pull it away, I give a little squeeze, and a large amount of oozing greenish goo comes out making me gag. Wiping it away, I glance up at him and see an expressionless face. So much for the grinning child at the tattoo parlor.

After cleaning both, I rub some antibiotic ointment on them, best I can, spinning the ring through it. I'm sure that was torture for him, but he took it like a pro. I'm not the type of person to make fun of something, so I do it all in silence. Wordlessly, I put everything away and he leaves. I would make some sarcastic response of 'no thank you?', but I can tell his pride is a little wounded. May as well not poke the bear.

Heading up to the bunkroom, I change quickly and take a minute to just sit and be. Sometimes, the best thing to do is have nothing going on and just sit for a moment. I talk with God, get my headspace all clean, and go out to find the others. They have a card game going.

"Want to join?" Logan calls over.

"What are y'all playing?" I ask.

"Bullshit," he yells at Johnny. Okay, that answers that question.

"Nah, not this one, but anyone up for a round of spoons next?" I prompt. I freaking love spoons, and usually I can get people into it, or at least the wildland guys at my last bunkhouse loved it.

They all nod their agreement and go back to hollering profanities to each other.

My friends and I growing up used to play with cookies, for more incentive. I quickly learned my family could not play with cookies because they would be pulverized in seconds. Crumbs flying everywhere, chocolate mashed into everything, nope not happening.

They continue yelling until Garrett wins, I swiftly grab three spoons from the drawer. It would be much more fun with more people, but tonight I will settle for my crew. Logan shuffles expertly, bridging them, sliding them through his hands. Three spoons lay in the middle, eyes dart back and forth.

Then it begins! Logan picks up a card, passes it, it goes to Johnny, Johnny passes to Garrett, and then to me. This continues for a few minutes, then a hand flies to the spoons. I snatch one quick, and poor Logan is still looking at cards while Johnny grabs the last one.

"Bullshit!" Logan cries.

"Nope, this is spoons, nice try though!" Garrett laughs. Next round begins, one eye on the spoons, one on the cards as they fly past. Garrett grabs a spoon! No! My chair flies back as I jump up. I grab the spoon the same time Johnny's hand lands on it. I rip as hard as I can, and the spoon comes with me.

"Woah girl. You about ripped my hand off too," Johnny chortles with a laugh.

"Sorry. Well, not really. But sorry anyway." I retort back. I mean, I kind of feel bad because it is Johnny, but then again, I am merciless at spoons. No empathy or compassion aloud! Yes! Just Garrett and me. The cards start, then he whips the spoon away. He ends up getting four in the first few seconds, how is that fair?

Next round! Johnny goes out without even knowing what happened. One-minute spoons were there, the next we all had them. As the cards go round and round again, two spoons are left. Logan grabs one, and as Garrett's hand lands on the other, I dive across the table. My hands clasp for it. Somehow, it ends up in my hand, though I think it was more from him being in shock of me practically tackling him.

We play round after round, laughing and having a wonderful time, then the tones drop. Everyone instantly goes into professional mode. It's crazy how fast you can switch from funny laughing to serious alertness.

We scurry to pull up our bunker pants and boots, hop in the engine and away we go. Johnny sits in the officer seat tonight, so Garrett and I listen to dispatch as we prepare med supplies from our jump seats. As I'm an EMT, Garrett is the lead. However, this is a CPR call, so it's all hands-on deck.

I grab a pair of blue med gloves and the vitals chart. Noticing Garrett is already holding the O2 bag, I grab the med bag and the monitor. As soon as the engine rolls to a stop we are first out. Parting the red sea of people, I push forward with my heart rushing. Why do people always crowd around a victim even if they cannot help?

"Start compressions, I'm going to ready the Oxygen and BVM," Garrett informs me.

"One and Two and..." I count as Queen's "Another One Bites the Dust" plays in my head. Yea poor choice, but it's what always plays in my head. At thirty compressions, Garrett gives two breaths via BVM. As I continue pumping, he readies the mask. I'm still counting and on my third round.

"Get ready to switch Kara," Logan prompts from behind me. After my thirty I roll to the side and Logan jumps into position. *God, please let her make it. Help her Lord.* I pray over and over.

Johnny continues taking any stats he can, so I move to relieve Garrett. I grab the OPA baggie from the med kit and fit one to her face.

"Switch Garrett." I place a hand on his shoulder and move into place.

While Logan pumps, I fit the OPA into her mouth and lean my head down towards her mouth to listen for breath sounds. A choke! A gagging sound and before I can move my face, she throws up. It splatters into my hair. *Yuck!* No time though.

I swiftly remove the OPA and get the manual suction as Logan rolls her on her side. The ambulance arrived at some point a few seconds ago and they came rolling down with a stretcher. At least the patient is breathing again. Thank you, Lord.

We lift her onto the stretcher as Johnny continues taking vitals. When the Ambulance is loaded, he passes the sheet off to the Medic on board and that's it. It's the last we will see of her. Sometimes, that's the hardest part of this job, never knowing what happens next. At least this time, we have hope for her, or at least more than sometimes.

Ugg, my hair. I can't believe I let that happen. That was dumb Kara. Think! They always gag with OPAs, I may as well just start off with an NPA, but no, I have to be thorough. Ugg. I should have known better. I'm such an idiot. This is freaking embarrassing and it's my own stupidity that led to it.

I sit in silence on the ride back to the station. Luckily the guys know me well enough in this short time to not make a joke about this. I grab some of the wet wipes and just do a quick wipe down of my hair. I don't want it to drip onto my gear or anything. This is legit so gross. But hey, she was breathing. It's worth it. All part of the job, and tonight was a success.

As soon as we get back, I take a rapid shower. I know, one would think I would want to take like an hour-long shower, but I've been in the shower before when a call comes and having to go on a fire or car crash or even a medical rescue with suds in your hair is the absolute worst! Especially if I'm on a fire and the sweat mixes with the suds, yuck. So, my rapid shower will be it for now.

Luckily, I keep some of my favorite girl items in my locker, and tonight, I need a face mask! I deserve a little self-care. I reach for my tube of blue peel off mud mask and inhale deeply, it smells amazing! Smothering it all over my face, I finally feel a little fresh again. No more puke hair. I hope the poor lady doesn't remember that, no she shouldn't. But I will probably always remember it.

"Ahh! What the heck is that?" Johnny yells. "It looks like a freaking blue version of ghost face, or Pennywise or Jason or something."

Of course, he would say that as Stephen King's "It" is playing. I burst out laughing. Well, I am a horror fan, so I'll take those references.

"I should have tried to scare y'all!" I chortle.

That would have been hilarious, yet I'm one of the biggest scaredy cats ever. Not when it comes to movies, I love horror films, I live for them even, but when it comes to jump scares, I'm a coward. Haunted houses, I'm the one screaming and running into walls. So, yea, starting any sort of scare war is not a wise idea.

"Hey, that looks fun, can I try?" Garrett asks. Of course, Garrett would say that.

"A face mask?" I ask, although I already know the answer.

If Garrett weren't so much of a man whore, I would almost hedge to thinking he was gay. No straight man should care about his looks as much as he does.

"Yea, a face mask, it will go well with my new piercings. Come on boys, let's do a face mask." Grunts of displeasure go between the other two, but sure enough, we all head to the bathroom, face mask in hand.

I hand it over to Garrett. He looks at it for a second, looks at me, then back at the tube.

"So, what do I do with it?"

How can someone smart enough to give tons of drugs to people for a living, not be smart enough to do a face mask? I give a laugh and just take it from him.

"See, it comes out like this, and then you smear it on," I instruct as I show.

I rub a glob across his forehead and hand him the bottle. "Here, you do the rest."

He gives me a look but accepts it. Before long, he has it over his mustache, down part of his neck and on an ear.

"Okay, then. You look beautiful," I proclaim holding back tears of laughter.

"Johnny's turn," I announce turning on him.

"Nah, I'm good," he claims, eyeing Garrett.

"Oh, come on, if you can get your nipples pierced and run into a flaming building, then you can surely put on a little face mask." His eyes shoot daggers, but soon the expression softens, and he accepts the tube. A small streak across the cheeks and a small dot on the nose and he passes it to Logan. I snatch a glob and smear it across Johnny's chin, covering his mouth and all.

"Hey!" He protests, a little bit of his inner lip now blue. I hope it tastes as good as it smells.

After Logan finishes, I make them all take a selfie with me. This is just too good to not share on Instagram. I mean come on, fire guys all masculine, sitting with blue face masks on.

Sitting in a circle with them, it certainly feels like a little pow wow. Why are guys such gossips? And who knew a girls' night with the guys would be so fun? Questions after questions. I'm learning things my little innocent brain would never think of, but I guess it's kind of cool to see the inner workings of a man's brain.

"So, Kara, where is the craziest place you have ever had sex?" Logan asks me, wiggling his eyebrows. I feel my face grow hot. Or not!

"P- Pass" I stutter, clearing my throat.

Why does everything come back around to sex? Not like there aren't a thousand other things one can talk about. Though, I suppose half of their conversation was about that in some form. I mean seriously, I've learned way too much about these guys and will never be able to think about some things in a non-sexual form ever again. You know what, I might also never be able to look any of them in the eye again.

"No!! You surpassed your pass limit!" He rebuts.

"Tell! Tell!" A chorus of voices shout at me.

Okay, here we go. I'm not embarrassed about this. I am not embarrassed. I am a proud Christian woman:

"I am waiting until marriage," I proclaim boldly, surprising even myself.

"Whoa! So, you've like never had sex?" Garrett probes.

"Well, yea, that's kinda' the point," I retort.

"So, you're kind of a virgin," he shoots back.

Like duh. Oh, my goodness. Now I feel like I'm talking with a twelve-year-old boy instead of a thirty whatever year-old man. Okay maybe late twenties. Here I was thinking he was all hot when I sat on his knee and I legit have zero idea how old he is. At least I know Johnny is only two years older than me.

"Yea, Garrett, yep, that would make me a virgin." I nod, grateful this is no longer embarrassing for me. I'm more appalled at how dense Garrett seems sometimes.

"Wow," Logan intones. I just look at him, glaring as hard as I can.

I am really glad I'm waiting, and no one will ever change that.

"No really, I respect that, I can't even go for like two weeks," he admits.

Johnny chokes, then bursts out laughing. "Yea, the fire department can attest to that." Johnny chuckles.

Hmmm. Am I missing something?

Garrett joins in on the laughter. Part of me wants to know the secret, but I decide not to bring it up, hopefully we can move on. And move on we do. Talking about foods and travels, everything besides that topic.

After a while, I decide my facemask has been on long enough, it pulls a little every time I talk. Beginning at the chin, I start peeling up, and soon hold the replica face of blue.

"Cool, can we take ours off? Not that I didn't love it, I actually might buy myself a bottle," Johnny claims, but even I can hear the sarcasm lacing his comment. I just nod and they begin tugging and pulling.

"Aye!" Garrett yowls. Startled, I look over at him and see him tugging on the portion near his mustache.

I burst out laughing. Of course! You can't put it on hair, I always avoid the eyebrows, it just didn't occur to me to tell them. Laughing so hard, my belly starts to hurt. My abbs tighten and I gasp to catch my breath. No way!

"It's not funny Kara! Help!" Logan pleads while it's stuck in his own.

Turning the hot water on, I look over at Johnny. He ripped at it and stands holding a blue face with hairs stuck on it and wide eyes.

"Kara, if this ruined my mustache..." He doesn't finish but he's looking at his mask in remorse. Luckily, I can't tell all that much of a difference, at least his was a short one. Really, he didn't really have a mustache at all, just a few stray hairs. But I decide not to argue that point at the moment.

Besides, I like my guys clean shaven, but I don't need to let them know that.

Ignoring him, I turn to the other guys. "Wet it with some hot water, and it should wash out," I advise and then watch them scrub. Luckily, in a few minutes, theirs comes out just fine. Thank goodness. I did not need three angry men at me. I know just how particular my own brother can be about any of his hair. I don't need that kind of heat from my fire brothers too.

CHAPTER 7

Days off always create a tough decision. Do I want to just stay in bed all day and watch Harry Potter, or do I want to get up and do something? The latter succeeds today. I decide since I moved all the way out here to Oregon, perhaps I should actually see what my new state has to offer me. Aside from where Johnny took me, I really haven't visited many places.

Starting off, I walk down to the ocean. Standing there, letting the wind rip through my hair and the waves lap over my feet, I feel peace. No thoughts flying through my brain, anxiety gone. Bliss. My feet sink deeper and deeper into the sand with each wave. I don't move until I feel nothing but peace, no stress, no worries, calm. Granted, by the time I do move, I'm sunk into my calves and my feet are numb, but I will take what I can get.

Walking back to my house, I start wondering, what comes next? Not just today, but in life. I have a solid job now, so where does life go from here? Am I supposed to get married and have three kids, or what if I'm never supposed to get married? Do I have a next step then? Or what if I'm in the wrong place completely? Nah, I feel like this is where I'm meant to be, it just feels right. But seriously, could God have a guy in store for me? Sometimes it feels like I'm forever meant to be alone. No guy could ever love someone as messed up as me. Nope, I am not going down that road, I just found my peace, lets focus on today. Today, I think I want a mountain.

Not wanting to drive all the way to Mount Hood, or the sisters or anywhere far, I settle on Mary's Peak. It's the closest mountain to here. Luckily, the road the fire department is on will take me all the way there.

Driving the curvy road my eyes skim the Alsea River. It twists and turns along with the road. Once it gets warmer, I'm definitely going to float that! One of my favorite things back home is floating the Blanchard River, and maybe a day on the river will help me not miss home as much, a little connection.

Finally, I start the winding drive up to the top. It's always funny out here on the coast, but in a lot of places out west too. People just camp along the road! On 101 there are always cars parked along the sides. National forests too! Granted, I myself have just parked in a national forest to camp, but they offer real dispersed camping too that's actually legal in designated areas. I mean how stinking cool is that?

My car finally breaks through the treeline, and I pull into the parking lot. I clamber out and walk to the edge. WOW! Just the view from here is stunning. I could just sit here all day and sketch or read a book, but I came to climb a mountain. I grab my pack and load my Nalgene's in it. Granted, it's a short hike, but I will want a snack at the top, plus I have my journal so I can just chill, and a small med kit just in case.

Deciding to take the longer, scenic route, I wind through trees. For a while, I'm even in a burn scar. It's crazy to see so many dead, standing trees, yet so much greenery on the ground. I love how after such a traumatic event, nature just thrives and come back stronger. I try to learn from nature. I bet this place is just absolutely gorgeous in the late spring, but today I will just take the fact that the rain stopped, for now. There's sunshine and for the moment, the view is clear.

Look at that view! My brain is instantly in awe from the breathtaking view. Thank you, Lord, for a clear day! Oh, my goodness, I can see for miles! Scanning the distance, I can see different peaks touching the sky. I know that one is Mount Saint Helens to the North, so the one standing faintly behind it should be Rainier. Adams is over there too, and I see Jefferson and the three Sisters with their distinct points, so that last one should be Bachelor.

Ticking them off one by one as I do the run down in my head. One day, I would love to hike them all. Goals. I love my hiker-trash self. I really am a dirtbag at heart. Always living for the next adventure, the next chance to sleep on the ground. I thrive. Mountains are my freedom rocks. When I'm on top of one, it is like nothing will ever hurt me or mess with me. I'm a badass up there and I feel like one too. They're all just so beautiful. As the wind whips around me, it steals all my dark thoughts and wraps me in a hug.

Plopping down on a rock, I pull out my journal. Filling pages describing my life so far out here, telling of the beauty, the homesickness, the brotherhood, and more. Who knows how long I write, but I keep staring off into those glorious miles and miles of earth before me. Slowly the sky starts to get greyer letting me know that I should head back down before the rain comes.

As I get back in my car, I ponder what should I do? I kind of wish Johnny was around this weekend. Or any of them! You know, not just Johnny. It's not like he would even want to hang with me on a weekend without them. Well, I mean there was that one weekend, but it was probably just to get out of the firehouse. Besides, as much as I would love to think he would want to spend time with me, I know the truth. I think I'll head to the ocean. I can't ever decide if ocean or mountains are my favorite. Well, it depends on which mountains because let's be honest, oceans beat the Appalachians hands down, but the Cascades out here, ooo that's a close one.

Finally, I make it back to Waldport. I can't believe how long it took since the rain has been coming down for a while now. I'm starving and I know just the place I want! I pull up to the Chubby's food cart and order a big chub. Yup, that's it, Johnny ruined me, and I now have a huge addiction. Thanks Johnny. Gosh darn it!

I think around each glorious bite of burger, fries and cheese.

After I get my burger fill, I decide I need to work it off some way, so the beach it is. After parking in my driveway, I meander through the woods until I hit the beach. Kicking off my shoes, I race to the waves. This is freedom. I always feel so at peace out here. The rain soaking me from the top as the waves saturate my pants. I fling my arms out and look to the heavens.

"Whhhoooahhh!" I scream. I love this rush. It might be freezing, but the waves always take my stress away. Is there anything better than the ocean? I just feel so free, so alive. The shock of the cold water melts all thoughts away. Perfection.

***

Today is going to be a long day. Ugg why did I volunteer myself for this?

Lily and I are heading down to the Oregon Dunes together to talk about wildfires. Well, she will be talking. I've been volunteered to be Smokey. Why on earth would anyone want to meet a five-foot tall Smokey the bear? Smokey is supposed to be a tall bear, like six feet, but oh well. They had no one else to play him today and I have a hard time saying no. Think of the kids, I'm here for them, I tell myself repeatedly.

I find the ride down interesting. It's the first time I'm really getting to talk with Lily. She's undoubtedly a very chatty lady. I'm guessing she's late thirties and just started with Mid Oregon Fire about a year ago. Apparently, I'm taking her spot-on shift. She switched shifts about a month ago.

"So why did they switch your shift?" I question. I hate the idea of switching shifts. I really love my guys. She gives a snorted laugh.

"I'm surprised working with him that you haven't heard yet." She pauses waiting to see if I know the answer.

I shake my head. Him? Which one? There are obviously three men I've been working with.

"Chief caught me sleeping with Logan," she reveals nonchalantly.

I gasp. "What?" I sputter. "How did he catch you, like really? Not like he shows up to our houses. Logan really... wow."

My tries to wrap around the idea, two of my co-workers sleeping together. I thought that only happened in movies! Logan? Oh, my goodness.

"Dude, he caught us at the fire department," she reiterates like I'm an idiot.

"Wait! At the fire department? Like in our bunks? How? Wasn't there anyone else on shift with you?" I shoot out.

I mean seriously! At work, plus like ew, we share beds with different shifts. What if she has the same bed as me? Okay, I know I have my own sheets, but like it kind of disturbs me. There are always at least three people on shift too, so I don't understand. What if someone walked in? Well, I mean, I guess someone did.

"Yea, well, we've kind of done it everywhere. You know how it goes. The fire engine, the ambulance, the office, the bunks, wherever." She laughs out.

What? Good golly! I'm mind blown again. This actually happens? "Wow... um that's a lot of sex. How long have you been going out?" I am fairly sure I saw a wedding ring on his finger at some point. Like 100% positive he has a family.

She snorts. "Girl, what fairy tale are you living in? I'm just banging him; he has a wife. And we've been banging for over a year," She declares almost proudly.

Married! My forehead scrunches with disbelief. What a scandal! Speechless, I fan myself. Wow. So, Logan and Lily, at the fire department, a lot, and the chief caught them! I feel like I'm on a prank show. Does this happen at a lot of workplaces? Like really! Welp, I guess that solves it, my life is officially a movie.

The trip passes rather quickly after that. Between her jabbering and my brain whirling, it feels like we're there instantly. Dragging the large Smokey suitcase with me, we disappear into the back of the engine. We had to bring our spare engine today, luckily Lily drove. I hate driving a normal car, the engine really stresses me out.

As I struggle into the costume, I find pulling up the sagging legs to be the hardest part. This Smokey is certainly stubby legged today. She zips up my back and sets the head on. Wow, you cannot see anything in this thing. Well, if I peer out the mouth, I can at least see my feet. Stuffy is about the only word I can use to describe how I feel right now.

She takes my arm as we head down the steps. I have to do high knees with every step to try to get the huge feet to move. You know, I'm really worried one of the feet might fall off, my feet are way too tiny for them, and I'm even wearing boots. The toe catches and I lurch toward the ground. Flying forward, she catches me in the nick of time. Jeez!

Scuffing the titanic feet along the sand, we walk campsite to campsite. Kids yelling and hugging my legs, parents getting pictures with me, and me sweating my butt off. I can't even wipe it from my face as it runs into my eyes. My eyes sting and I blink rapidly. At least she guides me everywhere, not like I need to see anyway. People everywhere offer Smokey a shot, a beer, alcohol of every sort. Like really people. All these Dune riders would fit in great back home, that's for sure.

Lily stands a few feet away talking to a few kids when suddenly my feet are lifted off the ground in a jolt. I try moving my head, but all I can tell is the fact that someone is carrying me like a bride or something. Rapidly, I smack the back of my assailant. Should I talk, I'm not supposed to talk as Smokey. My heart racing, what do I do? If he carries me much farther, I'm going to shout if needed. I'll scream! Is this a kidnapping? I smack around trying to get the criminal to put me down.

"Look, I caught myself a cute, little Smokey bear!" I hear a guy holler in a gruff voice. Well, he's probably just some drunk dude from the slur of his voice.

"Sir! Sir, I need you to put Smokey down!" Lily shouts, sounding like she's a bit of a ways off. Laughing he reaches a group of men. Through the mouth hole, I can only tell that they appear to look like young men, maybe like mid-twenties. Weight drops as I'm passed to another guy.

"We sure this isn't Smokey's girlfriend or something." Someone hoots. I squirm and manage to break out of his arms. Unfortunately, this lands me right on my butt. Thankfully, Smokey certainly has enough padding that it doesn't hurt.

I feel an arm help me up and turn my whole body to the person. I breathe a sigh of relief at the sight of Lily, thank goodness. She grabs my arm; says a quick goodbye and we walk away. Someone whistles a catcall.

"Hey, little darlin, when you get out of the bear, come back and see us!" One of them calls. Ugg, drunk people.

Lily leads me away, and luckily the rest of the day passes without further incidents. I actually really enjoy Lily's company. She just has a super quirky personality. A little gruff, but so bubbly too. Plus, it's nice to finally hang out with another girl. I could get used to this.

CHAPTER 8

Parking my bike along the outside of the firehouse, I walk in as normal. No one sits at the window this morning, interesting. When, shift starts, someone is always supposed to be there unless we're on a call, but even then, usually a volunteer comes down to cover it.

I round the corner and Johnny jumps out at me. Startled, a yelp escapes me, and my feet leave the ground. He starts laughing.

"You do startle easily." He chuckles. "Wait till you see this!"

He exclaims and whips out a huge syringe. My breath quickens on sight but then he jabs it at me, and a scream rips from my throat. He lunges and I fall flat on my back. Dying with laughter, he hunches over.

"Har-Har, very funny." I glare at him.

He throws his arm around me all the while still cackling. Ugg.

"Well thanks for the splendid time, but I'm going to go check my email," I grumble sweeping out of the room. I just need a little time to myself now. I can't believe I reacted like that.

My heart still pounds out of my chest, and I continue gasping for breath. I don't want this to trigger an anxiety attack or anything. I wonder what Johnny is scared of. I sit down at the desk and login. The great thing about sitting here, I can see the dispatch screen, the ocean, and the forest all from one chair. My heart rate returns to normal, and I breathe out a sigh. I know he was just having fun, and I will get him back, but that was way too uncalled for.

If I can remember right, I think he said something about not liking wildland because of the cardio and you never know when a spider might crawl in your mouth. I'm sure we have lots of spiders hanging out here to test that theory.

The fire background pops up and I scroll over to email. Seeing that I have quite a few new ones, I scroll through. A lot of them are junk mail, or my mom. Then, I see one from Mr. Marshan. Interesting. I only met the man once, but he was an FFA teacher at my high school back home. I had been chapter president back in my day, and the following year I came back to meet the new advisor. He seemed like a nice man, but it had been a while since I last talked to him. I click on the email and read.

Dear Kara:

I see that you have moved out here to the beautiful PNW. I am not sure if you know this, but I myself moved out to Washington about three years ago. I live up near North Cascades, and if you ever need anything, I am a lot closer drive than home.

I'm writing to see if you might be interested in a hiking permit up Mount Saint Helens. It's for August 15. A group of friends and I were planning to summit that day, but I am now, unfortunately, booked. That being said, would you want it free of charge? It would be a great trip and I am sure you would love it.

If you would be interested, shoot me an email back and I can work on changing out the name. I would just be glad it is going to good use. Keep living it up over there in the south state!

-Jack Marshan

Wow. First of all, I had no idea he moved out here, but that's so kind of him to reach out. And a freaking free hiking permit! Yes, please! I mean those things you need to sign up for like a year in advance and pay money. That's coming up so soon though! I mean my parents are coming out to visit in a week and then the hiking permit is only a week after that. Woohoo. I'm about to have a rocking month.

Looking at the schedule, I won't even have to trade shifts with anyone that day and it's only like a four-hour drive. I could drive up the day before and hike it then drive back that night. Piece of cake! I shoot him back an email about my interest and I'm practically shaking with excitement.

I almost forgot! The spiders! I start searching the corners, floors and ceilings. I find a few tiny ones and lots of webs. Then I see it. Not huge, nothing like the basement spiders at home, or tarantulas in Texas, but it will do. I sneak over to the little guy, and snatch! I hold about a quarter sized spider. I feel him crawling around between my cupped hands, and hurry to make my move. I find Johnny still over by the engines doing inventory. Not saying a word, I sneak up behind him.

"Spider!" I shout. He whips around and I toss the spider at him, it lands on his shirt and scurries around.

"Kara!" he screams in the highest pitched yelp ever, as his back smashes into the engines while he tries to escape it. Now it's my turn, I start laughing hysterically.

"Some big hero," I joke. He shakes himself down and squashes the poor little guy. Well, I feel positively bad I caused its death, but it's still kind of funny.

"Well, at least I'm not an EMT who's scared of needles," he retorts like a child.

"Hey, I have no problem as long as it is someone else," I claim defensively.

Really, I have come a huge way since EMT school. Before then, I would pass out just seeing someone else get stabbed. Now, I can deal with it for a job. Granted as an EMT, it's very rare I ever get to physically use one. However, I do unwrap them all the time for the medics and put them in the Sharps container and such. Five years ago, that would have never happened!

Not saying anything else, he goes back to work, I can still see the pink embarrassment along his neck. That is golden. Crossing the bay, I find Garrett and Logan with some paint.

"We finally painting lines today?" I ask.

"Yup, got it all power washed and ready. We could really use someone to go down on their knees to paint." Logan says.

A laugh burbles from my mouth. "Yea, I'm sure you do," I shoot back. Nonetheless, I take off my class B, and get ready to paint. We're just painting the parking lines so with three people it should go rather quickly.

And quickly it does. I paint, while Logan moves the stabilization board and then Garrett comes behind us to sprinkle glass pebbles on it to shine. We finish in no time, and it even looks great. We need a little fun around here. All work and no play makes Kara a dull girl.

Dipping my finger in the yellow paint, I run at Garrett and smear it across his arm. He wipes it off quick and mashes it into my face. I scream and dodge. Grabbing another finger full, I go to aim at Logan, to find he already has a smear in his hair courtesy of Garrett. We yell and run around painting each other, though being respectful to not get it on anyone's clothes.

"Hey! Get back to work!" Johnny yells, but you can tell he is only half serious. If it is not on a call, these guys are the goofiest goobers ever.

But when someone's life is on the line, or someone needs our help, it's all seriousness, and I love that. I walk over to Johnny.

"Sorry Lieutenant." I say acting like a scolded child. My hand springs out and paint slides across his nose.

"Oh, you are just asking for it today!" he yells running after me. He grabs me from behind and rubs his face all over the back of my hair all the while with me screaming. A laugh escapes me as pure joy rumbles through my body.

Woah... he's holding me from behind. Like way intimate. I suddenly become aware of every inch of our bodies melting together. My body tenses and then realizing that, his arms release. My body shivers and a small sign escapes my lips. Well, I sure ruined that moment. Great job Kara. Way to make things weird.

Clearing his throat he prompts, "Back to work." And walks out. After he leaves the room, Garrett and Logan start laughing together, snickering and hooting.

"Shut up." I say, but my smile feels tight.

Johnny was just lost in the moment, right? All part of the game. No way he would like someone like me. No, he could get tons of different girls. Don't get your hopes up Kara. Ever. But... A smile slides across my face and I try to hide it best I can. No. Kara. I cannot catch feelings for my commanding officer. Stop it. Besides, he doesn't like me, won't ever like me. I'm being childish. This isn't high school, I can't just go around teasing the guys and thinking they might like me, they don't. Let it go.

The rest of the day flies by. We went from call to call, and all awkwardness dropped the instant the tones did.

First a van fire. One of those old VW vans, some hippie couple lived in. I feel bad for them, their whole life was that van. You know, I finally had the guts to strip my pants off before jumping in my bunker pants. Oh my gosh! I totally get it now! I have way less swamp ass! Plus like the movement is freeing. So much less constraints. I can actually do lunges without feeling like I'm going to rip my pants. I love it!

Then we jump to a medical call, followed by a broken arm on the playground. Poor kid. He's only like five and his arm appeared to be in bad shape. All I could do was stabilize it and put it in a sling and swath till the kid got to the hospital. The mom opted to take him, which is fine, cheaper for them, but still. It's been one thing after another.

We sit in the engine heading back to the station and I think every single one of us is praying we don't get another call all night, at least for the hour. As we get our gear in order, I realize I still have ice cream in the freezer. Thank goodness! My mind simmers on the idea of ice cream while finishing my tasks.

"Oh, that looks good. Could I have some?" Logan asks as I grab a spoon.

"Well, you could..." I begin, laughing seeing his crestfallen face. "But yes, you may." I mean come on, he had to have known that was coming, he's a dad for heaven's sakes, and that's a hard-core dad joke. As it turns out, all of us end up eating ice cream. Yas, another girls' night at the firehouse.

"Hey, look, Hereditary is on Netflix!" Garrett exclaims.

Before, waiting to see anyone else's response, he clicks on it. I guess we're watching a scary movie. This calls for hot tea. I always love hot tea and movies, and it gives you something warm to hold onto during a scary one.

As my tea warms, the guys jabber about everything and nothing at the same time. My heart swells. I might have only been here for a little over a month, but these are my guys. My little family. The tea dings, I pour some honey in it and wander back over. Everyone goes quiet as the movie begins.

Throughout the movie, my hands remain in a constant state of clenching, my teeth are clamped shut, and eyes glued to the screen. No one has uttered a sound. The movie has every ounce of our attention. I don't think I have taken a breath the entire movie.

Bang! The door flies open. Before I even know what happened my mug is launched from my hand and hits the body that just walked in the door. A scream comes out of my mouth like a banshee.

"Woah, woah! Not cool!" a voice shouts. The body walks into the room and my eyes widen as they land on Titus!

"Oh, Titus, I'm so sorry!" I exclaim taking in his shirt with a wet mark down it. I hope the mug didn't hurt too bad. The mug, shoot.

I look across the room to the floor, well at least it didn't break. The guys continue laughing at what just went down. Well, at least I know if nothing else, I supply a source of entertainment for the department. But seriously, I could die from embarrassment right now. So much for the "I love horror movies and they don't scare me" fact. I've never had someone burst into the freaking room like that before either!

"What on earth did you think I was?" he asks taking in the scary movie.

"Uh, well, I'm not sure I was thinking at all actually," I admit, and truly, I wasn't. Even if he was a big scary monster, it's not like a cup of tea would have done much good.

We all laugh. The mood remaining light and fun for the rest of the night.

CHAPTER 9

Luckily, today went much smoother than yesterday, no needles, no scary movies, and no calls. The white cloud seems to be back at it. We clean engines, go to the gym, get some Chubby's, a typical day at the fire department. With the work done, we all lounge around and talk.

"Any big plans for your days off?" Garrett inquires.

"Well, I am actually supposed to have a date tomorrow," I inform him. His eyes spark up, and the other two guys turn their heads to join the conversation.

"A date, huh?" Logan asks.

"Yea, it's no big deal," I mumble, though, to me, it is kind of a big deal.

I've never really been on a proper date before. Well, school dances in high school definitely don't count for me. That guy never even opened a door for me, or even got the nerve to dance with me. I kind of think he went with me out of pity.

High school relationships are so dumb. People just say, *Ooo we're dating*, when in reality, you're still friends, he doesn't buy your food, and you have never once held hands, but yes, we're dating. Dumb. I only ever had one date to anything in high school, and it didn't end well. We *dated* for like two months, then boom, he turns around and dates one of my best friends. Yea, I didn't take it too well. Not like he ever took me to dinner, or a movie or anything. We just talked on the phone every night. Oh well, not like they lasted anyway, and I'm doing fantastic nowadays, but let's just say I've never really been one of those desperate girls who jump from man to man. I do perfectly fine on my own. Not that I could get man after man even if I wanted to. But I've learned to be quite content with the old hag life.

This guy, on the other hand, looks gorgeous. Okay, I've never met him in person, but we've been talking on Tinder for like two weeks, so that counts for something right? And he's been so sweet and just seems amazing.

"Who is he? Anyone we know? How did you meet him?" Garrett asks. I can't help but notice, Johnny hasn't said anything, perhaps giving me confirmation, he really doesn't care. My heart breaks a little, but he was never mine anyway.

"Um, his name is Kyle. I met him on Tinder."

Ugg, is that lame? No one actually expects to get a real date off Tinder, do they? I mean can I really find a Hallmark romance like that? Probably not. I'm totally being naive, aren't I? Well, one can hope right?

"Well, tell us more! I never would have pictured you as the Tinder type," Logan claims with a grin. Nope! Wouldn't want to give off that idea!

"No, no! I'm looking for a real date. I haven't really ever been on a date. But this guy is nice, and cute and he's in the Coast Guard! He kind of seems perfect. I'm so nervous though. I mean how are you supposed to greet someone you've only ever talked to online? Am I supposed to shake his hand, or is that awkward? Like that seems official right?" I spew it all out.

Logan bursts out laughing. "Kara, you can't shake his hand! You're supposed to go hug him or something, you know, be all flirty and cute," He encourages with a wink.

"Nope! I don't really do hugs and I don't flirt. I don't know how to flirt." He gives me a look like he's trying to convey that he knows different. What does he know about me? Before he can say anything else, Garrett says something to Johnny that I don't quite catch. Johnny launches at him and starts tickling him. Yes, tickling! Grown men tickling each other, what the heck!

"Stop! Stop, I'm going to fart!" Garrett hollers through his laughter. Not a second later, he rips the loudest, longest, juiciest fart ever. Even I start laughing. Oh, my goodness, how did we get here? Boys!

It turns into a full-on fun fest, we throw around a ball, shoot insults at each other and joke on and on. Eventually, we get some grapes out of the fridge and find ourselves sitting around the table again. I start throwing them into Johnny's mouth and he catches almost every single one.

"Your turn!" he announces. Before I can say anything, he throws one at my face and it bounces off my nose. Laughter. The next one I manage to catch and eat. Ew green grapes. The purple ones definitely taste better!

He launches a few more, some catching, some rolling away. The next one, he zings right at my mouth, except it goes right through my mouth. It catches in my throat. I cough once, gag and before I can do anything, it projectiles, along with other contents of my stomach right across the table.

My hands fly to my mouth. Ew! Oh, my goodness, I'm so embarrassed! Kill me now.

The guys begin howling and banging the table. Ugg why does this stuff happen to me.

As they all hoot with laughter, I get a cloth to wipe it up. At least none of the Chubby's came back up. No one made fun of me either, just laughed, so really, it's not all that bad. I can't blame them either, I mean come on, that was funny. How does that even happen? I guess I just have the best luck around, don't I? Shaking my head, I heave a sigh. Shame ripples through me at my own annoying, embarrassing, awkward self. Why do these things happen to me?

Kyle has been texting me all morning and I can't be more excited. He's actually driving down here from Astoria. How cool is that? I'm currently at work straightening my hair. Makeup is on point and my outfit is decent. For me, I think I'm looking pretty fly.

I hear a ping and check my phone. It's a message from Kyle. OOO, he should be here in like fifteen minutes. I open the message and have to read it twice. *Sorry, I don't think you would have been the right chick for me. I'm not coming.*

That's it? He's cancelling now? With one stupid, dumb sentence? Two I guess, but that's the lamest text ever. Why would he text me all morning and cancel now? How rude! Ugg. That's so unfair! I can't help it.

The tears start flowing. What did I do wrong? I mean I was even trying to look really pretty. I guess maybe I can never be a pretty girl, or maybe it's just my whole being that drives guys away. I sit there sobbing for a few minutes. I don't even bother texting him back. I just delete my Tinder account once and for all. I grab the closest sock and wipe the snot from my nose.

Trudging over to my movies, I pick out *'You've Got Mail'*, one of my favorites. Not even bothering to change, I crawl in my bed, dress and all, with my laptop beside me. The movie starts playing and I launch into the world of Meg Ryan and Tom Hanks.

By the time he finds out she's the girl he's been messaging, I'm already feeling a little better. My eyes have at least stopped leaking and I can breathe right again. I uncurl my body and lay there thinking. Really, what is the big deal? So, what if he didn't want to go out with me. I'm not desperate. So, what if he's the only guy who has like ever shown any interest in me, not a big deal. I'm fine.

Meg Ryan is lying in bed sick when I hear my phone go off. Well, I know it can't be Kyle, because I don't have the app anymore. It's from Johnny, asking how my date is going. Tears almost spring to my eyes and my heart squeezes.

Well, that's sweet of him to ask. A smile creeps across my face. No Kara. No hopes, remember? I text back, "He cancelled."

All of a sudden, my phone rings, it's Johnny. "Hey, that guy was a douche and doesn't know what he's missing out on," he insists. "How are you?"

"I'm fine," I mumble. Less is better, I would hate to start crying again.

"Uh, dude, I have a sister, I know fine is not a positive connotation word. What are you doing right now?" He asks. Okay... maybe some guys can be perceptive.

"Lying in bed watching a rom com."

"Nooooo! Come out with us! We will cheer you up!" He shouts.

"Aren't you in Portland?" I really am not going to drive three hours tonight just to have a little company. Even if the company is super cute and sweet.

"Nope, I'm crashing at Logan's. We're actually at the Flounder right now," he says.

Oh, the Flounder is doable, I can even bike there. Well, I could stay here and continue to feel sorry for myself while Meg Ryan meets her soul mate, or I could go see my friends. "I'll be right down!"

Okay, for once in my life, I need to choose to hang out with people or I know I will spend the rest of the night in bed, which will lead to crying. So, yea, I need to get out now. Running to the bathroom, I wipe away the running tears, and consider myself good to go. Somehow, my hair still looks great, and I would say I'm presentable. Luckily for me, it's like I planned ahead by not changing out of my dress, so I'll just go in it. I love this dress anyhow; it's a beautiful yellow dress and I adore it. Plus, it hugs my curves, and shows off my butt. Not that I'm super proud of it or anything, but hey all those squats definitely help in some areas.

Slugging my raincoat on, I head out the door. I pedal as fast as I can with my hood cinched tight, managing to reach the flounder before I completely look like a mess. I'm barely a foot inside the door and catcalls start from across the room. Startled, I glance up to see Logan and Johnny leaning out from the pool area. My face fills with heat, but a smile slides across my face. Those goobers. I sling my raincoat up onto a hanger and make my way over to them.

Johnny immediately wraps me in a hug making me want to melt into him. "Dude, I'm sorry about that douche bag. Don't give him a second thought."

You know what, getting a hug from Johnny, I doubt Kyle will cross my mind much at all tonight. I smack myself mentally for thinking that, ugg.

"It's all good. Thanks though," I mumble. I really don't think I'm too bad, at least I had friends to hang out with tonight. That's sure a nice change. I've never really had friends who you can just call in an instant. I like it, I could get used to this. It makes me feel kind of warm and fuzzy knowing they have my back. We play a few rounds of pool, they kick my butt every round, but it's fun, nonetheless.

"Hey, why don't you go pick a few songs out on the jukebox?" Johnny suggests holding out a couple of dollars for me.

Normally I would just pay for it out of my pocket and politely decline, but tonight I'm feeling bold. Okay, I'm more feeling the fact that he's being sweet but also makes a ton more money than me. But I'll accept his kindness, it at least makes my broken little heart beat a little faster. I bounce over and take the money. Plus, like, for one night I want to pretend that a guy can be nice to me, can like me. You know? Like just for the night, I want to believe I'm someone who can be loved, admired. Someone who a guy would buy songs on the Jukebox for.

Scrolling through the jukebox, I settle on some of my favorites. I really don't care what the bar is going to think of them at all. Shania Twain's *'I Feel Like A Woman'* comes blasting into the bar. Logan and Johnny look up at it and then strike a diva pose. Laughter bursts from me. Oh, these guys. It seems they like the song just as much as I do, and they prove it by screaming the entire song's lyrics making me smile.

After that one finishes, Hall and Oates 'You Make My Dreams Come True' starts up. A classic. I love this song. My shoulders start moving with the beat as I can't contain myself.

"Let's go dance," Johnny prompts, holding his hand out to me.

Like I said, I am feeling bold tonight, so I clasp his hand and practically drag him over to the dance floor. Not that the dance floor is anything spectacular here, but this twenty feet of floor is good enough for me. We do a bit of a swing dance, which actually goes amazing with the song. I follow his cues through twists, turns, swings and breathless fun the entire song. Somehow, the smile stays contained to my face, but really, I could not be any happier.

"I'm really glad you came," he murmurs into my ear.

The heat creeps up my neck again. I smile, but my whole body seems to be making a fist. Waiting, ready for the next punch. The next thing to go wrong.

As soon as the song ends, I break away. Don't get me wrong, I had a good time, but my breath is starting to come faster, and I'm semi shaking. I have no idea why.

I think I just did too much bold stuff too fast. Or maybe it's fear of Johnny actually liking me. I mean what if he did like me? I kind of like him right, so what's the big deal? Except now if he likes me then it would make it real, and then I might have to like to act on it or something. Or what if one of these days he tries to kiss me, or even worse, what if we would start dating? What if we dated for years and then broke up but I still had to work with him? Or what if he thinks I'm a girl like Lily? What if he wants that? Or what would be worse? What if I'm the type of girl a guy could never love? What if I'm destined to be alone forever? A thousand what ifs fly through my head as I make my way over to the bar. I need a distraction. Taking deep breaths, I head to the bar.

"Can I please have a sweet tea?" I ask the bartender trying to keep my voice normal.

"We don't have sweet tea, only iced tea," he replies.

"That's fine as long as y'all have Splenda or something," I state. Ugg, stupid West Coast not having proper sweet tea. I just want something to lift my spirits, some sort of comfort drink. Breathing deep, I work to keep composure. He passes me a normal tea and I dump three Splenda in it. Good enough. Better. Sipping my tea, I wander back over to the guys.

The rest of the night my brain remains preoccupied with thoughts of romance. I've never been a boy crazy girl, and honestly, I've always been too focused on my career to even give any guy a second thought. But now I'm out here, I have a steady job, I could fall in love. Right?

However, if I do find a guy, what if I get stuck out here. Do I really want to be tied to Oregon, more specifically the Waldport area? Though I suppose he does commute from Portland, but I don't really want to live there either. What about my family back home? Or more importantly, what about all the adventures I wanted to have when I decided to move across the country?

After a while, I excuse myself, my brain becoming too stressful. It's getting late anyway, and I didn't want to end up stuck as a babysitter for two drunk firefighters. Biking home, the rain seems a bit more bitter tonight, no longer the beautiful drops of happiness. Tonight, it seems to match more of my own tears and that just makes me hate it all the more.

CHAPTER 10

I'm so stoked to finally have mom and dad here visiting! This week has been a total Godsend. After that night with Johnny at the bar, my brain just won't shut off. Could he like me? Could any guy ever like me? Do I like him? Maybe I should lose weight. How am I even supposed to act if I like someone? Or what if I'm totally messing things up as always?

Then at our next shift, Logan was being all weird, but Johnny seemed totally normal. I think I'm reading too much into things. He doesn't like me, we're just friends, well more like he's just my Lieutenant. Things are normal. Nothing is awkward. Normal.

Stepping away for some travels with my parents was exactly what I needed. Getting my mind off boys and back onto adventure, and why I moved out here in the first place. It does make me really miss home though. Them telling me about the hot sun, the corn, and all the lake adventures makes my heart ache. I want to give living out here more time though before I decide I miss home too much.

So far on our adventures, we've hit all Oregon has to offer. We camped at Cape Perpetua and hiked Mary's peak. Walked to the Giant Spruce, the tide pools, and the waterfalls around the Siuslaw. We've had many beach bonfires across from my house. The pie irons the best part. I love pie irons; they always take me back to camping trips as a kid. Nothing's better than sitting around a fire cooking your sandwich in a little square pan. Nowadays, we even get hard core gourmet with them. Pizza pie irons with sauce, cheese, peperoni, and garlic. But the dessert ones are to die for! Mmm, bananas, peanut butter, chocolate, is there anything better? No way! Plus, driftwood fires look amazing. I love the colors of them, the greens and blues. Beautiful.

A few days ago, we hit up every lighthouse we could. The sights glorious, we found like six of them along the coast and we stopped at every single one. Yesterday, we did some hiking around Crater Lake and climbed up Garfield peak. So much snow still remained on the ground! It was absolutely beautiful, even if a little sketchy on the hikes. None of us had thought we might need crampons or snowshoes, and we made it without them, but they sure would have helped.

I can't believe it's summer and there's still so much snow there. I mean sure if it's like a 14,000-foot mountain but this is Crater Lake! After the hike we made the long drive up to Mount Hood. By the time we got there, it was dark, so under the light of our headlamps, we pitched a tent and went to bed.

In the morning, however, we got to wake up to the absolute most amazing view. We're at Lost Lake, looking up at Mount Hood, and she's a beauty. My family firmly believes in waking up super early to get on the trails before anyone else.

We're about halfway around the lake before the colors of the sky even start to really pop. When they do though, oh it's just stunning. Mount Hood standing in front of us, the colors reflecting off the lake's surface, this is what I am here for.

After we finish our little hike, millions of mosquito bites later, we all pile into the car and head to Timberline lodge. This is someplace I have wanted to go ever since I was a kid! *The Shining!* It's been my favourite movie since third grade. As an adult, it's not really scary anymore, but as a kid, ooo boy, it was a huge thrill.

The beginning scene was filmed on Going-to-the-Sun-Road, and I have been there quite a few times. Two years ago, a friend and I traveled out in Colorado, and we snuck into the Stanley, the hotel used in the movie. That sounds bad, but you had to pay money for a tour or big bucks for a night there and let's be honest, I'm not rich enough to stay there. So, we snuck in. It was fabulous. Unfortunately, they have changed the carpet since the movie, but I still loved it. We felt like such rebels. But now, I'm finally going to get to see where they filmed the outside.

"Red Rum, Red Rum!" my dad croaks out as we wind through the trees up to the lodge. Suddenly it looms before us and a grin pins across my face. Lots of skiers and boarders mill about as we walk up to the lodge. It's funny how they filmed the outside at a different place from the inside, but really, they couldn't have chosen a more beautiful setting. Besides, in the winter, I can totally see how this could be a place for a horror movie. But now, it's beautiful. We can walk around, but there's still quite a bit of snow around here. I bet in the winter it really does pack in next to the building. Scary stuff.

"Want to go for a quick walk before we head into the lodge?" my dad inquires. We all know a walk will never be quick with him and this will turn into a hike.

"Sure." I shrug. I've been dying to come here all my life, I'm willing to wander about. Plus, the PCT should go like right through here. We were on it for a tad bit yesterday at Crater Lake, then again near Government camp, and we stopped near Lost Lake too. It's crazy knowing we hit it in so many different sections. One day I will get to hike it through. Ugg, what a dream. The PCT takes over my mind as we head up the mountain. Seriously though, if I could just quit my job and go backpacking for the rest of my life, I would. Zero hesitation. Well, I do really like my job, don't get me wrong, plus the people are pretty darn cool. But the freedom of being on the trail, surrounded by wilderness, unbeatable. How about just a seven-month break?

There's still a lot of snow and for a while we sink in up to our knees. I hate walking in snow without snowshoes! Up here, it ends up getting like an icy crust and it really kills my legs as they sink with each step. Ouch! However, I remind myself, it's worth it as we can see for miles. Hmmm, Portland is that way. I wonder if Johnny is there today. I mean theoretically, he should be, it's not a shift day. Maybe I should have invited him over today to hang out. Nah, that would be awkward! Way awkward! Besides, this is my family time, time to focus on them!

Sludging through the snow, carefully, I step into my dad's footprints. Skiers whip down the mountain on the fluffy powder, and off in the distance, we see a few more lone peaks. Hey! It's like the lonely mountain, well it's not lonely because it has the whole range, but still, it could definitely be a movie scene right here.

We emerge cold, but sweaty to the lodge a few hours later. The heat feels great! Ugg, I definitely vibe with cold blooded reptiles. I love soaking in the heat. I'm always cold! Wandering the inside, it sure looks nothing like *The Shining*, but it's beautiful in its own way. Definitely looks like a mountain cabin type theme. I can really imagine how one would get snowed in up here though. However, the going crazy part, nah. I could be a hermit up here on my own forever. Although, I suppose the hotel had some influence on Jack's mental health, so I should give him a break. We head to the restaurant in the basement. How cool is that! Dad orders a beer while mom and I decide on the pizza.

"It's so good to see ya' honey," my mom reiterates.

"I can't even tell you how great it is to see you guys. I've been loving it out here, I have, but I miss home," I admit trying to sound like I do really love it, and sometimes I really do. But this week with my family, I needed it, a lot. Maybe I wouldn't make a good hermit like I've always thought.

"Tell me about it," she urges, looking into my eyes intently.

How do moms do that? How can they always tell when something's wrong even though you wear the happiest face ever? I launch into everything, telling her about how I thought I loved rain until it rains every day, how work is okay, but I miss the trauma work, we don't get many search and rescues here.

I tell her about Johnny and how sometimes I think he likes me, but maybe that's just because I like him. Then I remember he's my boss so I can't like him. I tell her I miss Elizabeth back home, I miss our sleepovers and always having her for an adventure. I miss Hardin County and my family. I miss the dumbest things like golf cart rides and movie nights. Holding back tears the entire time, when I'm finished, she reaches over and hugs me. At least dad still stands over at the bar, he doesn't really do emotions.

"Well, I don't really know how to help, Kara, but all I can say is, if it doesn't work out, you always have a home. As for the boy, he sounds amazing. I'm sure a lot of girls think that too, but he would be crazy not to fall for you..." I scoff and shrug my shoulders. She's wrong, no guy could want me, but she does make me smile just a tad at the hope. She goes on giving me pearls of wisdom. She continues, saying things moms have to say. But still, it's really nice to get everything off my chest.

Just then my dad walks over with an extra beer as the waitress brings the pizza behind him. Yas, carb therapy. I think calories are my soulmate. Really, or carbs or sugar, but maybe it's just an affair with all of them. Taking a deep breath, I urge myself back to happier things, my family enjoys our last meal out for a while. It saddens me that I have no idea how long I will have to go again before I see them. I won't get to go home for Christmas or Thanksgiving, but maybe Easter I can.

After we fill our bellies with pizza, well beer for my dad, we start the drive back to Waldport. They leave early tomorrow morning. My heart clenches just thinking about it. Talking and jabbering the whole ride home, keeps my mind off it though. It's dark and raining as we reach the coast, wow, shocker. We hurry inside my house and crash for the night.

I suck at goodbyes. Half the time I don't even bother with them, sneaking out in the early morning hours of a friend's house or whatever I can do to not have the awkwardness of those last words. I put on a brave face as I hug my mom and dad. For some reason this goodbye feels very significant, like I need to make each minute count. Something tells me to make these few moments last. I hug a little longer and say I love you a few more times. As they pull away, the sobs come. My heart breaks all over again. Why does this one hurt so much more?

My phone rings not long after, I see the chief's name flash on the screen. "Hey, Chief, what's up?" I suck up the snot, my heart rate instantly spiking. Is there a bad call I'm needed on? My brain goes through all the what ifs.

"Hey, Kara, I know your parents were supposed to be leaving this morning, so sorry to bother you. Would you be interested in going on a conflag with the forest service? The Siuslaw is sending a few people to join the Columbia Gorge crew up in Washington. They're expecting a big blow up and I know you still have an active red card," He states all in one breath.

I liked my time with the forest service, actually some days I really miss wildland over structure. Wildland wasn't a job, it's a lifestyle.

"Sure, I would be up for that. When would we deploy?" I prompt. I haven't packed a red bag in over a year, but my line gear should still be set to go. It's sitting getting dusty at the bottom of my locker here at the fire department anyway, just in case.

"You'll be meeting up with the Siuslaw up at their cache at 1400 if that works." Oh, wow, two hours. Okay, I will definitely need to get a move on! Woohoo! Wildfire here I come!

CHAPTER 11

Rampaging through my house, I look for all the spare undies, socks, sport bras, and foot powder I can spare. I'm actually pretty stoked about this. A wildfire, woohoo. I miss that life. Sleeping in the dirt, waking up in the wilderness every day, guess I am actually going backpacking. Well, backpacking with a very big purpose. But I miss being a dirtbag. That hiker trash life calls my name every day. It's a complete vibe that is missing from my soul. However, this is going to be very different than I am used to. I'm used to living, breathing, and working with my crew, here I'm going in not knowing anyone.

I finally have a bag packed, I had to search everywhere for my box of backpacking gear for my tent and sleeping bag and such. Typically, I never use the tent and lay my sleeping bag out on the ground, as do most of the guys, but you never know when it could start snowing in the mountains or the wind could be whipping through.

I decide to actually drive my car up to the forest service barracks after I grab my line gear from the fire department. I know I could have biked there, but with my gear, that would suck. Plus, by the time I get back from a wildfire, I'm usually too tired and take a shower and veg on the couch.

I haven't paid all that much attention to the forest service office yet. I know we have a bit of a partnership with them, but so far, I've never done anything there. We monitored the pack test about a month ago to make sure everyone was okay physically, vitals and such, but that's it. Driving up the hill, I pull into the office.

As I step out of my car, I take it all in. Cool, a bunkhouse, cashe, everything right here. Oh, I miss these days sometimes. I've spent many summers living places just like this. It kind of feels like I'm pulling into my home driveway.

"Hi, my name is Kara, I'm supposed to be joining the fire crew here for a deployment to Washington," I say to the man walking by. He's in green nomex and smoke jumper boots, so I know he's fire.

"Yea, you can head over to the cashe, Supe will take care of you," he informs me, pointing. "Oh, I'm Rock by the way," he shoots over his shoulder as he's walking into the office.

"Thanks!" I holler. I walk over to the cache where I already see some line gear lined up and a pile of redbags. Mine looks different from theirs, so I toss it on the pile knowing I will easily be able to pick it out later. The others all look like fancy, Mystery ranch bags, lucky.

"Hello!" I holler as I walk in the door, making my presence known.

"Come in!" a gruff voice answers. I nudge the door open to find a few guys in the office.

"Hi, I'm Kara with the fire department, I was told I would be joining y'all on your deployment." I declare a little nervously. All new people, I can do this. New people are not scary. These are my type of people. No need for anxiety. Calm down heart, calm down breath, I've got this. I put all my focus into not fidgeting and breathing normal.

"Sure, great to have you, we were just going over some things," he states. "As I was mentioning, there is a new start in the Colville National Forest, the Mill creek fire. We will be primarily a handcrew, joining engine 629 from the Columbia Gorge." He goes on listing the crewmates, squaddies, and tool line up.

"Kara, you will be where needed. I've heard you have served on forest service crews before?"

"Yes, Sir, I have been Helitack, Engine and hand crew in the Bridger Teton National Forest," I respond.

"Good, good. You will fit right in here then. You might be working more with Columbia than us, with the engine, but we will put you to good work," he enlightens me.

With that, we're dismissed and start loading the trucks. Welp, I'm already a part of the crew, thrown right into the mix. So that's at least a plus. It looks like about ten of us in total are going, which would mean Columbia will be supplying their own squad of ten, makes sense. I see Rock load up in the truck I'm assigned. Cool, at least I know one person. See nothing to worry about. Fellow dirt bags.

We roll out. I look around at the crew. I'm sitting squished between a large man who could be an MMA fighter, and a skinnier runner looking type. In the front, Rock sits alongside someone with a rad beard named Phil.

"Hey, I'm Corey," the blonde runner introduces himself.

This guy must be like six foot five but one hundred and forty pounds. A nerdy innocent kinda' cute vibe. But nowhere near comparing to Johnny. Not that I base my interest on looks, I'm way more of a personality person. But I can't help but notice sitting next to a cute guy with the entire side of my body smashed to his.

"Kara," I mumble awkwardly giving him a sideways handshake.

The guy on my right speaks up, "Hey, I'm Morty." I almost burst out laughing, this huge guy is named Morty. It's so goofy! I mean not a name I would picture for a guy who looks like him. I wonder what it's short for. Morticus? Mordecai? Morticia? Ha-ha.

Most of the ride they talk amongst themselves as music plays in the background. Right now, it's like sailor shipping tunes. Never would have called this my music, but I am kind of vibing. These guys all seem nice enough, but I can tell they're a solid crew. They're one unit and I'm someone on the outside of the group. At least they're not standoffish or anything. We wind through the mountains, into the farmland, then the more baren parts of Oregon.

Finally, we reach the Columbia Gorge crew's headquarters. It's getting dark now, so I guess we're to stage here for the night. It's a bit funny, us all laying our sleeping bags out in their offices' yard. What a sight we must be. At least we're far enough off the coast that it's not raining here, but boy it's sticky and hot. It's funny I was actually just up this way yesterday. Mount Hood is right around the corner. Yet, I feel as if a lifetime has passed since we left here just over 24 hours ago. Now I'm with twenty strangers, sleeping in a yard, on my way to a wildfire. Wow, how times have turned.

What a day, woke up at 0600 and started the drive from the Dahles to the Colville National Forest. At least I got to ride in the same truck, so I knew everyone. I keep seeing so many new faces. I barely have my truck down, let alone the Siuslaw Crew and now to add the Columbia Gorge crew... my brain is ready to explode.

Once we get there, we unload and grab our gear. Everyone slinging on packs and jumping into the line. Where am I again? Oh, yea!

I jump in behind Corey, as the line starts taking off without me. Oof, after such a long drive, these men appear eager to move. We hike at cheetah speeds. Man, the fire department has made me soft. I'm so not used to hiking this fast anymore. I feel like I'm sprinting to keep up. However, with the smoke off in the distance, I think we're all itching to get a move toward it.

So far, it's a lot different from the fire rolls I'm used to. Will I like Wildland or structure more? I love the rush and adrenaline of Wildland, living on the ground and the base camps, but I don't like how it constantly pulls you away from your family. Plus, there's never really a chance to breathe in Wildland, it's the life. Always moving. Wildland has been a part of my life for so many years, but I really do think structure was the right call for me. The fire department has just felt like home these last few months. And I love my brothers there. I'm content there, and honestly, I am kind of planning to call it home for a long time. Wow, look at me, kind of ready to commit. It's definitely awesome to get this chance to go back to wildland though.

Wow, structure firefighters need to work on their cardio more! Even my brain is gasping for breath as I think that thought. Why is wildland like all cardio and structure all muscle? Where's the happy medium? I struggle to keep up with these long-legged men. There's one girl on the crew, but she's a squaddie, so I probably won't work with her since apparently Rock is my squaddie. She looks like a rad, hippy looking chick with long brown hair and a nose ring. I wish I could pull that off! Maybe one day. I do have tattoos scattered across my body, so a nose ring wouldn't be far off. However, the whole hippy vibe? I could only dream of pulling that off. I have the crunchy, tree hugger soul, but I definitely like pop culture too much.

I'm dying, ugg. How can I be out of shape when we work out all the stinking time at the fire department? That's it. I'm putting in a suggestion to the chief for more cardio. These hills are kicking my butt. Even if we run up and down the stairs like twenty times a day with our gear. That would help right? Or maybe I'm just kidding myself and I'm not cut out for this anymore. Nah. Come on, if eighteen-year-old Kara can do it, so can twenty-two-year-old. My legs get an extra boost.

Colville looks super pretty, but way hot compared to the coast. Finally, we're starting to get a view of the fire. Big, torched trees, you can tell this fire is moving. Just since we've been here, it has blown up! Once in position, we separate into our squads, and head off for our assignments.

Rock is running point, as Phil is our lead sawyer. Morty will be swamping right on his tail as Corey, and I dig behind him. Our handline twisting and turning as the flames draw ever closer and closer. My brain just kind of goes into robot fire mode as I'm working a fire. Dig, step, dig step. Grab the logs, dig step. On and on it goes.

Before long, we're running a hotline. The fire right in front of us creeping across the ground. Phil felling tree by tree, as we hold the green edge. Working as one, we go on for hours. It doesn't matter where all we're from. When the fire is burning, we all have the training, we all work, and slowly we make progress. Brutal, blistering work, but my heart swells with happiness. This job really is great. I've missed this. Maybe not the out of breath moments, or the sweat dripping in my eyes stinging and making them cry. Not the steep hikes, the cuts, scrapes, and bruises. But letting my brain turn off and my body moving, just knowing what to do. Like this is what my body was born to do. The feeling of purpose. Of being a part of something bigger.

By the time another crew takes over for us, we're all dead on our feet, or at least I am. Now I remember why I switched to structure. Ugg. I feel like structure is like running a 5k. Yes, it sucks, and it takes more time than a sprint, but not as long as wildland. Wildland isn't just a marathon it's like an ultra-runner marathon. Today, I feel it in every bone of my body. Structure is hard, and in some ways much harder than wildland, especially the mental toll from victims, but today, physically, wildland kicked my butt. Yup, take me back to my structure firefighting.

We parked our trucks in a safety zone, so that night when we finally arrive at them, I'm starving. Everyone grabs an MRE for supper, devours it, and stretches their sleeping bags beside the trucks. Someone's body lays next to me, touching my leg, and my head brushes someone else's bag. Tight, close arrangements for sleeping, but a tight crew. I do miss this part. Of being a single unit, like we all compose one single organism. Each of us a vital organ in one body. My heart feels happy. My soul just completely vibing.

Not even seconds go by, and I'm out.

Today I wake up to a whole new day of fire torcher. Don't get me wrong, I'm loving this opportunity, but this might be my last big wildfire. We run more hotline, dozer lines, and everything else with lots of swamping and hiking. All the while, "Watch your footing" continues being called out every few minutes in this steep, slippery terrain.

The chafing feels like hell. At one point, on a break, I tried to put some duct tape between my thighs to help. It did at first, but now it's caught on my pants, and it rips away from the skin a little more with every step making me cringe.

Ugg. My bunker gear doesn't rub like this. Maybe I put on weight at the fire department? Muscle Kara, its muscle, I tell myself.

It is true, I mean I can drag and carry more weight now, and there that is a huge achievement, here though, more thigh muscle just means my legs chafe more. Ugg! Why can't I win?

Thunder crackles across the sky as fat drops of rain fall. So much for it being dry. I used to always picture wildfires as hot, dry, and sweaty. But I've tackled various wildfires. I've been hailed on in Idaho, wandered through swamps in Alaska, and even had a muggy, infernal one in Louisiana. We heard this fire started with lightning anyway, so maybe I should've expected rain. Luckily, our relief crew shows up just as we're nearly soaked through.

Bedtime! Yas. Tonight, we make the small drive back to the base camp. I shiver slightly from being wet, but the idea of food and a tent warms my thoughts. Base camp will at least have some sort of food rather than MREs. I appreciate the MRE's but catering at wildfires is better than I can afford back home pretty much every time. Or at least better than I can cook. A can of cream corn counts as a gourmet supper for me.

All our spirits lift as we get some hot food in us, sitting in some high school's cafeteria. Noodles, green beans, even a brownie. Yes, right here, now this is just what I needed. We all devour our food in just minutes.

"I forgot my freaking tent," Morty complains as we hurriedly set up camp. I glance over at him. Poor guy! My goodness, I have no idea what would happen to him. I mean, I really don't. All the crews I've been on would never let you sleep in the trucks unless everyone was doing it, so he would probably have to stay out here with all of us. I would offer to share, but mine's a bivy, barely big enough for me. I notice all my gear getting soaked through watching the conversation, so I need to move. I shove my bag into the small tent and shimmy in after it. Peeking out of the corner, I see someone helping poor Morty. Good. I wouldn't have been able to sleep not knowing if he had anywhere to sleep.

"I just never use them on wildfires," he explains as someone helps string up a space blanket to a rain fly. Well, it's not much, but at least he has a little home for the night.

Assessing my own gear, I find it sopping. Literally everything in my red bag feels damp making me grimace. I shiver as I crawl into my sleeping bag trying to get warm. I'm miserable. Ugg, who ever heard of rain at a wildfire? Okay, that's a dumb question for me. My deployment in Alaska was the soggiest, most miserable two weeks of my life.

Freezing and shivering, I drift into a sporadic sleep.

I feel like I've been digging hotline for years. My back is in a constant curved position. My arms swing and my feet shuffle without me even having to tell them to. My brain operates in low power mode for hours. My body knows what to do, and I don't even think my brain has been singing to itself anymore, which means it's just quiet, a rare thing. The fire has been barrelling towards us for a few hours now and with each thrown spark, my adrenalin jumps more and more.

"Embrace the suck!" Corey hollers. A honking laugh escapes me. No matter how long I've been digging, no matter how many countless fires I've been on, someone always says that. Embrace the suck. Yet, we all do. We chose this glorious life of living in the dirt and sweating with fire nipping at our heels. I love it though, as do all of us. The brotherhood, the adrenaline, this is living.

***

My favorite day yet! Mop up! Something I can do just as well as everyone else! Finally, no sprinting through the woods, digging hotline, felling trees, finally something I can do well. How did I ever do all of this for a living? I used to be out for weeks at a time, come back for two days and go right back out for at least two more weeks for months on end. How? I can't imagine this life anymore for a career.

These past few days have been great, but not for this long anymore. I long for a shower, a piece of garlic bread, bologna, chocolate milk, a bed, and Johnny. Give me my medical calls and rescues any day.

Corey and I worked together in the morning then Rock lead me, Phil, Corey, and Morty this afternoon. I really love this job sometimes. The guys are what make it great. Corey had told me; I am always there when he needs here. That he would be thinking he needed a hand, or someone to grab that log, or something and all of a sudden it was being done by me. I love when I just hit a groove with my partner and words aren't even needed. I love fire camp suppers and being part of a crew.

Although, I do really miss my crew at home. I have a pretty good crew there too. I miss Johnny's winks and laughs, and Garrett's teasing. I miss Logan and all his sarcasm. They're my crew now, my brothers. Okay, well not full brothers, because even here, nine hours away from him, Johnny still crosses my mind, and one doesn't think about a brother like that.

"Hey, Kara, do you know how to tell Indian time?" Corey prods walking over to me. Indian time?

"Um, like a sundial? I think that was way before Indians, like maybe the Greeks or Romans," I say with an awkward chuckle.

"No, no. The native Americans around here could walk by a pile of sticks, drop them, and they would know the time from it. It's a long-time skill, comes in handy out here. Here let me show you." He says as he stoops over to pick up some sticks and sits on the ground cross legged with the pile of sticks in his hand. Morty wanders over and sits beside him, so I sit across from him. This can't be real. It has no science behind it. Sure, I get the concept of shadows and reading the sun, but sticks? Skeptically, I watch him.

He throws the sticks on the ground and looks at them for a few seconds. What a joke. No way.

"I should tell you, Indians only had ten-hour periods instead of twelve," he informs me.

Interesting. I mean I just figured they had gone by the sun, who cares if there are numbers to go with it. But ten? Why ten?

"Any guesses?" He looks at me studying my face with intense eyes.

I count the sticks, one, two, three, four, five. "You've got me. Five?" I respond. I honestly think he's pulling my leg. I never trust wildland guys. They're always teasing and pulling pranks. I swear everything they say is either exaggerated, twisted, or a complete lie. He laughs.

"Two," Morty answers.

"Yup." My head swivels to peer at them.

"Round two." He tosses the sticks on the ground again. Is it divisible by something? What am I missing?

"Five," Morty states.

"Right again." This goes on for a few more rounds. Me guessing over and over, trying to figure out the rule. I don't understand. Sometimes he will add a stick, sometimes take some away. But Morty is always right. Unless... maybe Morty is in on it. This must be some sort of game like the stupid stick, right? These guys always play dumb riddles. One riddle took me four days to figure out! It was about a dumb cabin on top of the mountain. I was supposed to ask yes or no questions until I figured out how the men died. 'Two men were found dead in a cabin on top of a mountain, how did they die?' It took me four days! I hate riddles!

My eyes start watching Morty. He sees me watching and his eyes dart around. When Corey throws the sticks, Morty's eyes flash to Corey's thighs, then back on the sticks. There! Corey holds up the numbers with his fingers!

"Three!" I cry out. "Ugg, so dumb. What a stupid trick, no Indians told time like that! Ugh you idiots." I rant on and on, as they burst into laughter. Why did I fall for that? Ugg. What a way to waste ten minutes of my life.

***

Our next few days are filled with mop ups, gridding, and hose lays. I enjoy it when the guys are forced to slow down a little. I hate rushing through life, it really makes you feel like you miss things. But with this slower pace, I feel like I can still see the world. The mountains rolling, we pass streams, some greenery, my soul feels at peace. Everything just feels right when I'm out in nature.

Even though there's ash and black everywhere, it's really beautiful out here. The mountains loom all around us. There is just so much beauty out here. Nature is never angry at me or rushing me. Nature just is. It doesn't have emotions or judge you. It treats everybody the same.

However, everyone can take something different from it. I don't care if I haven't had a shower in how many days? How many days have we even been out here? Six? Seven? Sighing, I push my questions aside. I wouldn't trade this for anything. Maybe the west really is my home. Or well, the Pacific northwest at least. I really do love it out here.

Every day, I wake up feeling at home. At peace. I think I started forgetting that feeling in Waldport because I've focused on the rain and missing my family. I love the rain, though and the dense rainforests, the cushy green all around me. Even here, where it's black, the mountains still feel like my place. For the first time in a few weeks, my heartrate lowers, and I feel calm, tranquil. I'm home.

***

Thankfully, we finally have a day of just monitoring. All day, we get to sit and watch the black. This is my kind of day! The guys all complain and grumble, but once they start gambling, doing push-ups, and taking naps, I think deep down they're all grateful for a bit of a break. I'm enjoying the view for a bit, sitting, and staring at the mountains, while the guys continue talking, jabbering, and gambling behind me.

After a while, I decide it would be a fantastic time to catch up on some very missed sleep. Wandering over to the trucks, I find only a couple guys scattered in them and the whole back seat is free. Clambering in, I shut the door quietly, hoping I don't wake Rock. I lean my head against the door enjoying the warmth and fall asleep in seconds.

A jolt rocks me as I plummet to the ground. A hand catches my arm just before my face tastes dirt. The rest of my body pummels the hard, dusty ground. The shock still wearing off as my brain suddenly adjusts to what happened; I was sleeping and fell to the ground.

"Ugg," I groan and look up as someone helps me to my feet.

"Kara, I am so sorry!" Morty apologizes.

"It's not a big deal," I grumble, wiping down my pants. "At least you saved my face." I say and he laughs. One of my biggest fears is getting my teeth knocked in. I wore braces for eight years growing up, I'm never ever going back to them.

"Sorry, but we have to move. So, grab your gear and let's get going," he informs me. Giving myself a shake, straightening up, my mind is back in the race. Jumping in line, we book it, to where, I haven't the faintest idea.

We hike hill over hill, leaving our trucks far back in the distance. My mind goes into hiker mode where it remains silent, then sings the same song over and over, somehow always ending up saying the preamble of the constitution. We sang this dumb song about it in the fourth grade, and ever since, my mind goes to that. My head plays a steady mixture of 'Hips Don't Lie' by Shakira and the Gettysburg address. I'm pretty sure I would be committed the second anyone could read my mind.

"Holding!" The front echoes the words down the line as we suddenly come to a halt.

"Circle up!" Supe yells and we all move around him. "Alright, we are staging here for now. Nice work busting it over here. Take five," he instructs. In other words, we'll be taking like five hundred.

"Hurry up and wait." I hear a few people mumble. Isn't that the way for it all? Every wildfire, every medical scene, every search and rescue. There's at least some component to this. Granted at least when a house burns the waiting takes much less time, but somewhere along the lines after my adrenaline is already going, there's going to be some briefing, scene safety, some communication, or lack thereof, but something that will make us wait.

***

Luckily, the next few days pass without any more incidents. Monitoring, gridding, mopping up. We fall into a routine. I can tell the guys look bored with this work, but I enjoy it. Plus, we're still doing a very vital job by putting out heat spots and little spot fires. Very important.

Right now, I'm proudly sporting an ash beard one of the guys drew for me earlier. They were having fun drawing mustaches, beards, unibrows, and everything else on with ashen sticks. Even the other girl, Laura has a rad ash mustache like the monopoly man. I love how out here, no one seems self-conscious about anything. There's no society to tell you the norms, no one to judge you or make fun of you. I'm the most me I can be when I'm out on the line. I don't care how I look; I act exactly how I want and am just my happiest self. Why isn't everywhere like this? It should be. I should be. I love who I am out here. I am my best self. I'm going to try to make it a point to be this way everywhere.

Everyone here roots for you, they're your teammates, like at the fire department. We are all one. I really struggled climbing the dozer line and everyone cheered for me and helped me along. With them, I feel like I can do anything. There was no judgement, just absolute support from them. Granted, I never want to have to climb another steep dozer line again, back to structure for this girl.

I'm so back and forth about everything though. One minute, I think my mind is made up, but then I switch again. Do I want stability? Stay at the fire department, marry someone, maybe Johnny? My stomach flips, oof.

Just kidding.

But do I want to start a family? Or do I want to continue traveling, living out of my car, and having adventures? I feel like I'm being pulled to stay here, but I can't see any future down the road. Isn't that funny? Like I'm meant to stay at the fire department, but passed that, nothing. Like God just hasn't given me any idea yet. That's so new for me. I've always had the next plan in mind, working towards the next goal. Preparing for the future I want. Yet, I just don't see what's next.

***

Finally! After thirteen days of being sweaty, drenched in rain, dirt, ash, and everything else, I get a shower. Oh, my goodness, this feels glorious. The water runs over me, a sigh of contentment escapes my lips. Yas! This is exactly what I needed. All the tension leaves my muscles. It feels like a water massage, some mental meditation, and a little bit of a break from all the guys. I crank the water up to lava levels of heat and I love it.

We get to go home tomorrow! Home. Yes! Waldport feels more and more like a home I'm missing the more I'm away from it. I miss my fire department family, my little house, the waves, Chubbys, everything. This was a totally rad crew to work with, but I miss my own crew.

After showering, I lay out my sleeping bag one last time. At least it has finally dried out and will be nice and warm. Granted, if I sleep without a tent, it will be wet by morning from dew, but I want one night under the stars. Hopefully it doesn't rain, but I'm prepared to climb under someone's rainfly if needed. However, no rain looks to be on the horizon.

Staring up, I see the most amazing stars. They glitter across the sky, and I can't help but think of all the Creator plans for me. Is there anything better than being in a sleeping bag, surrounded by people who would do anything for you, listening to nature. I really am part of something bigger, aren't I? I needed this roll, even if I had moments I didn't quite enjoy. I needed to remember my hippie soul, to get back into my happy mind set.

I love being my crunchy, tree hugging self. *Thank you, Lord.* I drift off as contentment hugs my heart.

CHAPTER 12

Shock, the only thing my brain seems to be capable of right now. Jumping right back into the structure side of fire, my brain misses the peaceful serenity of the cascades. No one ever tells you that you have a mini culture shock going from living in the dirt for weeks to coming back to civilization.

I remember after my first season of Wildland, where I'd been out roll after roll for six months with less than seven days in an actual bed, I slept on the ground for days in my house. I recollect how hard it was adjusting to simple things like the fact I couldn't just go pee in the woods wherever I wanted or having to keep daily hygiene habits again. I missed the lack of civilization, not having to deal with society. I hate how society has tainted the world. Things that should be normal, or at least society claims are normal, but they aren't when you live in the woods. The woods seem easier, better. I would live in the woods as a little crazy hermit if possible. Or Radagast the brown, I would totally be him. Then, jumping right back into work on top of that, having to wear my uniform, and switch my brain over to EMS and rescue work, today will be a little hard.

Leaning my bike against the bay, I step into the office. Instantly, I'm mobbed. Arms circle around me and I am smooshed from all sides.

"It's good to have you back Kara," Johnny proclaims. Lifting my head, I see all three of my guys smiling at me. My heart feels full, I could cry, my little family. All the love. We jabber about everything and anything as we prep for the day.

***

It's definitely not a white cloud day. Not even an hour into shift we got an EMS call. The poor guy was long gone by the time I walked in. I checked his pulse, nothing, but his stone-cold skin, and rigor mortis was the big teller. When I lifted his shirt and already saw the lividity stretched over, I knew there was no helping this man.

Sometimes a victim's death feels personal, and it hits your soul. But after years of it, you grow accustomed to it, like a rock yourself, it doesn't even phase you. Sometimes I wonder if I'm losing my humanity, my soul, my heart when I cover a victim and feel nothing. Other times, I remember it's what had to be done. My brain should not think, not show emotions, or they will consume me. Keep myself numb, succumb to the void. When I was a cadet, I remember being a wreck. Always crying for the dead, taking it to heart, and thinking it was my fault, that I could've saved them.

My pager buzzes against my hip. Welp, no time to mourn. I leave the man for the medics, while I look at the dispatch log. Hopping in the engine, I find Logan already there as Johnny pops in the back. Garrett will have to catch a ride back to the station with the ambulance.

"Stroke victim. Female, age 64, onset fifteen minutes ago as known..." I read off the log to my partners. As we pull up on scene, Johnny rushes in with the monitor and med bag, while I grab the O2 bag and vitals chart, rushing after him. An ambulance should be coming behind us soon.

Once inside, I'm hit with a blast of hot air. I like warm weather, but what is it with old people having their houses at one hundred degrees? Okay, yes scientifically, I know they don't thermoregulate as well as younger people, yadda, yadda, but still.

Sweat instantly swims down my back. I take vitals as Johnny does everything he can for her. We get her strapped up to the gurney and ready to roll as the ambulance pulls in. She grips my hand and my heart squeezes for her. But at least she has maintained hand function for now. The ambulance will need to rush to the airport, and she will be life flighted. Our closest cath lab is in Portland.

Lord, please be with this woman, help give her peace, and be with her family. I pray. I wish I knew what happened to our victims after they leave us. But then again, maybe that would be worse, knowing the ones that made it and the once that don't.

Once back in the station, we finally get a chance to breathe and fill out a few charts. Thank goodness. My mind wanders to the lady every now and then. She gets me thinking about the man from earlier. I wonder if he had a family too. Or was he all alone? Did he know peace in the end? No! Kara don't go down this road. Every time I get in too deep thinking about the patients and victims, I always spiral downhill.

To get my mind off things, I go in search of some company. It's after hours, so I see Logan already in bed. I find Garrett talking on the phone with someone. Knowing him, it's probably his latest tinder date, or bar romance. It never lasts long, but he always has a line of new ones to pull in. So, Johnny seems to be my only option, but I'm not complaining.

"Mind if I join you?" I ask Johnny as I sit on the couch opposite him.

"Not at all," he proclaims pausing the movie. "How are you holding up today?" he prompts turning to me. Oh, I don't want to go down this road. Not tonight. I want an escape, not open the door.

"It comes with the territory. I'm okay," I claim avoiding the word fine. Not tonight. I don't share my emotions, and I don't let any of the men know this job gets to me sometimes. I don't need another reason for them to think I'm inadequate.

"Okay but know I'm always here if you need to talk," he reiterates. He pauses a few more seconds looking into my eyes. I look away and I'm sure my cheeks blush. I'm afraid if I look into them any longer, I will burst into tears. But his eyes seemed so intense. It felt like he could see into my soul. Ugg. How can I be one second away from tears thinking about them, then start blushing thinking about Johnny, it's so not right. I really am messed up, aren't I? The movie resumes and I stare at it, trying to pay attention, but honestly, I couldn't even say what genre it is, let alone a general plot line.

Noise. Loud noise. I jerk awake, looking around. I must've fallen asleep on the couch. The guys stride in from the bunkroom and I scramble after them. Tones go off all around the station. They all beat me to the engine this time. Hurriedly, I pull up my pants and jump in. Luckily, Johnny is officer tonight, already talking to dispatch, so Garrett and I are in the back.

I pull on gloves, grab my clipboard and med bag, listening to the readout. Senior male, age 82, fell in the bay at 0530. Wow, it's morning already, who knew. What is it with old people wandering around at the break of dawn? Ugg, stay in bed people!

We arrive on scene and Garrett, and I hurry over to him. He's conscious, holding onto a rock. That's a good sign. A younger gentleman crouches beside him.

"Sir, we are with Mid Oregon Fire, here to help you." He nods vigorously. I can tell he's been crying, and he's probably really upset he needs to be rescued. Hurrying over to the edge, I start doing my assessment.

"ABC's are fine, head laceration of three inches, early stages of hypothermia," I state, glancing at Garrett out of the corner of my eye as he does his own work.

"What's your name Sir?" I ask, but no response. He looks over to me and glances away.

"That's my father, Ken." The younger man from the side informs us.

"Okay, Ken, we're going to get you out of here, okay? Tell me if anything hurts," I instruct as I go through a primary assessment. Johnny and Logan wheel the stretcher over. We need to get him out of the water fast. Do we backboard and lift out or assist in helping him the couple of feet to the stretcher? It's about three feet out of the bay, the latter would probably be our best bet, but it's Garrett's call.

"Sir, if we help, do you think you can stand?" Garrett gently probes. Great, he's thinking the same thing! The man mumbles something and we take that as our go ahead. I figure we will be lifting out for the most part anyway.

"On three. One. Two. Three." With Garrett's last count, we gently urge the man into a standing position. Grasping him under his arms, we lift him up rock by rock. Making sure I have an even step with every movement, we take our time. The stretcher is waiting for us, one more step. Setting him down, he's still shivering violently.

"Sir, I'm going to need to get these wet clothes off," I advise as I take out my shears. I always feel bad for cutting people's clothes off. What if this is his favorite t-shirt? Then there's the fact I'm seeing people in just their undies... or worse. Way too intimate for my liking, but this is the line of work I chose, so I guess I need to get used to it.

Granted, I've come a long, long way since my first wilderness first responder class so many years ago. I didn't even want to touch someone's wrist to get a pulse at first. I was like, nope! That still felt like crossing a line, too intimate. Here I am years later, stripping guys down for a living. I mentally fan myself as I think of a Victorian lady talking about seeing a man in underwear.

The poor man tries to push my hand away. But we must get him warmed up. Even by ambulance, the Newport hospital will be a twenty-minute drive. As soon as I cut the pants and shirt free, I wrap a blanket around him. We tighten the straps and roll him over the grass. At least Garrett will be the one riding in the ambulance today. Ugg, I hate having to be a third and assist in the ambulance. I get motion sick as it is, but trying to write vitals, do CPR, or anything in the back of a moving ambulance sucks!

The rest of the day passes with ease. No big calls, just a lift assist and an allergic reaction but both went well and thankfully a quick fix. Well, thanks to Epi, but you know, all the same. Grateful to be off hours I'm melting into this couch.

"Hey, want to go pick up some meals at the Moose?" Johnny questions. We got to talking about it a few days ago and it turns out we're all members. Though coming from a small town, I guess it's not all that unexpected. Waldport is about the same size as my hometown, and the Moose has some of the best food.

"Ugg," I groan sitting up. I hate to get up, but really, the Moose sounds awesome. My brother is a moose member, as well as my father, my grandfather, and the rest of the family. They do a lot of good stuff, and the best part is they serve awesome food too! I follow mindlessly behind, my stomach leading the way making Johnny chuckle.

We take the engine over and park it outside. You know the Moose is raging when the engine sits out front. Logan swipes us in with his card and we all show our cards to the bartender, then make our way over to the food. MMMMM, it smells heavenly.

"You know, Kara, this is legit like an old man fraternity. What are you doing having a membership?" Garrett asks, arching his brow.

"I could ask you the same thing." I laugh out loud. "But actually, it is a family fraternity," I claim as sarcasm laces my voice. Sure, it's a family fraternity, but here in Waldport, it's all the old fishermen frequenting it the most. Back home, it's all the old farmers.

After heaping our plates with food, we all sit at a table. Mashed potatoes, steak, carrots, the whole works. Yum! I shovel a bite into my mouth enjoying the heavenly taste when our pagers all go off. I hold back a groan. Dang it! I mean gosh darn, couldn't I at least make it through one of the sides? But everyone goes into pro mode and sets aside our plates, shovelling one last bite in our mouths. We all hop up and head out. I cast one last longing glance at our meals.

"We will box them and leave them at the station for you guys!" Shouts the little lady at the back. Bless her. My heart swells, I love small friendly communities. Thank goodness, at least I have my yummy food to look forward to. Sometimes they even throw in a few slices of free pie when we need to rush out on them.

The sirens wail as we rush down the street. CPR code. Well, at least we didn't eat a ton. I hate working a CPR on a full stomach. My adrenaline spikes and heart rate increases as we draw closer. Pulling on gloves, the clip board and bags, my hands go through the motions.

"I want you to start on O_2 while I start on compressions this time," directs Garrett. My heart skips a little. I almost always start on compressions. Okay, I've got this. Deep breath. Really O_2 is less physical, but connecting hoses, sizing OPAs, making sure to squeeze the BVM in between, in theory it's stressful. Stressful, at least to me. Control, it's all about control, I remind myself. You know what to do Kara.

"Copy that," I state. We hop out of the truck and head into the house.

"Over here! over here!" Shouts a woman and we walk over to her. She steps out of the way as Garrett assesses, checking the airway, then starting compressions. My brain automatically flips a switch, and my hands know what to do without thinking. Tilt the head, BVM, find manual suction, BVM, connect hoses and O_2. BVM, size OPA, stick it in, size NPA because he will probably gag, BVM.

Before I know it, Garrett calls for a switch. In a heartbeat, I'm counting compressions, beats going through my head. We continue for who knows how long. Logan switches for me, and I take over for Garrett, all on a rotation. One and two and...

Gasp! All three of our hands expertly roll him into recovery, ready to suction. Success!

CHAPTER 13

Somehow, I find myself having new friends. I woke up this morning to a text from a few of the wildland guys at the forest service. They invited me over to the bunkhouse today for a river float and beach bonfire. How cool is that? Dancing around in excitement, I am a ball of joy.

Growing up in Ohio, I never had many friends, especially ones who would invite me to hang out randomly. I always had to prearrange it with friends, and I would have to make all the plans. These guys actually want to hang out with me.

I walk up to the door, but I don't even have a chance to knock, my hand poised when the door bursts open.

"Kara!" Morty hollers squeezing me in a hug. I laugh. Freaking fire guys. The scariest looking teddy bears ever.

"Hey, Morty," I wheeze. I see Corey and Phil in the background and try to wave. I'm totally shocked they're so excited to see me. But then, after you spend two weeks living and working with people out in the boonies, a few days away seems like a lifetime. I really love these guys, all my guys out here, structure and wildland alike.

"So, we were thinking about hanging out here for a bit this morning, then going over to the Alsea to float, and end it with the bonfire," Corey calls out.

"Yea Rock is still crashed out, but he should be up soon," Morty explains. Probably a hangover. That sure wouldn't surprise me out of these guys.

"We were thinking of taking out the bikes for a little bit," Phil adds. "You said you ride, right?" Woah... Okay, I'm not prepared for that. Maybe I'll just stay here. I have my Harley at home, but it's just a little sportster and honestly, Ohio is flat. I've never once in my life had to work a clutch in the hills.

"Um, yea, I do, but I don't have a bike out here," I declare. That should get me out of anything, unless I could ride behind someone, but that's a little too intimate for my liking.

"No worries, I have an extra bike," Morty offers.

"Nah, I couldn't. What if I wrecked it or something?" My anxiety spikes, running through the roof. I mean honestly, what if something did go wrong, and I've never ridden in the mountains. So many things could happen. And I know that many men think of their vehicles as their children. What if I wrecked his bike? Or worse, what if his bike wrecked me?

"Girl, a tsunami couldn't hurt that thing. It's just a big dirt bike I ride in the dunes," he claims.

"Come on, I'll even let ya' borrow my cool helmet," offers Corey. Okay. Okay. What's the absolute worst that could happen? I mean even if I did crash, at least there would be an EMT right there. Plus, I grew up riding, moped, to dirt bike, to motorcycle. A few hills won't kill me. Hopefully.

"Fine, but let's test it out first," I demand.

I guess this could be pretty rad. Like a little wildland gang. They lead me around the side of the bunkhouse where I see six bikes parked. I assume one is Rock's, and I can definitely tell which one I'm going to be riding. I am kind of excited. My heart rate racing, yet in a pleasant anticipation way. I haven't gotten to ride in a few months, not since I left Ohio, and even then, it was winter when I left, so not since last fall. Walking around to it, I can definitely tell it's going to be too tall for me.

"I don't know, it's a bit high," I hedge. I'm not a baby, just cautious. I was always taught to have your feet be able to touch and just looking at it, I would say it would fit my six-foot-three brother, not little five-foot-two me. Besides, there's nothing wrong with being cautious, or overly cautious.

"Eh, you'll be fine," Morty replies, shrugging. Okay there's no getting out of it. I've got this. Right? They all walk to their bikes, and I have to hop to swing my leg over mine. It leans heavily just so one of my feet can touch the ground. One by one we take off. At least this bike has an electric start. Heaven knows I wouldn't be able to kick start it with this lean.

With a rumble it comes to life and slowly letting out the clutch I twist the throttle. I have to give it enough gas to get me upright, but once it's going, I'm golden. Now I'll just hope there aren't too many stops. I follow them out, over the speed bumps from the office, onto 101 and southbound. I grin up at the sky it's finally a sunny day, and heading south, we should avoid rain.

The four of us rattle along the coastline. Oh, what a beautiful day. We ride south to Florence, passing many beautiful areas. I see the lighthouse Johnny and I went to, the Dunes, and more. Finally, Corey in the front motions and we make a loop through a parking lot and head back north to Waldport.

I may have been hesitant, but this trip was just what I needed. Riding is something I didn't realize I missed. Luckily, the helmet has a full-face mask so as a smile plasters my face, no bugs fly in. I love this. It feels like freedom. I always kind of feel like I'm flying when I ride. As free as a bird gliding through the air. Like nothing can stop me.

Following the guys, we loop back into the forest service lane. It's over so fast. Then I stare up, speed bumps going up a hill. My stomach churns, anxiety spiking, I'm nervous all over again, I'm going to have to slow down for those speed bumps, but it's a hill, so I can't slow down too much. Crap!

The bike wobbles as I bump over the first one. Two more. I give it a little more gas and practically jump over the next one. Squeezing my break, I slow up for the last one. The front tire makes it and then the bike stalls. Shoot! It's tipping, tipping, and it crushes me to the ground!

"No!" I cry. Ugg. I guess a speed bump can stop me. Why couldn't I just have the guts to make it over the last one. I try wiggling out from the bike but before I can make it far someone hauls it off me. Looking up, I see Phil reaching a hand down to me as Morty holds the bike.

"Little tumble there, ya alright?" Morty asks. Wow, no one makes fun of me or anything. I expected laughing, judgement, but nothing. Just like on the fireline. My heart feels full as I breathe in a sigh of contentment, I love these guys.

"Yea, I'm okay. I'm so sorry about the bike. I've never ridden in the mountains. My part of Ohio doesn't have more than a two percent slope anywhere! I'm so sorry," I babble on as I choke back tears.

"Girl, no worries." He pats the seat and I move around to take the bike. Only as soon as he lets go, it flattens me again. I huff in exasperation.

"Arg. This is embarrassing. I give up. I'm just going to walk it back up the hill," I grumble. Morty on one side, and me on the other, we walk the bike back to the top.

"What happened?" Corey asks as we near the bunkhouse. Morty doesn't say anything.

"I stalled on the speed bump," I whisper.

"Ha! No worries, I can't tell you how many times I tripped over one of them just walking back from the bar," He reveals and chuckles. Okay, a smile finally crosses my face.

"Y'all finally ready to go float!" Rock hollers from the porch. Oh, so now he's ready to go. We all chuckle. Morty walks back down to ride his motorcycle back up. Piling into Rock's van, we wind through the forest. The Bay turning to the river and snaking through the trees. We dance and sing to the music with the windows down.

As soon as the van pulls off along the road, we fall out. Grabbing the inner tubes out of the back, we sprint to the water. It's a bit of a slope down to the river, but worth it. Oh, my goodness, now that we're off the coast a little, back in the woods, it's definitely warm enough to swim. Ugg. I'm practically dying with this heat. Aside from the wildfire, I haven't had to deal with heat for months. My body was made for the Oregon Coast. But it's nice to finally have a different temperature.

At the water's edge, the boys strip their shirts. You know, I'm definitely not interested in any of them, but I can sure appreciate the view in front of me. My face flushes with my thoughts. The guys all jump in yelling and hooping. Timidly, I wade in. It's quite warm yet refreshing. Closing my eyes for a moment, I listen to the water, and the boys jabbering around me. Soaking in the peace, the sunshine, and all the good vibes. Finally, I jump the rest of the way, wiggle into the floating donut and float towards Corey and Morty.

"Hey girl! Thanks for hanging with us today!" Morty chimes.

"Thanks for the invite! I was pretty stoked when y'all texted and asked. I honestly don't have much of a social life aside from when one of the fire department guys stay in town after shift," I reply.

It's true. Most of the other guys are on shift when I'm off, Garrett and Johnny live in Portland, and it's not like I'm going to go hang out with Logan and his wife, especially with everything going on there.

"So, give me the scoop. You must have more of a social life than you say. Dates, boyfriends, hook-ups. Details!" Morty digs. Dang, why are these guys like hard core drama queens? I swear men gossip more than women and they only make up that women are gossips to hide the fact that they're worse.

"Oh, um. Not yet. I'm still kind of getting settled in," I mumble, and he snorts.

"Dude, I move every season and still have time to have on average two girlfriends a summer," Corey chimes in.

"Well, yea, but I'm like looking long-term, not your random hook-ups." I shoot back. I love my fire brothers, but so many of them are man-whores.

"Nah, girl, hook-up wise, average is like fifty a season," he explains as if it's nothing. Ugg, men, I roll my eyes.

"Well, isn't there anyone who has caught your eye?" Morty prods.

"Hmmm, I mean, well, yea, but I'm not going there." My face flushes none the less.

"OOOOOO, do tell!" He scoots his floaty over to me and Corey tunes in.

"Nah, there's no one," I hedge.

"Bullcrap! Now spill!" Corey adds.

Ugg fine. I mean I would love to talk to someone about it. I am kind of dying inside. Plus, these guys don't really know the fire department dudes so there isn't much crossover. I can tell them, right? I mean after two weeks on the fireline, we're practically family anyway. If they can see me peeing, they can see my heart. "Well, there is this guy at the department. My Lieutenant..." I trail off.

"Dang girl, get it!" Morty exclaims.

"Scandalous!" Corey chimes.

"Well, no, I mean we're not a thing. He's my boss and doesn't like me like that. Probably doesn't even give me a second thought."

"You're like the whole package, of course he thinks about you like that. Plus, didn't you say on the roll that he invited you out? Yup, I ship that," he declares as if that's the end of the debate, and I let it be. Although, I know he could never like me. Well, I'm still clinging to my one percent chance. But I'm not getting my hopes up too much. There's no point in arguing with a guy though. Ever. Well, unless it's like life or death, which my love life, or lack thereof is not.

The rest of the afternoon we spend floating around. Floating down river and having to paddle back up. Adventures of rope swings, craw dad gigging, and laughs. I'm so thankful for these guys, for all my friends out here, I really am.

Once the sun starts sinking, the air chills. Climbing back up the banks to the van, we pile in fly down the winding roads to home. Wow, yea, I guess Waldport is home. Finally, it feels like it. I think I could be okay with staying here the rest of my life. With the mountains to visit, rivers to float, ocean to splash in, it really has it all. My perfect state.

Once back at the bunkhouse, we load up our arms. Full of supplies for pie irons, smores, camp chairs, the whole works. Now, working with the fire department, I'm not sure how legal beach bonfires are here. Maybe that's something I should look into, but after tonight. No way am I missing this.

The little jaunt takes all of five minutes before my feet begin squishing through the sand. We plop the supplies down and the guys go to work on the fire. Knowing they're going to have a ball playing with it, and certainly don't need my help, I wander over to the waves. They lap over my feet and before long, my feet tingle with numbness. I inhale deeply, relishing the chilled waves and crisp air. Nothing better.

The sun starts dipping into the clouds as vibrant pinks and oranges stream across the sky. I wonder how God does that? How can he paint those colors? Orange hits the dark blue waters and shimmers over to me. With the tide all the way out I can walk around the mini braided streams far out across the sand.

Glancing back over my shoulder, I see that they have a tall tepee lit on fire. Great. If the fire department gets called, I'm screwed. I'm so running for it. Hearing no sirens in the distance, I meander back. I know technically even if the tepee should fall over, the sand and water will put it out, but why does it have to be so big? As I see the guys laughing and wrestling around, I know they wouldn't have a fire any other way. Those goofballs.

We go to work making the perfect pie irons. I smother my bread with butter and mash it into the irons. Then loading it with cheese, spaghetti sauce, and pepperonis, I know this will taste like heaven. Getting the iron level in the fire is the hardest part with such a big fire. Ugg, don't these boys know you're supposed to let the fire burn down before cooking on it.

Looking over at Morty, I notice a little bit of his beard looks singed. A laugh escapes me. These men are professional wildland firefighters, and they still play with fire like children. Checking my pie iron, I bang it on the ground, open the clasp and peer in. MMMMMM. Looks like heaven. I dump it onto my napkin and pass the iron off to the next person. I wiggle with anticipation, it looks so good, and bite into it.

"Oh ahh!" I let the scalding hot piece fall from my mouth, but the cheese stays stuck to my lip, and I have to scrape it away. Ow.

"You good," Corey asks with a laugh. I nod.

"OOO, you got yourself a blister there," Morty states pointing at my now swollen lip. Great, it will end up cracking all over this week. Oh well. I give it another minute and test my sandwich again. Okay, definitely cool enough now. It still tastes like heaven, even if a little extra crunchy from sand.

The night feels perfect. We spend it watching the flames of the fire then running into the ocean, warming up next to the fire and watching the stars. There's no better place or better people.

"Next time, you should ask that fella from the fire department to join us," Corey suggests and bumps his shoulder into mine. The fire warms and heats my face. Don't question it. It's for sure the fire, I tell myself, not believing the lie.

"Uh, maybe. We'll see," I mumble my typical standoffish answer. I like the idea of inviting him, and honestly, he would be the type of guy to say yes, just to hang out with people. But would it mean the same thing to him as it would to me? Probably not. Besides, I come from the Midwest, where I'm still a firm believer in the man taking the lead. I should never have to ask out a man. If he doesn't have the guts to do it, then he isn't the one for me. Besides, I'm not the one going to make things awkward if he doesn't like me.

Listening to the roar of the waves and the crackle of the fire, my mind wanders to the plans of the future. I'm starting to think it will always be here in Oregon. Maybe this will be my last adventure and for once, that's okay.

CHAPTER 14

It's finally here! My Mount Saint Helens trip! Once, I got off shift this morning, I packed and drove up to Washington. It was a beautiful drive, and I actually went right through Portland. I thought about giving a shout out to Garrett and Johnny, seeing if they wanted to come. But they just got off shift too and were probably drinking or sleeping or something else. Besides, they just spent forty-eight hours with me at the department. I'm sure they need a break from me. I would need a break from me.

The drive really didn't take that long, and it was gorgeous. I even arrived early, so I can explore! I twist and turn through the green peering up at the mountain when it pops through the trees. Seeing a sign for Ape canyon and caves I decide to head that way.

Once parked, I grab my backpack filled with snacks, water, headlamp, and other things I may need. I don't know about this cave, but I went spelunking in West Virginia once, and it taught me to never go on any hikes without at least one light source. Let alone the three I have in my pack now.

I love all the green. There are no words to describe it except fantasy like. As I come up to the hole leading to the caves, it looks like it belongs in Lord of The Rings. A staircase leading to indescribable darkness stands in front of me with moss growing over all the steps.

As I descend into the staircase, I keep the headlamp off. I want to experience this without a light first. As I feel my way down step by step, the rocks become slick. Finally, there are no more steps, and it feels like I'm on the solid rock floor. Peering up, all I see is a circle of light, the rest complete darkness. A little shiver courses through my body as goose bumps pop up on my skin. The darkness consumes me as a smile tugs at my lips.

Switching on the headlamp, I sweep it around, the light only illuminating a few feet in front of me. I make my way over to a wall and follow it. It's wet to my touch and kind of icky. I walk on for a mile or two before the cave starts getting narrower and narrower, before finally I'm crawling. It is kind of exciting. Not quite knowing where I'm going, my body feels the way. Moisture soaks through my clothes, everything around me damp.

Finally, the ceiling begins cramping me enough that unless I want to soldier crawl, then I can't go any farther. This looks like the end of my road. Deciding to take a break, I flip over on my butt and use my backpack as a back rest.

I switch off my headlamp and let darkness engulf me. Doing this reminds me of when I'm driving and I get lost, I turn down the music because somehow that makes me see better. Turning off my vision almost makes me experience everything else a little more too. Being surrounded by pitch black is actually making me a little claustrophobic though. But it's such an experience. It feels like when it's dark at night and the clouds are over, but this is extreme darkness. Nothingness. A void.

As I sit in the void, I can't help but think about things. What sort of things are looking at me from the dark? Are you in a big cave? Or in fact a little hole? What would it be like to have another person with me? What if Johnny was here? Would I be more aware when he slid an arm around me? Or would I feel it just the same? Would all my other senses be heightened? Or perhaps there's a vampire looking at me from the dark now and I'll never make it out alive.

Finally, after I can't stand it anymore, I switch back on the lamp and munch on a granola bar. I wonder if there are bats in here. I mean I'm sure there are. I saw some signs for white nose syndrome coming over to the caves, but I haven't seen any yet. Poor babies. It's rather calming to just sit and be with the nothingness. However, I should get going back soon. Scootching forward I say a goodbye to the void and head back to where I started.

It seems that I find myself back to the beginning of the cave far more quickly than it took me to get to the end, but that always seems to be the way. Soon enough I see a light growing closer and closer. The hole looks so bright now. I step up out of the darkness one foot at a time. Wow. My eyes squint even though it's still a grey, rainy Washington day. Incredible.

Afterwards, I find myself hiking around the rest of the evening. Across a swinging bridge, overlooking a canyon, waterfalls, everything I can find. Each view looks even more breathtaking than the last. I just love it out here. It's nice to get away from Waldport for a little bit too. Don't get me wrong, I love my home, it is just that the fire department takes a lot out of me. Mentally more than physically. It is nice to step back and remember how great it is to be alive.

There's always this special feeling when I leave society. It's just me and nature. The stress just leaks away. When I don't have to worry about work, or house payments, or boys, I'm finally able to breathe again when I didn't realize I was holding my breath for so long. I could almost collapse with relief.

Finally, it starts getting dark. I had better start my drive to the hiker's bivouac. I honestly don't know if I'm allowed to camp there, but I plan to sleep in my car anyway and that way I'm right there to start my ascent in the morning.

When I arrive at the top, I find that there are some people actually already camping there. Cool, at least I know I won't be arrested or something. However, I don't want to go and just hang out with strangers, even if they're like-minded to myself. Don't get me wrong, I hard core vibe with all my hippie peeps, they just always have to make friends with me first. I'm an introverted hippie soul, which makes things hard. I pull off, away from the rest of the cars and park next to the trailhead sign. Cool, front row seats.

Doing a quick Chinese fire drill, I hop into the back of my car. This car is legit perfect sized for me. I have just enough room in the back that with the seats laid down, I have a little bed. I dig my little cooler out from under some of the pillows. Luckily, I packed some awesome camping food. Okay, not that awesome, but I don't cook. This big bowl of chopped up boiled eggs doused in yogurt ranch is gourmet for me. Yum. I'm glad I made enough that I can have it for a late lunch after my hike tomorrow too!

It's quite dark outside as I finish my meal. I hop out real quick and pee behind my car before the rain gets me too soaked. I love being back out in my element. Rain or no, nature calls to my soul. Snuggling under my sleeping bag, I settle in for some sleep before my big climb tomorrow. Okay mediocre to small climb.

Crinkle, crinkle. My head jerks up. What was that? Listening, it's all quiet. Sighing, my head falls back to the pillow, and I try to drift off again. *Crinkle!* My head jerks up again. It's too dark to see anything. Staying still the crinkling continues.

I move to reach for a flashlight, and it stops again. I huddle back in my sleeping bag, heart racing. The vampire from the cave! Okay but seriously, something is very close to me. A few seconds go by, and I hear it again. I jerk up and flip my flashlight on. Nothing. I flip it back off. *Crinkle.* I jerk up again. Nothing. I have to say, I'm a little scared. My heart races as if it can win a derby. I know there's no monster in here, but what is it? It's really freaking me out. I lay there, hand on my flashlight.

Then, I feel it! Something runs across my hair and over my arm. I scream and point my light at it, ready to throw it if needed.

It's a stupid little mouse! Ugg. How did a mouse get in my car? Great. A groan comes from my mouth as I try to slow my racing heart. Either way, with it crinkling things I'm not sleeping in here tonight. I peek at my watch. Just after midnight.

Opening my door quietly, I peek out. It's lightly sprinkling but nothing terrible. I gather my sleeping bag in my arms and drag it outside. I lay the space blanket on the ground, then my sleeping bag and burrow into it. Then it starts pouring. Awesome. I jump up. Well, I'm not getting any sleep here tonight. I may as well start my hike.

I look at my watch again. Almost 1AM. Not terrible. At least with the cool moisture throughout the air it helps me shake off any lasting sleepies. I jump a few times wiggling around and my brain is ready to go. Hiding under my hatch back lid, I gather my stuff. Headlamp, raincoat, backpack, snacks, trekking poles, water, all the necessities. I know I'm going to be sweating my butt off in this raincoat, but I need it anyway right now. It's a warm, muggy night here in Washington. Though, it was about ninety here yesterday, so it doesn't surprise me all that much.

Keeping my headlamp trained on the ground in front of me, I head towards the sign in post. My permit is sealed in a Ziplock in my pack thank goodness. Otherwise, it would be toast by the time I got up there. Bouncing on my toes as I sign my name and grin. The trail snakes me through the trees. Every now and then I hear signs of some animal out there in the rain, but for the most part it's a nice steady downfall.

Finally, around three in the morning, the rain stops. Although, I seem to have just made it above the treeline. I think that's what it looks like as my headlamps sweeps over lots and lots of rocks. Sitting down, I decided to take a break for a few minutes. Physically, I don't really need one yet, but I've got to stop and smell the roses, you know? I feel like every single day I'm hurrying to the next thing, so I'm going to make this last. The trail was a low percent grade which was nice. But I know going up, soon I will need this little break anyway. Plus, a little less darkness would help. At least in about an hour there will be signs of dawn.

After my legs feel satisfied, I start up again. For a while I weave around through the small rocks. Just as some light begins spreading across the sky, I come to the boulders. Ooooh boy. Taking off my pack, I strap my trekking poles to it. I know some people swear by them for everything, but no way am I using them for boulders.

I scramble up over boulder after boulder. Breathless as I reach the top of each one, and scurry to the next. On and on. The sky a light gray now as I emerge from the boulder field.

As colors pop around the sky, I stare up at the last two hundred yards or so. I mean up. The last part of the mountain looms above me. At least a sixty-degree angle of little volcanic pebbles. Taking a step up only to slide down halfway. *Ugg*. It's like hiking in the dunes. My worst enemy. The wind whips around me, chilling me. From the dried sweat and the wind, my body shivers as it steps again and again through the tiny rocks.

This last stretch seems to take twice as long as the whole hike to get here. Woah! The colors look amazing. I made it to the top just in time to catch the sunrise. Ironically, I'm kind of thankful for that little mouse. Don't get me wrong, I am dragging, but seeing this sunrise on the top is freaking fantastic. The view alone was worth every step. However, this hiking high, the adrenaline, the feeling of accomplishment, this is what I live for.

Looking out, I'm above the clouds! A mountain stands up across the clouds from me. I actually have no idea which one that is. Jefferson? Adams? Who knows, but this, this is unbelievable. Like cloud city in Star Wars, only mixed with the lonely mountain of Lord of the Rings. Wow. What a vibe! I could just stand here all day. Floating.

I only have about thirty feet to the top, at least, I think. I thought I was almost there a little bit ago but then I got there and all of a sudden, I had more to go. Stupid teasing mountain. Finally, once I'm shivering, sweaty and out of breath, I make it to the edge of the caldera. Wow, it's incredible! The ridgeline snakes around the edge of it, and I make my way up to the little peak of the ridge.

Slinging my pack down, I plop beside it. Huffing, I enclose my arms around me. It's breathtaking up here but freezing. I see a couple of people working their way through the boulders. Wow, I can't believe I came up that! It looks worse than the steps to Mordor. But man do I feel accomplished.

That was sure brutal. But I have seriously relished in every single moment. Besides, I've been on plenty of dozer lines that are much worse to climb. At least this was fun without a pressing timeline.

CHAPTER 15

Why didn't you invite me?" Johnny whines as I scroll through the pictures of Mount Saint Helens.

"Well, I thought about it, but wasn't sure if you would be interested or anything," I drawl awkwardly. I mean, I don't want to be one of those annoying overbearing friends. I feel like I'm constantly bugging my friends, and one day it will just be too much for them. Ugg. I hate talking about thought processes and feelings. Yes, I know I'm awkward.

"Dude, I'm always interested in an adventure. Next time, invite me! No matter where it is." Shaking his head with a slight groan as he leaves.

Ugg, see this is what I don't get. Does he just want to go on the adventure, or does he want to spend time with me, or both but as a friend level? Probably just the adventure. Right?

Attempting to push thoughts of Johnny aside, I complain to Lily. I am enjoying having her at the fire department today since she switched shifts with Logan for the week. It's odd having a girl around. I mean yes, the guys always seem to be gossiping, but she's a little bit drama. A bit of like a fire diva.

"So, your hair keeps getting all tangled under your helmet? Want me to cornrow it?" she offers after an hour of jabbering at me about everything in her life. Her and Logan are still a thing every now and then, but she has an awesome new boyfriend. Go her. Heck yea, I want cornrows!

"Actually, that sounds awesome. Thank you." I'm touched she's willing to do that for me. Giddiness makes me wiggle as she brushes my hair out, I can't help but want to grin like a little girl. I love getting my hair done, it's such a rare event but there's always something so sweet and intimate about it. I love the feeling of her fingers running through it, massaging my head. That is until she starts yanking to get the hair into fine little braids making me flinch. I grimace and grit my teeth the whole time but I'm still dancing inside.

"Dang, look at that little chola," Johnny bellows peeking his head in the office at us.

I grin. "What do you think?" My heart squeezes in anticipation.

"Makes you look like a little bad ass. Not that you weren't already," he amends. I just smile as he walks away.

"What was that?" Lily prompts.

"What was what?" I turn to look at her.

"I think that was you and Johnny flirting with each other."

My face heats up. "No way," I defend. Nope, I can't be seen flirting. Besides, I wasn't flirting. Was I?

"Girl, I'm like the queen of flirting, and that was hard core."

"Um, well I guess I kind of like him, but he would never like me," I whisper.

"Well, what I'm reading there was that he already digs you," she claims.

"No way!" I retort a little too loud. I don't want to believe it until he makes a move. Don't have any expectations and you will never be disappointed right? Luckily, she doesn't argue anymore because Garrett walks in. I hope he didn't hear any of that.

"Hey, we're going to take a trip to Ray's," he announces and heads out.

Okay, you know what that means! Food run. If we're on shift and someone needs to go to the store, most of the time we all ride along. That way if we get a call, we can just leave from there. Otherwise, if two people stay behind, then we need to worry about taking another vehicle and what not. We like efficiency.

Besides, I like running to the store. It always feels so normal. Back home in Ohio, sometimes me and friends would just run to the store for something to do. Not like we had any big stores near home, the closest Walmart was thirty minutes away, but it feels like a little bit of home vibes. Something so simple, but it's the most it's felt like home in a while.

"So, what are we thinking tonight?" Johnny inquires to no one in particular as we hop out in the parking lot. Not bothering to answer, Lily and Garrett walk off, already on their way to get their own things. He looks over at me and asks, "Any cravings?"

"Hmmm, you know I just got back from that trip to Washington. Every time I go backpacking or on a fire roll, I always crave chocolate milk and garlic bread. But right now, I'm really feeling a fried bologna and cheese sandwich."

"A what now?" He questions scrunching his face. No way!

How can someone not know what a fried bologna sandwich is? "You know, like a grilled cheese with bologna in it?" I legit eat it all the time at home. It's my idea of gourmet cooking. My grandma used to make it every day when I got off the bus from school, so it kind of became my comfort food. Like a hug I can eat until it envelopes my heart.

"I mean it doesn't sound all that great, but I'm honestly down to try it for supper tonight," he mentions.

Ooo boy. Am I about to prove him wrong! These babies always hit just right! "Awesome!" and my mood instantly spikes a little more. Yass! I love fried bologna and cheese. I pick up some chocolate pudding for dessert too because it sounds good. I'm down for a bit of a fat kid's night. Do I need anything else? Maybe some Reese's cups or cake?

"Do you have to sprint everywhere you go?" he hollers after me.

Oops. I didn't realize I was walking that fast. I slow my pace down as he catches up. Once up to the conveyor belt, I see he got some Tillamook ice cream too. Oh, my goodness, yum! I put the little space bar between his ice cream and the food. He reaches over and slides it back in the rack, scootching the food up to his ice cream.

"Nope, I will get my own food!" I demand.

"Nah, I've got it. This is all mine," he tells the cashier.

"Dang it, Johnny. I will get it next time then!" I fuss, but really it means something that he's getting it. I'm honored. I mean not a lot of people buy my food. Even my close friends and I get our own checks. Family, right? My soul dances with absolute joy.

***

"This is actually quite good," he admits taking another bite of the sandwich I made for him.

"I told you they are the bomb," I defend. Ugg, now the next step would be shredded chicken sandwiches. How do they not have them out here? That's like a Midwest staple food. Instead of hamburger or hot dog, it's shredded chicken or hotdog.

As we're cleaning, I turn Pandora radio on. I have this one station that I listen to all the time based around the song 'You Make My Dreams Come True' by Hall and Oates. It plays all the best music and it's mostly appropriate. I sing and move along with the rhythm as I wash dishes.

Garrett sits in the living quarters watching TV and Lily is down in the bay talking on the phone. I feel a little self-conscious knowing it's just me and Johnny but go about doing things just as I would anywhere.

Snap! A crack whips across the back of my thighs. My feet leave the ground and I jump as a yelp escapes me. Turning, I see his eyes laughing as a towel dangles in his hands.

"OOOO you are so asking for it!" I cry as I wring out the washcloth. It may not be as big as the towel, but since it's wet, I'll be able to get it to snap. He darts around the edge of the kitchen snapping his towel at me every so often. I swing mine out and it gets a good crack at his stomach.

"Yowl! That was a good one! Truce?" He proposes. The sink is right behind me, and I dip my hand in searching for some suds. I feel them slip into my hand, a little mountain of bubbles. He extends his hand to me, and I smash the bubbles on his head, fighting a grin. Only then, I take his hand.

"Truce. But I still think I win," I pipe with a wink. Aww, I remember my first adventure with Johnny, the seaweed, and splashing. I love that every day with him is still filled with childlike fun. My chest heaves with a quick intake of air. Oh, my goodness, Kara. I think maybe I was flirting. Yep, I definitely was flirting. Holy smokes! I mean, it's the twenty-first century, and I'm a strong, cool lady. Why shouldn't I flirt? Well aside from the fact that someone like him could never like me, but still. I'm kind of proud of myself.

***

Ugg, I'm dripping with sweat, completely soaked. I have weight strapped on, plus full gear and I've been doing stairs for the past hour. Ugg. I hate training but know how rewarding it is. Plus, I know the consequences of not training too. Besides, after that wildfire, I'll take all the cardio and such that I can get.

"Alright! Time!" Johnny calls and I hurry back down the stairs knowing I have to drag Logan across the bay. That's our deal. We need to be able to drag the heaviest guy in the department with full gear. I go as fast as I can over to him and link my webbing around his shoulders. Luckily there isn't too much friction on the bay floor, and he slides with me as I heave. I'm huffing and puffing by the end, but I did it. My legs feel like half jello, and I sink to the floor.

Argh. Why is the forest service wildland all cardio and this all strength? I get it, you don't have to explain it, but still. I'm dead. After a few minutes of sitting, my breath evens, my pores stop leaking and I realize I do actually feel pretty decent. It was a good workout, and I'm glad they pushed me.

I barely sling my SCBA off when the tones drop. Instantly, I have energy again. I grab my water off the back and load up. Car crash. Going through scenarios, I try to mentally prepare. While the guys get their gear on, I read off the charts. Not a lot is known because a bystander called it in. But it's a bad one. The ropes team had to be called too, meaning there's a good chance at least one vehicle went over 101. There are two known victims. Woman around fifty and a young boy. Composure covers my face, but my heart pumps.

We arrive on scene and pop out; I can tell we're all a little on edge. To the public eye, nothing but calm, confident work, but this is a big call. The car went over the rocks' edge, and luckily went over in a sandy area. With so much of the Oregon coast around here Basalt rock, it could've been much worse.

Logan takes care of the engine and getting the ropes team on response. Making my anchor, setting up my ropes, and getting ready to repel all in a matter of minutes. Check, double check, and give the signal to Johnny. He is working on setting up his own system. Slowly I lean back into my rescue eight and harness, creeping backwards towards the edge of the face. My breath stops as I take the first step over the edge truly testing the set up. I sigh out as I start walking down the rocks in a repel. Johnny starts lowering above me a few feet to the right. As my feet hit ground, I radio IC.

"Off rope, on ground!"

"Copy, off rope on ground." I unclip and study the landscape around me. As Johnny unclips, I ready for what comes next. Slowly we scuttle along the narrow edge to the car.

Testing some weight on the front, we find the car is stable.

"Go to work on them, I will check out the car!" he yells over the wind. My heart is racing. At least I find the woman semi-conscious. I go into triage mode, check her ABCs. They're stable enough, so I move on to the boy. Moving around to his side of the car, I test the door, grateful it at least opens. Check for a pulse. Nothing. Taking a deep breath, I prepare myself for the upcoming battle.

"Johnny! We need to start CPR, help me get him to the rocks!" I cry. I know the backboard is still minutes out, but this boy may not have minutes. I stabilize the head and neck as Johnny scoops him up to lower him to the ground. I know it is not a safe maneuver, but he can't wait for the ropes crew. I start compressions. My body automatically going through the motions. Johnny at the head radioing the ropes crew for rapid evac for the boy.

It seems to take hours. One and two and.... Thirty! Two breaths. And repeat. Nothing. I continue on and on. In one quick motion someone slides him up onto a board while I continue compressions.

"Switch, Kara." Johnny's hand on my shoulder. I move out of the way and try to catch my heart from breaking from my chest. My chest feels so tight, I focus on the lady. The ropes team already has her loaded on a backboard getting ready to haul up.

"My baby. My baby," She keeps mumbling. My heart breaks for her looking back at the boy. We must have been working on him for a while. I see three other people there to help Johnny with CPR, so tap out and scan the scene.

Looking around the car, I make sure everything's okay, before I peer in the back seat. My whole world shatters instantly. The back door won't open, so I climb through the front. When I finally wedge myself back there, I pull up the crooked car seat. A baby. This one, I don't need a medic to know it won't be coming back. The poor little girl. My mind goes numb as my body goes through the motions of draping a blanket over the baby and hauling the seat out. Looking up, I see Garrett standing around the boy with Logan and Johnny and someone from the ropes team and I pull Garrett over.

"Garrett, I found another victim," I huff choking back tears. I have to hold down all emotions on scene. My body kicks them into numb mode. No emotions. Okay. I can do this. My emotions drop into the void. Body on robot mode I go into routines I've done on a hundred similar scenes before.

The rest of the call is blank. Johnny pronounced the boy expired a few minutes later. We get the car secure. Clean everything, hours pass. Finally, we make it back to the station. By now, my brain has gone into zombie mode. Absolutely showing nothing.

I strip off my coat and hang it, hang my helmet in the engine, strip my pants and squish them around my boots, suspenders laid on top. Perfect. Now what? It's off hours, so technically I can go change. I don't feel like changing, but I sure don't feel like sitting here with everyone. Plus, I know Logan has charts to fill out and I don't want to go back over any of it. I need to keep busy, keep my brain distracted, but there's nothing else to do so I trudge up the steps to the common room and disappear into the bathroom.

I take one look in the mirror, staring into my eyes and lose it. I grab my towel off the rack and huddle in the corner. Continuously wiping the snot from my face with my towel. Curling in a ball, I lay in the corner sobbing. Choking, gasping for breaths between the cries of pain. My whole body is consumed with the grief. I cry out all my pain for the boy and the baby. Praying for God to keep them and take care of them. Praying for strength for me. Praying for the poor mother. I cannot fathom her grief. I hope she's out of it for a few days before it sinks in. She doesn't deserve the physical and mental pain she's going through. No one knocks on the door, no one bothers me.

Finally, the tears stop. I wash my face and rinse it with cool water until finally my eyes return to a semi-normal whitish color. Slowly, I open the door and step out. The coast looks clear. I can hear snoring from the bunk room, so someone is in there. I head down to the office hoping to get some peace. Maybe I'll read a book for a little bit. I certainly can't handle much thought process right now. Something to take my mind off things.

I round the corner of to the office and smack right into Johnny. Crap. He steadies me as I peel my face from his chest and rock back on my heels. I look up and he stares at me, his eyes piercing into mine, seeing everything I don't want anyone to see.

"How are you doing Kara?" he gently prods, gazing into my eyes. I look down. Hold it together. Hold it together.

"I'm fine." I monotone and glance up. He's still staring. It takes all of two seconds before I break down again. I don't even fight it when he pulls me into his arms and holds me. A slow rocking and him rubbing my back. I can't help it. It's not just that they're gone, it's that I feel like I let them down. What if I could have saved one of them? Maybe if I had gotten to that baby girl first, or if I had done more compressions on the boy. The poor mother. I can't imagine all the pain she must be feeling, the loss. My chest tightens and I can't breathe. Choking sobs wrack my body as I fight for air. He pulls me away from him and holds my shoulders at arm's length.

"I need you to breathe, Kara. It's okay. It's not your fault. Just breathe." He takes exaggerated breaths with me. I didn't realize that I was getting extremely lightheaded until it all comes rushing to my head. Oooof. Hold it together girl. Come on. I need to be strong.

With a shake, I get some normalcy back in my system. I wipe at my eyes, nose, face, getting it clean. I can't believe I lost it like that. Especially in front of my Lieutenant, in front of him.

"Thanks. I'm um, good now. Thanks," I stammer avoiding his eyes. I'm still not great, but I am better.

"No problem. I'm always here, okay?" He says sincerely. I nod. "So, what type of ice cream should we get into?" he asks lightening the mood.

"The mudslide. Definitely the mudslide," I declare, glad we're moving past all of this. We sit and talk for a good hour eating ice cream and laughing. Learning a lot about him, I find out he actually grew up near Portland, his favorite color is yellow. What boys favorite color is yellow? Don't get me wrong, I love a nice sunny color, but still, him? He loves Hallmark movies, he's not a fan of classic rock, he listens to emo pop, whatever that is and hates mangos. What a guy.

"Well! I definitely have a few Hallmark movies in my case upstairs," I inform him after I've already forced him to listen to some Poison, Queen, and Foreigner.

"After that torture, yes, please," he mocks the classic rock, how dare he. But I just laugh.

"Well come on then." We head upstairs. I show him my Hallmark section and let him pick one out. I have to say, I'm seriously doubting he actually likes Hallmark movies. He picks out the nine lives of Christmas.

"You picked that because it has a firefighter on the front, didn't you?" I challenge as I specifically plop on his couch. Tough. It's the comfiest couch. He doesn't always get it.

"Hey! Hey! Nope. That is not yours. Off!" He comes over and tugs at my arm.

Ugg. What a child. I laugh. "Nope, go sit on the black one." I point over at the ragged black hard mass.

"Kara, that is my couch. No way am I being a pushover!"

"Tough." I laugh again. At some point he's just going to give up. Maybe, just maybe if he gives up nicely, I will let him have it.

"Not happening!" he yells and in one motion has me scooped up in his arms.

What? I gasp, feeling every single inch of his arms supporting my body. "That's cheating. Put me down!" I squeal.

He spins me a few times and promptly drops me onto the hard black couch. I feel like I'm in a Hallmark movie myself. Being spun around by the sexy firefighter as my arm circles around his neck. Only damsels in books get carried all cute like this. I could cry, I love this. This moment, I feel absolutely special. I laugh, but then remember where I am. My face floods with heat, breathing fast, and heart racing. Oops. At least the bunk room is way across the building. Hopefully I didn't wake anyone up. Blushing as I hit play, I really am thankful for him at least. As the movie begins, I realize I'm extremely worn out. Exhausted. I don't even remember seeing the commercials before I'm out.

CHAPTER 16

Hey, what are you doing for your off days?" Garrett inquires.

"Um, I don't know. Maybe stopping at the library? Going to the Moose for some pie? I know, I have big plans." I laugh at my own lame life.

"Why don't you come up to Portland tonight and go out with us?" he suggests.

Hmm. I mean maybe. After last night, once again, I can't get Johnny out of my head. He must like me, right? Why won't he say anything? I think I might really like him. Look how nice he was to me. Like a knight in shining armor. Gosh, I'm completely falling for him. Yet maybe, he was doing just that, only being nice. I can't be falling in love, what if it never happens, my world will be on a dinosaur level extinction crisis.

"Ehhh, I appreciate the offer, but I don't know."

"Nope, it's settled. You can come up, we will go out, and you will crash at our place," he declares with authority.

"Yes, officer!" I salute and fake mock knowing he's joking. He grimaces but goes on.

"Cool, I will text you our address, and we'll see ya' at our place at about 7:30?" he prompts.

"Uh, yeah. That will work," I mumble preoccupied. "Will Johnny be okay with this?"

"Of course!" he proclaims as if it's settled.

Okay, well I guess I am going to Portland tomorrow. Okay, that's about a three-hour drive, so I will have about three hours to go home and nap, then four to get ready. I laugh. Yup, plenty of time. Johnny peeled out right at the end of shift, so I don't have a chance to tell him I will see him later or anything, but Garrett can tell him. I'm actually super stoked to be invited. I really love spending time with people. Sometimes ha-ha. I mean, it has to be the right people. Only a select few actually. However, I think they top that list.

Being so far away from home can be very lonely. I miss having someone around all the time. My family, my wildland crew, my bestie. Before I moved here, I always had someone. Then it all disappeared when I moved away, and I felt utterly alone. I don't want to need anyone, needing people is overrated. No one will ever be there for you all the time except God. Yet, I feel myself starting to rely on these guys. Depend on them, love them.

***

Hoping this is the right door, I knock again. Suddenly, the door opens wide, and Johnny stands in front of me with a grin on his face.

"Kara! Garrett said you were going to be joining us!" He seems excited. Maybe... nope, don't get your hopes up. But after last night... maybe.

"Yea, so where are we going?" I ask.

"Well, you are from the country, right? Like all you Ohio people are hillbillies and what not?"

"Wow, um okay, people where I am are probably more redneck than hillbilly, but whatever." I'm sure some people would really get offended. Hardin County people take pride in being rednecks.

"Uh, sure. Anyway, there's this bar called Bushwackers. Like a country line dancing bar. Garrett thought you might like that," He reveals. That sounds really cool.

"Yeah, I come from a small town in Idaho, so I get missing home and stuff. Thought it might be fun." Garrett chimes in.

I hadn't even seen him. The couch looks so big he almost melted into it. Dancing sounds amazing. I practically bounce around in excitement.

"Well thanks. Can I just set my stuff somewhere?" I do miss home, but moments like this, with friends who can practically read your mind, this seriously is home.

"Oh yea, uh, you can use my bedroom," Johnny offers.

"Oh nah, I can just set it out here. I'll probably sleep in that corner or something," I say pointing to a little nook beside the TV.

"Well, I can always take the couch and you can have my bed," Johnny retorts.

"Nah, I'm used to sleeping on the floor. Wildland background ya' know," I say and plop all of my stuff in the corner.

I brought a sleeping bag and everything. Totally ready for a sleepover. However, I wish I had known we were going to a line dancing bar. I had no idea what to bring to wear, and I mean it is a city, so I brought a dress. Oh well, it will just have to do. At least I always wear my little fat baby Ariat boots so I will be half country.

Garrett, being the sweetheart he is, made us all spaghetti for supper. Oh, my goodness, I can't remember the last time I ate spaghetti. I love it! Plus, like when has a guy ever made me supper? Granted I wish Johnny made it, but hey, I'll take what I can get. After we finish having a quick bite, I think I better go get ready.

No need to ask where it is, I excuse myself and head to the bathroom. I like the layout of the apartment; you can tell just where everything is at. I put on my dress. Yup, this is definitely more of a clubbing dress, but it will look fine, maybe a little odd with the boots, but it's all good. Well at least it's my idea of a clubbing dress. A knee length flared skirt with a high neckline. I suppose in LA this would be fitting to meet someone's grandmother, but my knees show! How revealing, such a scandal, I think laughing to myself.

Fluffing my hair and swiping some mascara around my eyes, I think I look pretty decent. When I took the corn rows out the other day, my hair looked hard core kinky. Now, it still has more body than it used to but at least it's back to its blonde sleek self.

I slide my boots back on and stride out of the bathroom, then I remember I actually have to take much smaller steps with a dress like this. Ooops. A whistle sounds down the hall and I see Garrett. A half smile spreads across my face. I never know how to feel about guys whistling, I especially don't know how I feel about Garrett doing it. I still remember the first fire with him. I don't think I like guys catcalling me at all. Like part of it kind of makes me feel good and special, but also like ew. Then I kind of feel all sleazy. Plus, I don't have any of the looks that deserve to be cat called. I step out in the living room and see there are a few other guys here too. Twins by the look of it, and one other guy.

"Hi, I'm Kara," I announce as I wave awkwardly. I catch some names, Collin, Noah, Scott, but who's who, I don't know. I see Johnny sitting by the table in a polo and khakis. Crap, did I overdress? Oh well, I may as well show off these fire legs. Although if I'm going to show them off, maybe I should have shaved first. Oops.

The guys all finish their beers, take a few shots and we head out. I can't believe we're taking an Uber when I offered to be DD. Like come on guys, let's save some money. Unless they didn't trust that I wouldn't be drinking. But I come from a line of alcoholics. That saying of *Alcoholism ran in my family until it ran into me*, like, yup, hard core. I'm not giving alcohol a shot to do that to me. Let's be honest, I'm addicted to sweets too much as is, I can only imagine what would happen if I did alcohol or drugs? I would probably be dead in a week.

As soon as we arrive at the bar, I know this is my type of place. The first thing we see walking in is a mechanical bull. Good thing I wore spandex under my dress! A huge dance floor spans the whole south side of the building.

"Yes! This place is awesome!" I shout above the music.

"I figured you would like it!" Johnny states. I don't even hesitate. I want to try the bull. Grabbing his arm, I pull him over to the machine.

"You or me first?" I ask.

"Heck no, you go! I haven't had near enough to drink for that," he claims. I push him inside of the ring with all my might. Luckily, he's off guard, or I would have never budged that freight train. The crowd cheers. He shoots me a look but hops up to the bull.

He gets jerked around for a few seconds, even shouting a few times himself before being launched into the mats surrounding it. I run to help him up. Extending a hand to him.

"See, that wasn't so baaaad!" I squeal as he pulls me down. I practically land on top of him. My legs straddle his waist as I push myself into a sitting position, staying there for a moment, his eyes captivating me.

"Your turn country girl," he tells me, grinning.

Breathless, I roll off him and stand up. Blushing as I realize a ton of people just saw that little awkward moment. Ope. The crowd goes wild as I climb up on the bull. It starts off slow, then rocks faster.

"Yee haw!" I yell as it whips me all around.

Suddenly, it rips out from underneath me, and I'm flying. I land with a flump on the hard mats. I jump up and yell as my hands fly in the air. That was great! What a rush! Running over, I slap Johnny a high five.

"That was totally rad!" I yell with glee, and it was. I loved the rush! I'm radiating with absolute excitement. Life sure is good, isn't it? Its freaking fantastic!

"I'm going to get a drink. Do you want anything?" Johnny asks.

"No thanks. I'm going to go over to the dance floor," I tell him hoping he will say something about meeting me or save me a dance, or something. He doesn't, but I head over anyway with disappointment. I find Garrett dancing with a beautiful blonde. Shocker. The twins each have a girl, and the last guy I don't see. I like the twins. They're hard core funny. Johnny grew up with them here in Portland. Such characters! Plus, they each downed like three shots each before we left the apartment. Dang.

After the song, I find Garrett. He already ditched the blonde and he's talking to another girl at the bar. Thank goodness I never developed a crush on him, he's definitely a heartbreaker for sure. I already get my heart broken day by day with this current unrequited love crush. I wiggle my way through the hoards.

"Looks like you've been having some fun!" I shout over to him as he downs a shot of some brownish liquid.

"You know it. How about you?" he questions.

"Yea, I love it here. Definitely my type of vibe. Thanks for suggesting it."

"So, you see anyone worth your time?" He laughs.

"I don't quite have the line up as you do." I chuckle, but deep down, it's true. I will never have guys lining up the way girls do for him. Speaking of which there's a girl right behind him who's been eyeing him. But seriously, guys almost always want the pretty girl, and I'm not that. I will never be that.

"Nah, just start asking guys to dance and you'll have plenty of choices," he suggests casually. A laugh bursts out like a honk.

"Sure! Anyway though, I think your next move should be on the redhead behind ya'. She's totally into you." I whisper nodding my head in her direction. He glances over and looks back at me smiling. What a womanizer. I almost feel bad sending him in the direction of any girl out here.

"I just might. Thanks. Now go for it, girl, and hey, I'll save ya' a dance or two as well." He downs another shot and makes his way over to the redhead. She lights up as he starts talking to her. Surprise. I mean to be honest if a guy like him came up to me in a bar, I would probably die right there. My turn. Of course, he gets all the girls. I decide to be bold. I can do this! I am a firewoman!

Walking up to the guy next to me I tap him on the shoulder. "Would you like to dance?" I ask.

"Sorry, but no," he replies and turns back around. Oh well. Now I'm a little dejected. But I'm not giving up that easy. I tap another guy and another. Getting various answers of 'I'm here with someone', 'no thanks', 'I don't dance' and so on. Gosh darn, it's like asking guys to be my homecoming date all over again.

Finally, someone says something else. Thank goodness! "Do you know this one?" he asks. Suddenly I realize the song changed and they're doing some sort of round robin now. I watch the steps for a second, grapevine, left, sway, right, two step.

"Well, no, but I think I can pick it up," I say, flashing him a smile. Where I come from, line dances are a staple, this is a basic step, just with moving around a floor.

"Alright then, let's do it." He holds out his hand. My eyes sweep the room for Johnny, but I can't find him anywhere. Garrett however catches my eye. He grins and gives me a thumbs up. Ugg. Embarrassing. I can't help but grin anyway. The first lap around the floor I watch the man's feet intently.

Finally, I chance a glance up and he looks down at me. Dang, what a smolder. I want a cowboy! Can I keep him? Ha-ha. My heart melts as our feet move around to the steps. He doesn't really say much, but then again, I'm not sure I could concentrate on the steps if I were trying to have a conversation with a cute boy. The song ends way too quickly.

"Thank you so much!" I say with glee.

"My pleasure," he says and tips his hat before walking away.

No way! I can't believe that just happened! I had a real-life cowboy romance, well for three minutes, but still! I thought that sort of happiness only came about in movies.

"Nice going, Smokey. May I have the next one?" I turn to see Garrett. Not quite the Romeo, or should I say Johnny, I was hoping to ask me to dance, but I'll take it. Just another almost Hallmark moment for me. This song is a little bit more of a swing dance. My face flushes as he holds me tight. Okay, okay, he's a complete babe.

He spins me out, and in, twirls, twists, and turns, ending in a big dip. My leg kicks out and laughter escaping as the song ends. Oh, my goodness. I'm so blessed to have such good friends in my life.

Lifting his hand to his lips he gives it a kiss before spinning me out again. Ugg. Why can't a real guy treat me this way?

Footloose comes on next. Then *Cotton Eye Joe*, and on and on the line dances come. Surprisingly the step patterns are not all the same from back home. I would've thought it would all be universal, like the cupid shuffle or the electric slide.

I learned all these line dances at 4H camp back in the day, but with the steps changing it takes me a second to catch each one. Even so, they're easy to pick up and for the next hour, I laugh and dance, forgetting any of my cares or worries. Finally, after song eight or fifteen, who knows, I'm parched. I head over to the bar to order a tea.

"Here, I thought you might want a sweet tea," Johnny offers, extending a cup to me.

"You totally read my mind! Thank you so much! How did you know?" That's so sweet of him! Well now I wish I came over here earlier! Honestly, wow. I'm touched he got me a tea, well and that he knows me well enough to get me a tea.

"You kidding me girl? You are constantly drinking sweet tea. I'm surprised your body doesn't sweat it."

"You never know, it might." I laugh. We find a table and sit and chat. Well, even if he won't ask me to dance, I will take a sweet tea. Plus, at least he didn't try to sneak in alcohol. I hate when guys do that. Like no, I asked for a sweet tea, I will know there's alcohol in it. I'm not a drinking kind of girl.

"So, did you have fun tonight? A little bit of home here in Oregon?" he inquires, leaning towards me.

"Yeah, it was definitely a needed night of country. Believe it or not though, Oregon is becoming more and more like home. This was just a cherry on top, ya' know? But y'all definitely help make it home." Awkwardly my arm gives him a weird side hug before I pull it back in embarrassment. A grin bursts out over his face.

"Great, so um... would you ever... uhh. Anyway, so, you see any guys out there meeting your fancy? I saw you got a few different fellas to dance with you. Garrett and you were fantastic," he says.

What was all that about? My mind reels. How am I supposed to answer that? I mean, does he know I like him? I could be like one of those flirty girls and say something about how he's the only one who has my fancy. But what if he doesn't like me like that? I can't ruin our working relationship.

Besides, the guy needs to make the first move! Come on, make a move, Johnny! Please.

"Oh yea, some of these guys really know how to dance! It was so much fun, but no, I don't think I will be seeing any of those guys again. Well, except Garrett, you know with work and such." I laugh. Was that casual enough? I don't want him to get the idea I'm into any of them, but I also don't want to be desperate or anything like that. I can't do the whole hint thing either because I can't lie, and my face would end up telling it all.

"Yea. So, anytime you want someone to hang out with, I'm always around. We can make this more of a habit." He trails off.

Is that him asking me out? No. He would just come out and say it, right? Like please be blunt! I need straight up asking! Should I make a move? Or should I be a proper lady and wait? What if I'm reading into it all again and he actually doesn't even want to hang out with me? I mean who would? I wouldn't. Maybe they just hang out with me over pity.

Nope, I can't go back to over thinking all this again. I will cause myself an anxiety attack just trying to figure out if he likes me.

What if he does? What if he doesn't? What if he does and will never say? Or worse, what if I like him forever and he never likes me back. So many possibilities. Too much thinking! Nope, turn it off!

"I think I'm going to go dance again. Want to join?" I ask my hands fidgeting and wringing each other out. There I made a move. Oh my gosh, that was a huge step for me. I mean it's the twenty-first century, I'm allowed to ask a guy out. Shoot, that wasn't like actual asking out, but asking to dance is my way of asking him out. I mean I can't just blurt out 'Go on a date with me!' you know? My breathing is so rapid, I hope he doesn't notice I'm practically hyperventilating. Golly.

"Oh, um, no thanks," he answers.

Well crap, I heave a sigh as my body sags. I blew it. Dejected, I head back out to the dance floor. Give up Kara, he doesn't like you. No guy could ever like you. Just stick to being you. All I need is me and God, right?

Luckily, it's the Cha-Cha Slide, no partner needed. My mood instantly picks up as my feet fall in. Dancing makes everything better. Yes! I live for this! I don't need no man. Life is good.

As I dance the night away, I forget about my boy problems. Dancing with random strangers, watching people fly off the bull, setting Garrett up with more girls, it's fantastic.

"You are the bestest wingman ever... or is it wing woman? I got so many numbers!" slurs Garrett. He's absolutely trashed. He and I sit in the very back of the Uber with a bowl of French fries in my lap. Johnny sits in the front and the other three guys are in the middle section. How I got the back with Garrett, I have no idea.

"Oh, yeah? Well, you suck as a wingman, but thanks," I say wedging another French fry in his mouth. I just really hope he doesn't hurl again. Luckily, that was before we got in the car, but good golly, this boy.

I hate when guys get all drunk, but my mind goes straight to mother mode. I had to be the team mom for a lot of the drunk guys at home, well and girls. I just don't understand why people let themselves get this way. I guess from a mental standpoint I get it, losing yourself to the alcohol, letting it take over. I understand in theory just as well as the next person. A release. Losing yourself though along the way. But the whole physically getting sick thing, and then proceeding to do absolutely idiotic things, that's what I don't get. Isn't there a happy medium?

"Well, I know someone I could set you up with," he slurs back leaving his mouth open for more French fries. I roll my eyes. Goodness, it's like feeding a toddler. I laugh.

"So, thanks for coming out with us, Kara," Johnny pipes up.

"Of course! I loved it so much!" I proclaim as we pull up outside of their apartment. Practically pulling Garrett out of the car, I wonder if I'm going to have to carry him up or something. That's when I look over and see their friend Noah in a shopping cart. Where the heck did he get a shopping cart? Johnny gives it a push and it rolls down the parking lot hill.

"No! Oh my gosh!" I scream and chase after it as they laugh. He leans steering the cart like a skateboard, narrowly missing cars. It crashes into a curb as he and the cart fly forward. I rush down, assessing it all.

"Are you okay? Stay still for a moment," I urge trying to look him over.

Ignoring me, he jumps up shouting, "Woohoo! Let's do that again!" He screams. His twin is just as excited and jumps all over the place. Gosh darn, it's like the personalities of the Weasley twins. Luckily the other guy just got in an Uber to go home, so I just need to get this lot up to the apartment.

"No, no, let's not," I prompt grabbing his elbow and leading him up the hill. I can't believe that just happened! We find Garrett sitting back on the sidewalk and Johnny patting Garrett's back. Well, at least he's being a little more of an adult now. Jeez! I really do feel like a mom looking after four little boys.

Finally, we get all the little drunks up the stairs and to bed. The twins share a pull-out futon in Garrett's room, so I have the living room to myself. I still feel awkward about sleeping on the couch. It's out in the open making me feel all exposed. Sleeping at the firehouse is one thing, it's normal, but this just isn't the same without all the guys. So, I make a tiny little set up in the nook, hidden and protected. As I lay down in my little cove, I can't help thinking it might be easier to drag an unconscious body out of a burning building than get four trashed guys up eight flights of stairs.

CHAPTER 17

This really is the most beautiful place with the most awesome people. Johnny and I have been texting on and off all day. A lot of it is just sending GIFs. My heart jumps every single time I hear my phone go off. Part of me knows how silly I'm being. Just friends. It will never happen. He's just a guy I work with, but then again, how can you really know if you like someone or are just good friends? I'm pretty darn sure that I like him... more than I should. But is it unrequited love that will never be returned? Like if I love a celebrity, or think I love a married man, that love will never be returned. Or is it love that could one day be mutual? That is the million-dollar question isn't it.

However, I'm not good at this whole texting thing. Like I love that he's messaging me, my heart keeps fluttering and all that jazz, but we've been at it for hours. I've run out of things to text and GIFs to send. Couldn't we have like just called for half an hour instead or something? Or better yet, let me just send him letters and we can meet at some ball. I hate dating nowadays. Okay, we aren't dating, that's just wishful thinking. But this whole texting thing is hard. I just want to meet someone like back in the movies. Is that so bad? Ugg. Why does liking someone have to feel like work? So much stress constantly courses through my body. Ugg! This isn't working. I'm just going to be in my head all day if I stay here.

Picking up my phone, I think about who to call. Johnny or Garrett would be fun, but that wouldn't help me get my mind off things, so I dial Corey.

"Hey girl what's up?"

"Are any of y'all down to do something today? Anyone off?" I add. I forgot that people work normal hours too, or well as normal as wildland dudes can get.

"Actually, me and Morty are both off, we were about to go crabbing with our Squadie today. Wanna' join?"

"Heck yes! Be there in a few!" I reply as I am pulling on my boots and hopping on my bike. Crabbing wouldn't be my first choice by any means, but it will get my mind off Johnny and besides I miss my wildland guys. Anything feels like an adventure with them. I pedal fast and hard. I'm there before he even had a chance to finish his morning beer and eggs.

"Wow, starting early today?" I ask him.

"You know it, got those kegs and eggs," Morty chimes in. My head just shakes in disbelief. What a riot. These guys crack me up.

I can't believe I'm on a dinky little boat with three big men. Don't get me wrong, this is awesome, but I feel like I'm in some sort of movie, something like The Three Stooges. I'm definitely waiting for all three to go to the same side and tip us. Yet, everyone knows what they're doing. Mostly I'm just watching as expert hands hook the bobbers, sling the rope into the pulley and heave.

"You want to try?" Troy, their squaddie asks.

"Nah, I'm okay," I say waving him off. Really, I'm enjoying just being on a boat and the fact that it's currently not raining.

"Come on, Kara, you're losing your wildland muscles, come pull a crab pot." Morty hypes.

"Yea, Kara, quit making us do all the work," Corey counters. Dang. Called out! I hop up from my seat and wobble over.

"Okay, what do you want me to do?" I ask.

"First, you will hook it, you can either do that with your hands or the hook, but since you're not wearing gloves, I suggest the hook." I take it from his hand and get ready. The bobber comes racing towards me and miraculously, it catches, then starts trying to drag me back the other way.

"Now you latch it in the pulley!" I heave it towards the pully system, but I can't get the dumb rope to start weaving in. Before I can cry for help, his rough hands help me pull it into the wheel.

"Now as the basket swings up, you will swing it over here to dump in the pot." I swing it over towards me as my boot catches and I slip towards the ground. Luckily, it lands in the boat. Not so lucky, the crab pot swings sideways, the latch opens, and crabs fall down on me. They scurry all over the boat as I scream and jump up. The boat wobbles as Corey's hands steady my shoulders. Booming laughter escaping from all three men.

"Well, that's one way to get them in the boat!" Troy jokes. I can't help it; laughter escapes me too.

Turns out, crabbing does get easier. As we're here sitting at the Moose, I can't help but be thankful for all my friends here. It's nice that I have two groups I can go to. It's also awesome that Troy is a Moose member, so we each sign in a guest, Morty with me, Corey with him.

"Can I get a Shrimp Daddy Delight?" Troy asks the bartender. I look over at him.

"What the heck is that?" I question. Ew, shrimp? That sounds disgusting and my face must show it. He laughs as the bartender slides him a drink.

"It's pretty much a Fuzzy Navel with some raspberry Schnapps, a splash of Sprite and some Grenadine," he explains as if it means something to me.

"But why is it a shrimp daddy?" I ask.

"I am Shrimp Daddy and I made up this drink," he announces proudly. My turn to laugh.

"And why are you the shrimp daddy?" I inquire. I mean seriously? I know many of the wildland guys have weird nicknames, but this one might be towards the top of the odd list.

"Because I own a company called Shrimp Daddy so I can label myself as I please," he enlightens me with a smirk. Oh, well, dang. That's actually pretty rad, owning a company and wildland firefighting. Is this guy for real? But I'm sooo not calling him Shrimp Daddy. Sounds like some freaky pimp thing.

"Oh, that's pretty cool."

Is all I can say. The guys must like the drink too as they both order one. I mean if I were a drinking person, maybe I would give it a try. One day, just a sip or something. Actually, I've been exploring the idea of drinking, just a tad, for the experience.

"You want to try one, Kara?" Corey asks.

"Nah, I will stick with my tea." Even if it's not proper sweet tea. I chuckle as the bartender even sticks a few cherries and an umbrella in their drinks.

"So, any new developments with that Lieutenant of yours?" Corey probes, wiggling his eyebrows. I try to hide my smile, but my face goes hot anyway.

"I told you, there's nothing there." I claim.

"Why do I get the feeling that isn't true?" He mumbles, nudging my shoulder.

"Ugg. Okay we have been texting a little. But I went up to see them in Portland this weekend and Garrett danced with me more than Johnny! Actually, Johnny didn't dance with me at all," I emphasize, moping.

"Well maybe he doesn't know how to dance..." Corey replies. My stomach clenches. I hadn't thought of that. Here I jumped right to him having zero interest in me. Well, I know he can dance some, we danced that night at the bar. It felt so amazing, and magical. But they were all just like normal dancing, no line dances. Maybe he doesn't do those. Or maybe he was nervous or something. Or I mean he could just not like me. Yea, probably the latter.

"Oh, you know I never thought of that! But I mean he would have asked me anyway, right?"

"Kara, just because you're confident, doesn't mean the rest of us are," He proclaims as a snort escapes me.

"Confident? Me? Heck no! Who do you think you've been hanging out with?" I challenge, shocked.

"No, honestly girl. You walk around like you absolutely know yourself and it's intimidating. You may not think it, but you sure do have a confident aura. Even some of us guys on the crew were intimidated by you when you came to the fireline. I mean heck, this five-foot-two woman is willing to travel with nineteen guys she doesn't know and still be a badass on the line. Yea, that's hard-core intimidating."

Wow. I'm speechless. Never in my life, would I have thought myself to be intimidating. That's just not me. I'm always the shy one, the loner, the wallflower. And here, people apparently think I'm all confident and stuff. I burst out laughing. Wow, honestly that was a self-esteem booster I didn't know I needed.

"You've got to be kidding me. I'm the least confident person ever. But hey, I guess I will just go with it. That's kind of cool that people think that, but it's totally false. Well anyway, if I'm all confident, want to dance?"

He laughs but sticks his hand out to me. It's kind of hard to dance to people singing karaoke, but that's what we do.

A large variety from *'Friends in low places'*, to the *Dixie Chicks*, to *Chuck Berry* plays. We dance to them all for at least a good half hour. Then we join the others in a game of darts, followed by pool and before I know it, we've wasted the whole night. Dang. These guys are awesome. I'm so blessed to have such rad people in my life out here. No more stress weighing on me tonight. I feel free again.

As I pedal home, it really weighs on me how much I love the Pacific Northwest and my life here. Don't get me wrong, I do miss watching thunderstorms on the front porch with my family. I miss the seasons, and little things like mowing the lawn. I've only been in Oregon for like half a year, but I can't imagine moving home anymore. The lack of adventure, the lack of adrenaline.

I've gotten to go to Mount Saint Helens, Mount Hood, Crater Lake, Wildland fires in Washington and just all over. This is my home now. Sometimes, I miss the idea of being a little farmer's wife, having six kids and cows. But I think I want the adventure more. Keep my adventurous spirit alive. A new sunrise every morning, rad experiences every day and a different sunset every night.

Something keeps pulling me more and more into the life here. I love having friends and really the fire department is my family. Plus, apparently, out here, I'm confident. No one in their right mind would have ever called me confident back home. I was always taught to let the man speak, to be a follower. In high school I broke down crying when I had to read a paragraph in front of my class. Here, only a couple of years later and apparently, I even intimidate wildland guys. Crazy!

CHAPTER 18

I can't believe I'm on my way to another wildfire. I'm pretty stoked for it, but I had thought my wildland days were over. But here I am being a squaddie for the fire department. Luckily, I will only be leading a truck, so there will be three guys working under me. Even better yet, it's Logan, Titus, and a guy from Seal Rock. Unfortunately, Garrett and Johnny are helping cover shifts back home, so I won't see them for a week or so. My heart actually squeezes thinking about missing shifts with Johnny. Sadness cripples my poor heart. But this is huge! A squaddie! I'm so excited!

We're heading to the Kincade fire, somewhere east of the Bay area; San Francisco that is. Just a few hours ago, we drove right past Mount Shasta, and we could see it right from the road. What I wouldn't give to just get to stop and go hike it right now. My family actually went on a vacation there one time, and it feels strange to spend it with a whole new family. I'm pretty stoked about it though.

Supposedly, we will be doing less physical work than the forest service hand crew. Here we will be with the engine, putting out hot spots. Luxurious. Having water readily available is not something I'm used to. I am a squaddie however because out of these three guys, I have way more wildland experience. I guess my IC5 and trainings will come in handy. An odd feeling being in a leadership role to my captain. Luckily, I will still be answering to a Supe. He's from Newport Fire and he's a totally rad dude.

On this fire we're working twenty-four-hour shifts, however the night shift will be monitoring, which is freaking awesome. Working twenty-four hours on and then you get twenty-four hours off! Plus, on our days off, we get to sleep in a trailer. Freaking cake walk compared to sixteen-hour days on the front line sleeping in the dirt! I've never been on a wildfire like this. Part of me wishes I was about to be hiking far into the wilderness to be sleeping in the dirt for two weeks with my nineteen other guys. But hey, this is a new adventure, and I can't wait to see how the spoiled firemen live.

Thankfully when we roll in, dinner is being served. I'm pretty sure these guys were about ready to start eating sticks if we had to go directly to the line. I don't think they would survive more than three days on an Alaskan fire.

Inhaling deeply, I moan in appreciation. Yes! Fire camp is serving lasagne tonight! I'm a sucker for Italian food. This is legit the biggest, most awesome fire camp I've ever been to. I guess that's the difference between Cal Fire and the federal government. We always got the low end of the deal.

After supper, they show us the shower trailers and the sleepers. Good golly, legit I feel like a queen. I've never ever been on a wildfire that had portable showers and a real bed! At least not that I've known. I'm sure the bigger ones I've been on have had them, but we have always been spiked out pretty much or camping in tents by some school. I can't believe I'm getting paid for this, well, vacation. Woah! I know we are going to have to work, but I never buy nice food, or beds when I travel, so it kind of feels fancy to little me. We file into the sleeper trailer.

"Oh, heck no, you are small! Shorties take the top bunk!" Logan grumbles. And so it begins. The wildland fire grumps. Oh, well, I used to always like the top bunk as a kid, right? Only there are three beds stacked. The gap between the beds is so narrow that I have to use my whole body to shove the bag in. I wiggle myself in between the red bag and the walls. Very cramped, but hey, you won't hear me complain. Better than being soaked in the rain freezing all-night. Morty will testify to that!

***

"Girl, don't you ever run out of energy?" Logan questions as I dance to the music while we work our way through the breakfast line.

"Nope. It's a good morning!" I sing. Mandisa playing in my head. I used to listen to that song like every morning. I would drive my friends nuts with it. Sleepovers, five AM mandatory gym practices, FFA competitions in the rain, I was always bouncing listening to that song.

"It's four AM. Save some of it for tonight. Twenty-four hours is a long time." He grumps along.

"Yeah, yeah, I know. Besides, shouldn't I give you lectures now?" I taunt as I dance around him. I know I'm walking a fine line. Because really, even though I am a squaddie, he could pull the captain card any minute since I am technically here with the fire department. Well, or he could make my life hell back home. So maybe I should reign in just a little.

"Let's make a deal, you don't talk until I've had coffee. Deal?"

"Fine," I reply, knowing not to push anymore. I know better than that. But the music still plays in my head and my hips still move along.

***

"I need you guys to dig deeper! I'm still finding heat," I command. I'm not trying to be mean, but every time they think they are done, when I climb down and stick my hand in the hole, there's still heat. Not like they're digging real fast or hard either. Like come on! Wildland guys would have had these heat spots done and been three miles ahead of us by now. These guys were just covering it up and spraying water on it. What the heck do they teach these guys wildland wise?

"Ahh! Shoot! Gosh darn it. I'm probably standing on a freaking body right now!" I hear a yelp and someone cursing. Titus. I look back and see him standing in a hole.

Unfortunately, we're mopping up in a cemetery. First for me too. Usually, I am so far out in the boonies that we don't see signs of people for days. Here though, the fire ripped right through town. Some of the town was spared, some wasn't. Luckily, there are a lot of vineyards and such around here, so it burned quickly and not too hot. It didn't even torch most of the trees in our area. We all burst out laughing as Titus clambers up.

"Watch out for those tree roots," I warn through the laughter. "The trees are tall here, so their roots stretch wide. That's why we're having to dig so deep and our trenches snake like rivers. We're following the burnt-out root systems now," I state sobering. I know this is serious, and we're in sacred ground. Actually, it is kind of a peaceful setting. The smoke still lingers, the ground gray and black with ash. Headstones stick up amongst the cloudy air. Almost like a black and white movie.

I don't really like this whole being boss thing. I mean I do, but I don't. I know what I am doing, it's just I have a hard time telling them what to do. Nah, actually I'm kind of enjoying it. My confidence is showing a little and growing as the day goes on. I kind of like it.

I point out more heat spots along the way and we dig as a team. Within a few hours they've learned quite a bit. Looking for the fire bugs to spot heats, smelling for heat, and seeing it. They actually get down to feel if it's still hot before trying to move on. My heart feels happy. It feels like I'm a momma watching her kids learn how to take their first steps. My boys are growing up and they will make some fine wildland firefighters.

"Take lunch!" I shout out to them. No MREs for me today, the fire camp packed us sacked lunches and dinner. This is a luxury I seldom get. Yum!

"Ew, Broccoli" Patrick the Seal Rock guy complains, tossing it to the side.

"I will take it if no one else wants it," I say and he launches it at me. Suddenly two more pelt me. "What's this? My crew not eating their veggies?" I laugh as I dig through my own. I fish out an Uncrustable. "Bingo!" I say tearing it open. We munch along enjoying ambiance of the fire life. We all put our extra food back in the engine. I shove all my broccoli pouches in the side door for safe keeping. Yum. Those should be a good snack sometime.

***

"Take thirty and sharpen your tools a little. Give them some love," I tell the boys after we've sat and hydrated. These guys weren't even going to bring files in their line gear. Like jeez! In the Wildland world, these tools are your best friend, your responsibility. You get one tool, and you take special care of it. We even name them. The guys typically choose some sort of girl name, it's their baby. My first year, my Pulaski was named Roland. Roland definitely got special care every break.

I get that it's not quite like a gun in the military, it's not going to save my life from an enemy or something like that. However, if you take care of your tool, it will take care of you back. Work smoother, faster, enabling you to work more efficiently. Sometimes we are initial attack with a fire right at our heels, so in a way, it could save your life.

***

The rest of the afternoon is spent cutting snags, digging out hotspots, avoiding stepping on the front of graves as best we can, and making the best mud pits ever. Once the sun starts dipping, we've all been assigned our own property to protect. AKA rich people's houses.

As we snake our way up the road, I can tell this person must have one heck of a job. Some sort of plantation like farm. Growing what? Who knows now. But I can assume what it was. Supposedly this house and property is an 8.4-million-dollar place. Like holy cow! I don't actually know what the little place I am living at is worth, but considering all it has is plywood for flooring, it can't be more than like thirty thousand tops, ha-ha. Maybe I can marry one of these people one day. Nah, I need a man to take care of me, like a certain firefighter I know. I would take him any day over some billionaire.

It's completely dark as we make our sweeping rounds. Basically, our job is just to make sure that no trees torch on the property and that there's a cold line around the house. Easy peasy.

"Alright, I want a solid five-foot cold trail around the house, and a thirty-foot perimeter around it feeling the bases of trees." We grid off the house first, then the trees. The headlamps shine through the lingering smoke. You know, I can't quite see the house, but considering it takes us a good hour just to trail around it, yea this is a nice one.

"Give a hoot!" I yell. Hoots and hollers echo back to us from our right. Titus and I walk in that direction. Soon enough we see their headlamps and we're reunited.

"Good work! I want one last trip around our line, then we will take shifts of two sleeping. How's that sound?"

Choruses of "copy" and "good" resonate. Sweeping along, it seems this back yard is bigger than we previously thought, even going up a large hill.

"What the heck is that?" Patrick exclaims. We hurry along and all shine our lights in his direction. I follow the fence line up. Holy smokes! This fence has to be like thirty feet high with spikes pointed in. A tree had fallen across the fence ripping a tear down the whole side.

"It looks like a freaking T-Rex cage!" Logan hollers. I mean, he isn't wrong. Who knows what sort of weird stuff rich people buy? I'm sure he doesn't have a live dino, but a tiger or something? I mean if he did have a dinosaur, it would be pretty darn rad! But we should all learn a lesson from Jurassic Park, humans and Dino's are not meant to live together.

"Well, whatever was in it, isn't there now," I state. Not that I'm all that worried, but this is California. I mean who knows if this millionaire had a lion, tiger, bear, or something else. Hopefully it escaped the fire. Most importantly, hopefully it doesn't eat us in the middle of the night. But I don't think any living being would stick around a wildfire blazing through, it's probably long gone by now.

Holy smokes, it's legit freezing. My teeth clatter together, and I shiver all throughout our walk. Now that I'm not digging and rolling around in the ash looking for heat, I am no longer sweating. In fact, I'm pretty darn cold! Why is it cold on a wildfire? I've honestly never been this cold on a wildfire before. Being wet and damp in Washington was still alright because it was hot. But apparently, October in Northern California is not nice for winter camping. I thought California was always supposed to be hot!

"Logan and I will take the first shift. We will wake you guys up in four hours. How does that sound?"

"Copy, sounds good," they say as they climb into the trucks. I'm going to so be that person, but I grab my bunker gear out of the compartment. I am just way too cold. For now, I just slip on the coat and hope it will be enough to keep me warm.

"You're not supposed to wear bunker gear on a wildfire," Logan teases.

"Har-Har. I never would have thought I would be cold on a wildfire," I concede, teeth still chattering. At least I'm warming up a little, even if it's slow going. "Okay, once an hour, we're going to take a lap around the house to check for heat. In between, we can just sit and monitor." Really, I want to take the lap around the house more to keep me active and awake than anything else. It will be good to see on the other side of the house every hour, just in case, but this ground looks all black, it's about as safe as you can get wildland wise. One foot in the black always, except we are miles into the black now. My brain is at the point of tired that it doesn't know if it should shut down completely or laugh at everything. My teeth chatter uncontrollably then the giggles come. Come on Kara, compose yourself. You are a leader here.

"So, you got a guy back home or anything?" Logan asks.

"What is it with everyone being so interested in my dating life all of a sudden? What if I say I'm a nun doing community service out here? Or what if I was secretly already married to a prince in Nepal or something," I prod laughing harshly. Seriously, back home no one ever asked me about dating, even my family, but out here, it's like a crime to be single.

"Well, then I would say you just blew your secret with the prince. Does Nepal even have royalty? But yea, I would say you would make a decent nun," he claims with a chuckle.

"I don't know about Nepal, but thanks on the nun. But nah, I wouldn't actually be cut out for it. I had thought about it for a while, when I was a kid, I did want to be a nun. But I also wanted to be a rock star and an artist. For the nun, I unfortunately like many of my pop culture things way too much, but I also totally want a Hallmark movie romance. However, the problem is finding a decent Christian guy," I reveal. Really it is hard.

It's hard to be a female in my line of work and have a guy actually like you. I'm counted as one of the guys way too much. It's even harder to find a guy who doesn't drink constantly and believes in waiting until marriage. One who's sweet, kind, and an all-around just awesome guy. Pretty much doesn't exist. Not that I'm actively looking. I mean I can think about Johnny, but that's it. And that's because my brain is always thinking about Johnny. I don't need a man to take care of me. Don't get me wrong, I want a man to take care of me, but I actually do really well by myself and somehow, I guess I'm a very confident lady. I'll just keep telling myself that, and it will be, right?

"Well, have you ever thought about Johnny?" He asks. That's it, I lose it laughing. Of course, I've thought about Johnny. I've thought about him like fifty percent of every day for the last six months. But I can't let my captain know I have feelings for the lieutenant. Crap, what if he already knows and I'm about to get in trouble.

"Nah, that boy ain't for me." What? Why did I say that? I could have said anything else. Now what if he tells Johnny I'm not interested in any way. Should I say something else? Crap. Nah, just play it cool, brush it off. It's not desired for a girl to seem too interested anyway. That whole desperate thing or something. "I'm, uh, going to go look for heat spots," I say and wander away. Crap. I might have just blown my chances forever. Gosh darn it! Oh well, I needed to move anyway. My eyes were starting to droop as is.

One more hour to go. I sit back beside Logan, eyes heavy. He seems wide awake now, I don't understand how. We're on hour nineteen and some change of our shift. Plus, I don't think any of us got a good sleep last night. I'm going to sleep like all twenty-four hours of my off day tomorrow.

"Just a little longer and we will wake the others for shift change, okay?" I mumble. My head keeps dropping and waking me up. Keeping myself alert, I bounce my legs, pinch my hands, whatever it takes. If I were digging line, I wouldn't be having this issue. I've worked thirty-six-hour shifts on a hand crew with no problem. But that's when the adrenaline was flowing heavily. Now, just sitting here, I'm struggling, and I hate that! Luckily, with my bunker jacket, I'm no longer cold. That at least makes this night much better. I think I will fold up the pants to use as a pillow in the truck.

"Kara, it is shift change." Logan nudges me. My eyes had been staring off in the distance for who knows how long. Looking at nothing but watching it all at the same time. The million-yard stare. Ambling up to the truck, we wake the others. Looking ready to go, they hop out of the truck with too much energy. I hop in the back, knowing Logan will take the front. That's fine with me, I can stretch out across the back.

"You're doing a good job, Kara. Just remember you don't have to have this whole leadership thing down pat. You're allowed to be tired too," he says.

"Good, because I'm exhausted," I mumble, my eyes already closed as I drift off.

"And you know, it's okay to like Johnny. I'm sure the feelings might be mutual." Huh? My brain doesn't process. All I heard is something about Johnny. The fog is too thick.

"Yea, he's pretty awesome." I sigh out as the darkness takes over, hearing one last chuckle.

Morning rolls around and our replacements come. We start down the mountain before dawn even arrives. Too bad. I won't ever get to see the T-Rex cage in the daylight. Hey, we get twenty-four hours off now. That's crazy. I fully intend to sleep the morning away at least!

Like a zombie, I walk through the breakfast line, and devour the food. What did I eat? You know I'm not even sure, but I bet it tasted decent. I about slip trying to get into the top bunk, but Logan catches my foot and props it into the bed. Yes. Bed. Then, I'm out.

***

The shower feels like heaven. It's only been a little over a day since I've showered, and this feels amazing. How do I normally go two weeks without one? Honestly, as I stand there letting the water pour down on me, I can't imagine it. What a luxury. I feel like a queen. Thank goodness.

When I arrive back at the sleeper, I see many of the guys playing cards outside. Luckily, I brought a book. I'm going to lose myself in Middle earth. Sometimes I wonder if I would actually be strong enough to go on a quest like that.

I struggle with just waking up for wildfires and I actually do enjoy working on them, for like sixty percent of the time. Well, I like the job, does anyone really enjoy digging hand line and swamping? No, don't answer that because I know some of the guys do for sure!

***

"What's that terrible smell?" Logan announces as we load back into the engine. We ought to roll out to get to our post on shift change, us all climbing in the muggy, aroma filled box.

"Good golly, it smells like a wetland pond mixed with decaying vegetables," Titus complains.

Vegetables.... Crap. I dig in the side pocket and produce four containers of wilted, slimy broccoli. "Um, I think it's my bad guys. I'm sorry!" I say sniffing the container. "Yup, it's definitely my bad." Well, at least I'm not with the forest service. They would make me do like one hundred push ups for something like this. These guys all grumble and groan, but no one says much else. Small mercies. They might hate me for a few hours, but that's okay as long as no physical punishment is on its way.

We arrive at our post for the day, mopping up some yards here in the valley. For the most part it was all grasses and scrub shrubs so many of the structures remain in great shape. It's still so weird to not have to walk like twenty miles a day, digging hotline and swamping when your life depends on it.

Here, we are working at a more mellow pace and with far more water. This is the life. We do have to pack in some hose, but what else is new? I will trade that any day for having to pack in a QB, and bladder bag for miles on end.

CHAPTER 19

I hear you're getting back today?' I read a text from Johnny.

'Yup, sure am. It was a really good roll though' I text back smiling.

'That's great to hear. Would you want to hang out when you get back? I will be off shift in the morning. We could go on an adventure.' He asks. An adventure with Johnny, sounds amazing. Yes! My heart starts beating faster. Am I breathing normal? This is huge. I mean he texted first, is he making a move? Or just friends hanging out? Either way, I am so there.

'That sounds amazing. Hey, I've really been missing the fall vibes of home. Know anywhere to see some colorful leaves?' I text. And I have. It doesn't feel like Halloween should be here. I mean from the rainy Oregon coast, to dry, Cali, back to the coast, this isn't fall. Where are my leaves, and crisp foggy mornings? I need those vibes.

'You bet! I can pick you up at your house as soon as I'm off shift.'

'See you then!' Even my soul is smiling right now as I wiggle around in my seat. I glance up and see all three guys looking at me, even Logan in the mirror as he drives.

"Who you texting?" Logan asks as if he already knows. He doesn't, right?

"Um, no one. Just a friend."

"Sure...." Titus adds.

Ugg. Men. Patrick doesn't say much, and another guy from Seal Rock, Clancy sits in silence too. Apparently, our engine had more room and hey, I can't say I blame him for not wanting to be squished.

The rest of the ride remains quiet as all three of us in the back fall asleep on each other's shoulders. There's always something so intimate about being on a wildland crew. It wears you to the bone, exposes your true self. Makes you rely on others to the extreme and forget about boundaries. It really scared me at first how close I had to become with people, now leaning against Patrick's shoulder, with Titus passed out on mine, I wouldn't have it any other way.

I've grown to trust and rely on people through wildland, let people into my life and heart more. I had never felt like anyone could ever be there for me growing up. Like I always had to be capable of being on my own. Too emotionally damaged and all that. But with each fire roll, my soul gets healed a little more each day.

***

A knock at my door sounds. I swing it open and before I can even breathe out a hi, a boa constrictor hug engulfs me. He swings me around and plops me back on my feet. My heart pounds, giddy with hope.

"It is so good to see you! I feel like it's been a lifetime, and the fire department just hasn't been the same without you. I have no one to pick on." He fake pouts. I pat the top of his head.

"Aww poor Johnny. I know, the awesomeness just follows me, life is like pizza without cheese without me in it." I roll my eyes.

"It really is. Like a fat kids' night without ice cream," he says as he slings an arm around my shoulders and practically gets me in a headlock. We head over to the truck, and he opens the door for me as I boost myself in.

Belting out white girl jams the whole way, I feel at home. Maybe home isn't a place, but more of a person.

***

"Whoa Johnny! The colors are absolutely beautiful! Finally, a real fall!" I exclaim as we wind through the trees. The vibrant oranges and yellows mixed with the dense green look just breathtaking. Different from home, but my heart feels happy. This is home now. It really is. I just needed this last little bit over the edge. Oh, my goodness. Who would have ever thought deciduous trees in a rainforest would look so amazing?

"Okay! Will you tell me where we're going now?" I beg Johnny.

We drove for like two and a half hours and just now pulled into a parking lot. Granted, he could just be bringing me right to this parking lot and I would be happy just getting some colorful leaves.

"Nope, it is a surprise! But I am glad you're liking it so far."

Before I unbuckle my seat belt, Johnny rushes around and opens my door. What a gentleman. I could get used to this kind of treatment. I just wish I knew if he was doing it as a friend, or if maybe, just maybe he does like me. Face hot, I step out.

"Well, thank you." Just now, I see he was holding a hand out to help me step down. Oops, oh well. I mean if I had taken it, it would have been weird right?

"Alright, so we will be hiking a few miles, just to warn you," he says.

No worries with me, I had no idea what we were doing, so I packed anything I might need to summit a mountain, let alone just hiking through the woods. It's so great to be away from the coast and not be on a fire. It's been way too long since I just wandered and enjoyed life. My soul needs a little wandering and adventure every now and then.

"Deal, let's get going. I'm stoked." He starts walking.

Before I head after him, I close my eyes real quick and lift my arms.

Thank you, Lord. Thank you for giving me a home out here. Thank you for the peace this brought to me. Thank you, Lord, thank you. I open my eyes and see that he had looked back and is watching me. I give him a smile and follow.

I'm not really sure how long we've been hiking. No one needs time when you're wandering. Time doesn't mean anything. Being in the moment is what life is about. Living for the now. And the now is pulling me in with every colorful leaf I pass. I love the silence, the tranquillity, the peacefulness of just walking. Then, I hear it. I hear the rush, the roar. Louder and louder until it's almost deafening, then I see it.

"Oh!" I gasp. A waterfall, breathtaking. The colors blending all around it. The giant water rushing to the ground and crashing to the rocks below. Like something from a movie. That's it, I live in a movie. I am sure of it now. "Johnny this is amazing!" I rush up to the waterfall, letting the mist envelop me. "Woohoo!" a scream escapes me. Freedom. Absolute freedom.

"Yeeeeaaa!" Johnny screams and I look over and see him standing half in the waterfall and half out. What a goober! Aww but I love that. This is contentment! Wow, I just can't believe a God who made such wonders made me. How amazing is that? It's nice to know that no matter what, he has a plan for me.

Johnny comes running over soaking wet. I know exactly what his plan is going to be and scurry away. Countering the move, he runs behind a tree and catches me around the waist before I can think about running in the opposite direction. He shakes his hair off on me and wraps me in a big hug, the water soaking through instantly.

"You looked like you needed a cool down." He chuckles. I laugh anyway, this moment is way too amazing to do anything besides be happy.

We sit on the rocks for a while, gently the mist falls on us. No society, no civilization. Just us and nature. Luckily, I packed two sandwiches, and we share them like a little picnic. Drinking out of the same water bottle, and munching on some peanut butter, life is good.

As I stare at the waterfall, I feel his gaze on me. Slowly my eyes look to the corner and see him staring. The most intense look in those eyes. My head swivels to look at him. He gives me a smile as his arm snakes around my shoulders. His head turns back to look at the waterfall, as does mine, the smiles on both our faces apparent. Now this, this really is my Hallmark moment.

***

Gosh darn. I hate haunted houses. Okay, really, I love them. But why am I such a scaredy cat? I live for horror movies, yet if this was one, I would be the first to die. We're almost up to the door. I can't believe he brought me here. Actually, I'm really excited. I am, I repeat trying to convince myself. I haven't been to a haunted house in a while. My best friend Elizabeth and I used to always go to one back home. She's a complete maniac. Seriously. She laughs... the entire time!

"Just so you know, I'm so not going last! But I'm not going first either. So, we're going to just have to mush up behind the group in front of us," I tell him with a serious face. I think my whole body is shaking already. My heart is legit going to beat out of my chest. Am I having a heart attack? Every ounce of my body is just waiting for the moment something pops out at me. Breathe, breathe. It's all just for fun. I know I have to calm myself or I'll go into an anxiety attack. I can't do that, especially not in front of him.

"Aww, is little Kara scared?" He laughs but then sees my face. I must really be freaking out. Because instead of making fun of me he looks directly into my eyes and puts his hands on my shoulders.

"Hey, it's okay, I will be right here. It will be fun," He encourages me as his eyes stare to my soul. He gives my back a pat. Fun. Yea, it is supposed to be fun. "I'll be right with you the whole time. Breathe," he reiterates but looks away. My breathing slows a bit. Johnny will take care of me. It will be okay. I trust him. Okay. Okay. He pulls me into a hug and my face mushes to his chest. I pull the biggest breath in, his cologne enveloping all my senses. Safe.

"Okay, with you, I can do anything," I declare and attempt to wink back. He laughs and gives my head a little pat.

It's our turn to go. They separated us too far from the group in front. Crap! My whole body starts to shake again. I can do this. Come on Kara. You're a firefighter. You go into dark, burning buildings for a living. All this is, is a dark building. Just then something pops out at us.

"AHHHHHHHEE!" I jump and jerk back smacking right into Johnny. I hear a muted chuckle and feel his arms on my back.

"I'm right here," he repeats over and over. Every noise, movement, and touch I jump. But at least I have him.

A chainsaw. I hear a chainsaw. I know I work with them all the time. I used to legit work with them for over fifteen hours a day, they shouldn't scare me. But here, in a dark building. It freaks me out all the more. You know how many trauma patients there are on the fireline due to chainsaw accidents? A lot! Nope, these people are freaky people with no training. They shouldn't have chainsaws! There it is again. Closer. I look around but all I can see is darkness. I've stopped dead. I can't move. I can't even lift a foot. My whole body trembles.

VROOOOOOOM! It whirls right next to my face as a clown lights up with it. I bolt. I pass people and through doors, running as fast as I can until oooomf, I hit a wall. Bringing me to my senses, I now have no idea where I am. Great job, Kara. Ugg, why are you such a scaredy cat idiot? I'm too terrified to call out to Johnny. My voice might bring the monsters too. Breathe. Breathe Kara. Just like that entrapment practice, life is all about control. I can control me.

Okay, Kara. You're trained to get out of dark places like this. I put my left arm against the wall I just ran into and follow the wall back in the direction I ran from.

"Johnny?" I whisper. Nothing. Was that a footstep behind me?

"Boo!" A voice yells. My feet start to fly again but hands hold my shoulders back. I can't escape! It's got me! I swing back trying to hit it, but it holds me in its grasps too tight. A booming laugh comes from my captor.

"Calm down, Kara, it's just me."

That's Johnny!!!! I almost start sobbing with relief. He must sense to comfort me as his arm slides around my shoulders.

"You idiot! I hate you," I grumble and smack his arm.

"Nah, you love me, you know it," he proclaims nudging my shoulder with his. He starts guiding me back through. I still jump at everything but keep my eyes shut and burrow deeper towards him with every scare.

"Kara, it's too narrow. We're almost out, but we need to go single file." My heart is pounding, my breath shaky. I can do this. I've got this. Strobe lights flicker on and off.

My brain wants to shut down, ugg. I hate strobe lights. The little tunnel spits me out in a psychedelic nightmare. A freaky Victorian bedroom with tons of ruffles. Just then a sound comes from the other side of the room. Dolls. Like ten life sized dolls jump off the shelf. I start to back away from them.

"Want to play!" A shrill voice sounds from behind me.

"Noooo!" I screech as I tumble down. With the flashes, I realize, I fell into the life-sized doll bed. I roll to one side to get up, a doll pops up! Cackling, it inches towards me. I scream and wiggle to the other side. They have the bed surrounded! I'm shaking all over again. Rapidly breathing, desperately sucking air. Am I seeing spots or is it just because it is strobe lights? I can't move. One reaches its hand towards me; I try to melt into the bed. It grabs my hand, and with a gentle pull, I realize she's just trying to help me up. Oh...

***

"So, I have one more stop I want to make before heading back to your place," he states.

Once again, no details and my curiosity runs wild. The leaves and waterfall were just absolutely gorgeous, and I would go back there every day with him if I could. The haunted house on the other hand... while yes, I enjoyed it, I'm not quite itching to get back there anytime soon. I need a solid like 365 days first. We pull into a farm. Driving down a gravel lane, bumping along. Looking around I see it littered with orange polka dots.

"A pumpkin patch!" I exclaim. I've never actually been to one of these. My family always grew our own. This is so exciting! See didn't I tell you earlier, I really do feel like I am living in a Hallmark movie or something. Now if only the guy would fall in love with me. Hopping out of his car, he first takes me over to a little stand.

"Want some apple cider or something?" He asks.

Oh, my goodness, Heck yea I do! Apple cider is a superior drink, second only to sweet tea. "Yes please!" I say eagerly.

"Two apple ciders, and two apple cider donuts," he says to the young girl working the stand. Yummm! Donuts. Could this guy get any better? Munching on our donuts and holding some warm apple cider, we start walking down the rows looking for our favourites. I think I want a normal sized one. I mean some of them here are ginormous, and some are tiny. I love the tiny ones, but I want just a nice normal one today. Johnny on the other hand points out all the titanic ones, ones a dog could fit inside.

"I thought we could, uh, carve them when we get back. Maybe, if you have time," he stammers.

"Yea, that would be awesome!" Walking along I take it all in. Suddenly, like a butterfly, his hand brushes mine. Instinctively, my hand jerks away. Shoot! I look over to him, he's looking the other way at pumpkins, so maybe it was an accident. But if it wasn't, then I just ruined the moment. Why did I pull away? It was just a reaction! Maybe I should just take his hand? Crap! No, I can't do that. What if he doesn't like me? Or worse, what if I tick off my Lieutenant? I would just make things awkward right?

Like it never happened, we continue along the rows. He ends up picking like a two-foot diameter one that consumes his whole arms, while I pick a more modest one. Perfectly content, we head to the checkout counter. He sweetly buys mine. Okay, well if there's something there, then maybe I haven't ruined it, and if there isn't then at least he is a very, very nice brother.

Pumpkin sitting on my lap, singing the words to one of my favourite songs, I feel like there's nothing better. The car ride home is great. He lets me pick the music and I scream and sing the whole way home. His poor ears. I'm surprised he hasn't revoked my music privileges with my singing assaulting his eardrums like this. But he doesn't say anything, just smiles and sings along, which makes me want to sing louder. We pull into my driveway much too fast. Part of me is actually sad, our day together is over so soon, but we do still have pumpkins to carve.

"What are you going to carve on yours?" I ask as I hunt for knives. I really don't own any kitchen supplies since I eat canned food or Chubbys for every meal. Oh! I do have pocket knives though, like big, nice ones for wildland. I go and fish two out of my wildland pile. Yea, I don't really have a place for it, so all my gear sits in a pile by the bathroom. I am one heck of a house lady, aren't I? Judge me!

"Um, I was thinking maybe just a typical lantern face. That's about all I will be able to do, and I don't even know if I will do that well," he admits.

"Well, if it's terrible, then it might be scarier which means you actually did awesome. I think I'm going to be a clown," I state.

He makes a face. "Ew, a clown? Why?"

"Well because I kind of like the idea of clowns, but for some reason they scare a lot of people, so win, win."

"Gosh what a little freak," he says with a laugh. We go to work stabbing our pocket knives into the pumpkins, scooping out the goop, until I fling a little glob at him.

"If you don't want your kitchen to be a mess, I say we stop there," he warns as he dabs a chunk of pumpkin guts on my nose.

Hmm. I set the goop onto the newspapers but wipe my hands across his arms.

"I'm done, I promise," I claim with a smile. Ugg. Why do I always act like a toddler around him? He just like brings it out. I never act this childish, but it's so much fun to pick on him.

We sit in silence, enjoying each other's company. My clown doesn't quite turn out how I wanted, but you can still tell it's Twisty from 'American Horror Story', so good enough for me. I spin it towards him.

"Can you tell it's a clown?" I don't expect Johnny to have ever watched American Horror Story.

"Heck yeah, dude, that thing is terrifying. Can't wait to see it lit up!" He spins his to face me, and I burst out laughing. The poor thing. His jack o lantern has circular, triangular eyes and an almost smile.

"It's cute," I say, gasping for breath. Oh, my goodness, I can't believe that. My brother even carves better pumpkins, and he's like the least artistic person I've ever met. Okay, I'm being mean. He tried hard on it, what if he was really proud of it? Composing myself, I shut off my laughter.

"It looks good. Like the candle will definitely be the cherry on top," I state solemnly, but my face feels taut with my forced serious face, a smile ready to bust.

"It looks like crap, but thanks." He says then he starts laughing, so my giggles burst out again too. I shove his shoulder.

"So, candle time?" I ask, he nods, and we carry them to the porch.

"I feel bad yours will live on my porch; do you want to take it home? Or we could take them to the fire department? I feel like they're going to rot uber fast out here on the coast," I tell him. It's just so moist.

"I don't mind if it lives here, you will give it a good home, and I certainly do not want it at the fire department."

"Okay then, it shall live here. What are your plans now?" I prompt hoping he doesn't say that he has to leave. Maybe I can make something up to get him to stay, or we could watch a movie or something! Anything for a little more time with him!

"Well actually, I wanted to talk to you about that. I was wondering if I could go to church with you in the morning?" He inquires shyly.

"Absolutely! I would love that. Actually, we're pretty lucky our day off falls on a Sunday this week, but my church has mid-week mass too, so sometimes I can go to that. Where are you staying tonight then?"

That's awesome that he asked. Honestly, I wasn't sure if any of the guys are Christians. I mean Logan has a cross tattoo, but obviously his marriage isn't totally rooted in Christ. That's harsh, I'm not judging, I'm a sinner too. But that's one of my big reservations about liking Johnny, I didn't know if he was a Christian. That's like my only big must on the boyfriend checklist. Don't get me wrong, I would love if he's into Lord of the Rings and nature and such, but those are wants, not necessities.

"Well, Logan is busy with his wife and kids tonight, so I guess I will be staying at the department."

"Nah, you don't want to do that. You can stay here if you want." Oh, my goodness, did I really just offer that? I mean I'm just being nice, I never get good sleep at the department, especially if I'm not on shift, then there always seem to be more calls because I feel like I should go on them. I was just offering out of politeness. You know. Absolutely not for any other reason. That Midwest nice, trying to convince myself.

I look into his shocked eyes. Guess I took him by surprise too. "I mean not like... you know anything like that, but you could have my bed, and

I can sleep on the couch," I amend. I definitely don't want to give him the wrong idea. Especially since he asked to go to church with me in the morning.

"Of course, that would be really great. Thank you... except I am still not taking your bed." We argue back and forth with me finally saying that if he didn't take it, he could stay.

"Awesome, now that that's settled are you hungry?"

"Starving."

"Chubbys?!" We say at the same time and burst out laughing again.

Not minutes later we're back at my house, two Big Chubs in hand.

"Want to take this down to the beach? The sun should be setting soon." I ask, wanting a little sunset picnic.

"That sounds awesome," he replies. I gather up a blanket and a spork for me. Let's be honest, I know I'm eating this thing with some sort of utensil, so a backpacking spork works as good as anything else. Kicking through the sand, we wander over to the water's edge. Just enough away that the blanket won't get wet, but close enough you still feel like you're part of the ocean.

As I set up a little picnic spot, I think of how similar this feels to our first day together. I mean picnic on the beach and everything. I just wish I knew where I stood with him. I'll give it another week or two, but then I might ask. I don't like undefined things. Everything has a place in my life, and half dating someone who may or may not like me doesn't have a place. A boyfriend, or just a friend would. I need to know. I feel like I'm floating in between two roads, and I would rather just be walking one, no matter which road.

Once we finish our fantastic burgers, he pops up. Reaching a hand down towards me, he leans over to help me up. I slip my hands in both of his, as his warm hands encircle mine. In one giant heave, I'm on my feet with practically no effort. Loosening my grip, my left-hand drops but not my right. He is still holding it. My head whips to look at it. Yes, he's actually holding it, I'm not hallucinating. Okay, okay, this is a big development. He was trying to hold my hand earlier! I can do this. I can hold hands with a guy. At least he's pancaking my hand and not waffling it. Not like too much commitment then, right? Just enough. I'm sure my face is on fire; it feels like it is. Actually, it kind of feels like the fire is spreading from my hand up to my face. Am I holding his hand correctly? Can you hold a hand wrong? Am I squeezing too hard? Or maybe not enough? Can he tell my breathing is way faster than normal?

He tugs and we walk along the shore. The waves lapping at our feet and God painting the most beautiful sunset ever. Wow. The water rushes between my toes and takes my anxieties with it. This really does feel like a romantic movie. He drags me a little further into the surf where the water swims around our knees.

"Kara, you're really amazing. Do you know that?" He says and I stare into his eyes. Those eyes, they're a whole world. My whole world. The blue captivating me. Is this really happening? He starts leaning down, slower, and slower, his eyes closing. My breath catches before stopping all together.

"S- S- Sorry, but are you going to kiss me? I've never kissed anyone before. Make sure you really mean it, otherwise don't." Ugg. Way to ruin the moment, Kara. That was the dumbest thing anyone could have ever said. I mentally beat myself to a pulp. What a dummy. Now he definitely doesn't want to kiss you. I've destroyed any romance, any chance. He lingers for a second, and then, his lips are on mine. Heat instantly warms my body as it practically melts into his arms.

"Oh." A sigh escapes me into his mouth. He kisses harder for a moment and then pulls away.

"Of course, it's real. I've wanted to do that for months," he says.

My lips a tingling, burning mess. It takes a few seconds for my eyes to open. They want to stay in that moment forever, actually all of me does. My arms fling out without my brain knowing, my body lurching to his, fully intending to kiss him again. Except, I take him off guard and we crash down in the water. He starts laughing and gives me a kiss through the laughs. Saltwater mixing in with his lips. Just a quick one, but enough to know that this is real.

Splashing back through the waves we head to the blanket. How does one act now? Am I supposed to take his hand or something? Ugg. Maybe they make like a guidebook for this. I need to do some research. We plop back down on the blanket and watch the last of the colors. Absolutely gorgeous. I inch closer to him a little, just enough for our arms to touch. His arm instantly moves away. I start to scoot back over until his arm snakes around my shoulders. Okay, very new development. I lean into him letting my head rest on his shoulder.

Am I breathing normal? Can he smell me? Woah... he smells amazing. Is this how all guys smell? It must just be him because good golly, you can't make a smell that good. Heaven.

Lord, please let this be real. Don't let me make a fool of myself Lord, please. Help me always, keep you first. Thank you, Lord, thank you. Wow.

***

Oh, my goodness, I'm not even in the same room as Johnny and all I can hear is his snoring. That's okay, my brain keeps running way too fast for sleep anyway. I legit can't believe I'm the girl to get a prince charming. A firefighter, someone to take care of me. Okay, slow down, Kara, it's just one kiss. I mean, it's not like we're officially dating. Or are we? Do we have to verbally define it to be officially dating? Either way, I think it's official, he likes me. I think. My mouth turns in a smile at the thought.

***

Nope! Nope! Nope! All of these dresses are wrong. I know it's church and I wear all of them every time I go to church, but this is different. Now my maybe boyfriend is going to church with me. This is a big deal. Johnny has never really seen my church me. He's seen work me, and weekend me, but church me is the true me. Church is where I feel closest to God, where I'm truly me.

I settle on a blue and white dress. It reminds me of an old-fashioned teacup, like fine china. I kind of feel like china today. I feel priceless, yet maybe a little breakable. I don't want to get my hopes up too much about Johnny. What if he changes his mind? What if it didn't mean the same thing to him? Yet, I know that because God made me, I am priceless. I am worth it. Just like fancy china.

We walk the half a block over to the church. I love living so close to my church, I just wish they kept the doors open besides Sundays and Wednesdays. I would love to be able to just stop in every night and pray, or sit, or whatever I need to do. Sitting in church makes me feel as peaceful as standing on a mountaintop surrounded by nature. I just feel his presence so deeply when it's just me and God. Johnny and I don't hold hands on the way over, we don't talk about the kiss or anything. We joke, we laugh, we play a little game of tag, perfection anyway.

"Okay, so once we enter, this sanctuary isn't really a talking place, okay? Have you ever gone to mass?" I ask a little nervous.

I've never really gone to mass with anyone. I became a Christian in college, my faith was wholly mine. I've never had to deal with the fact that someone might not know my ways, or traditions. Typically, I go early to pray and just be with God, then the church prays the rosary before service starts. However, I am just bringing him to service, so I will have to make up for that in my own time.

"No problem. Uh, I've gone to church services before, but not like traditional mass."

"Ooo boy. Well buckle your seatbelt and hang on for the ride. This is a very traditional mass. But I'm so glad you are joining me." And I am. I'm so glad to have someone to share this with.

I walk in first, dipping my fingers in the holy water and making the sign of the cross. Johnny follows as I make my way down the aisle, kneel, then slide into the pew. I pull out the kneeler and bow my head.

Lord, you have given me so much to be thankful for. Thank you. Thank you for the life that you have given me. For my friends, my job, my family, my home out here. Thank you for loving me unconditionally no matter how much I sin. Thank you for sending Christ for me. Thank you for making me who I am. I love you Lord so very much. I want each and every day to be for you. Lord, my life is yours, use it for whatever plans you have. Take the wheel, Lord, we both know that my driving is terrible. Thank you, Lord, thank you.

I sit back in the pew and glance over at Johnny. He's looking right at me. My face grows hot, but I push it aside. I'm here for God. The rest of the service, I focus, and don't glance at him again until we've said the final prayers. When I do finally glance over at him, his head is down saying his own prayers. I look away giving him and God their privacy and send one last thank you to God.

I feel his weight shift and see that he's done, so we kneel and exit.

"So, what did you think?" I prompt looking at Johnny. We stopped walking as soon as we got out of the church. I love this church; it has a view of the bay and everything.

"Can I be honest?" He inquires.

"Of course!"

"Well, I've never been a huge church goer. I mean I believe in one God and Christ, but like church, not always my thing. However, I'm used to like church bands with lively people. Your church is, well, very formal. I kinda' liked it, but I'm not sure what I think yet. It was just different for me," he explains as if he's scared to say it out loud.

"No worries, everyone worships differently. As long as you share the core beliefs, there's nothing wrong with liking a praise band over an organ."

He smiles and the look he gives me almost stops my heart. "You know one of the things that drew me to you is how close you stick to your faith. You have a really strong walk with the Lord, and I admire that," he reveals. Wow. I didn't think anyone ever noticed me, let alone my faith.

"Oh, um, well, thank you. But really, I just want to show God. He deserves all the credit. Any way that you see him through me is his work."

Humbled, I almost can't believe someone was watching me in my walk. Wow. Thank you, Lord. You know, talking with Johnny, seeing him build his faith, is actually building mine too. As his grows stronger, it inspires me to want to be a better daughter, a better Christian. Maybe, just maybe he's the one the Lord has planned for me. I will just have to continue to pray and hope a little.

"So, um, about yesterday..." He pauses. Oh goodness, he's going to take it back! He changed his mind. A painful tingle passes through my heart. Did I mess this up already? "Would you like to be my girlfriend, then?" He chokes out.

A sigh of relief passes through me. "Yes! Absolutely!" I affirm and throw my arms around him. He twirls me around and plants another kiss on me. Girlfriend, wow. My Hallmark movie ending.

CHAPTER 20

I don't think I've ever heard bagpipes in person until today. I know I should be focusing on paying my respects, but honestly, they are wearing kilts. Is that even a real thing here in America? I've got my snazzy class A uniform on today. It's quite rare that I get to put this on. Granted, it's not my favorite thing in the world to wear. Having to shine my shoes, make sure my hair sits just right under my hat and everything, it's rather stressful.

But today is the fallen firefighter memorial for all of Oregon, both structure and wildland alike. Somber, the mood for the day. Logan, Titus, and a few others came from our department, Johnny and Garrett are staffing and when I get back, I'll go on shift too. This was important for me to come to though. I had no idea they would be honoring wildland guys too until I received the announcement for my friend, Alex. We had been on the same wildland handcrew all those years ago during my rookie season. He became a smokejumper out here in Oregon until that day it went horribly wrong.

I shed my tears for him weeks ago when he passed, here we're honoring them, a remembrance. Keeping my face tight and neutral, professionalism is what he would expect. I solute, take my hat off, click my heels all at the right times.

Titanic flags hang from the ladder trucks, and a hundred or more flags line the drive. One flag for every fallen firefighter. So many. We as firefighters come to accept death early on. We see it every day, then even in our dreams at night. But it's not as often that we think of it amongst ourselves. I make my way through the service and before I know it, we're back in the spare engine driving home. I strip off my jacket and take off my ascot, tie thing. Unpinning my hair and shaking it out, putting my sad feelings in the rearview the best I can.

The guys are on a med call when we return so I ready my turnouts and change back into my class B uniform. Much comfier. As they pull the engine up outside, I know exactly what's next, it's washing time. Striding over to the far end of the bay, I fill two buckets with soap and grab the brushes. Then I stretch the hose around to the engine and start spraying. As Johnny clambers out, I shoot a quick mist at him. Not enough to even get his hair wet, just to startle him. He jumps a little, but a smile crosses his face as he sees me.

We decided no hugging or any signs of PDA at the fire department, keeping it professional and all that. I have to tell you though, the urge to run up and hug him is almost overpowering. My foot takes a step. No! Be strong Kara. But after this morning a hug just sounds so nice. I've never really had a person who would be there for me before and now that I do, I just kind of want him to hold me while I cry. Is that cliché? It sounds like something a blond dressed in pink with a little chihuahua would do. I'm a firefighter for goodness sakes.

I swallow the lump in my throat and go back to spraying the engine. I don't need anyone. Needing people is overrated, but it's nice to have someone. Maybe someday I won't be ashamed to show emotion. You know like when we're at home or something, then I could run to him crying. Just the thought of having him someday to hold me, makes my mood a little sunnier.

Suddenly, I feel a splash of water from behind. My head whips around and I see Johnny pretending to be scrubbing the engine. A spark ignites in me. I then full-on blast him with the hose. Just at his legs, but still. It does the job. He lobs a glob of soap foam at me, and I grab the other bucket. He darts around the engine, and I chase after before switching sides to cut him off. He rounds the corner and I smack the foam on his head.

"Can we please try to be a little professional?" Logan booms from behind us.

Slowly, I turn, all the life draining from me. Oops. Am I going to get a write up? Then I see the twinkle in his eyes. All is forgiven. Thank goodness. We go back to a nice engine wash. No more water fights. Although occasionally I'll spray water a little too close where it ricochets off the engine and gets him just a little. The fire in his eyes igniting the one in my heart. Sparks fly, enough to start a wildfire.

Supper at the firehouse is an easy ordeal for me. After my first couple of shifts, everyone pretty much banned me from making supper. They realized I might be a decent cook, but I don't make what they want. They're big men who want meat. Meat! Practically every meal has some form of steak, hamburger, or something. Don't get me wrong, I certainly don't mind not having to do any cooking, but still, can't we have some variety? A nice lasagna, or alfredo? At least they usually have potatoes with their cow, or pig, or whatever. It feels like I'm back in Ohio sometimes. Meat, with a side of starches, with a side of carbs. Yum. No wonder I've gained weight since joining the fire department. Well, and the fact that we always have a stash of ice cream here. The deal is if one of us end up in the newspaper, we have to buy ice cream. Lately the chief has been in there like once a week. The glory of a small town.

I'll hand it to these guys, they do certainly know how to make everything taste good. Tonight, we have garlic and butter on the steak with some heavily buttered potatoes and rolls. I can feel the extra five pounds already. Nevertheless, we all fork it down, with them having seconds and thirds.

After dinner, we go and do our own things as always. I see Garrett reading a book; Logan is doing who knows what downstairs and I find Johnny watching a movie in the living quarters. Deciding to be bold, I sit right next to him. Leaning on the arm, I curl my legs up beside me, feet angling toward his thighs. He glances over with a little smile.

"Rebellious, aren't we?" He chuckles. We don't hold hands, he doesn't put his arm around me, but my right foot sits barely touching his leg. Just enough that I swear there's a tingling there. My foot certainly feels hotter than the other one. It's enough though. I'm content.

We all slowly make our way to the bunks. Garrett first, then Logan. Part of me could stay watching a movie with Johnny all night. But I also know I still have a full day of shift tomorrow, so it's off to bed I go. Slowly, I peel myself from the couch.

As I stand up, I reach out and give his hand a quick squeeze, then amble over to my bunk. I walk in, hearing Logan already snoring like a freight train. I need to make sure to fall asleep before Johnny comes in, or between the two of them, I'll never get any sleep.

***

Tones! I jump up and my feet fly out the door.

"Holy Smokes!" Garrett hollers.

At the same time Logan cries, "Gah! That girl's got the devil in her. Goodness! Give us a heart attack!"

What? Oh! Oops. I guess I do have a tendency to jump out of bed really fast. It's a habit though. As a kid, if I heard footsteps on the stairs, I would jump out of bed to let my parents know I was up. That way they didn't have to come into my room to wake me. If they did, they would've just complained about how messy my room was and demand I clean it. I guess it became tradition and now it's just how I wake up. Although, maybe

I should give myself a little more time. There have been instances over the years that I jump up too fast only to find myself on the floor seconds later. Putting my body into shock or something, I would shake and fall to the ground with blackness coloring my vision. I never lost consciousness though and it only happened a handful of times, so it's all good. Right?

"You know you talk in your sleep too!" Logan hollers.

"Johnny, Oh, Johnny!" Garrett whimpers and they both laugh.

Ugg. Men. Heat spreads across my cheeks. I've always known I talk in my sleep. You don't really think I was talking about Johnny, right? I would die from embarrassment! Maybe I should start sleeping down in the engine. Although it's not like it's a big secret. I mean maybe from the Chief, but all three of these guys already know. Why should I be ashamed of liking someone? Nope, no shame from me. I push the thoughts from my head.

I get down to the bay and have my turnout pants pulled up just as the guys make it down. Wow, that was fast for me, I should start timing it. A laugh escapes me. I look at the call log. Almost five in the morning, not bad. That's pretty much a full night's sleep for around here, I'll take it. Reading through the call log, I find that it's a fall. So, we'll probably take the mega mover and need the stretcher with the med bags. I get the med bags unstrapped, and myself strapped in by the time the guys hop in, and away we go.

We arrive on scene of a tiny little house on the bay. Cute setting. I follow Garrett in as a woman directs us. She steers us right towards the bathroom. Great. I see a pair of feet sticking out the doorway. Garrett shuffles in and I follow after him. My eyes immediately sweep the room, and instantly regret it. I mean, at least it's not a hard-core trauma. Small Mercies. Garrett leans down to assess the very large, naked man. This guy must be four hundred pounds!

"What happened?" I ask the woman, as Garrett finishes the assessment. I mean the guy is breathing, and conscious, so I would guess it's a typical slip in the shower.

"Well, he was just getting out of the shower and slipped. I tried, but I couldn't help him up. But he did hit his head pretty hard in the fall too, but he stayed awake the whole time." She's blubbering. Poor lady. Yup, we're definitely going to need the mega mover. Five other men to help would be nice too, but at least there are four of us. That's only like a hundred pounds each, we've got this. I take a step in, my boot slips across the slick floor.

The ground rushes up to me in the tiny bathroom. Twisting I catch myself on my hands, my hands straddling the man's thighs, my face bouncing slightly from his abdomen. Slowly I open my eyes. AHHHHH! Not what I wanted to see! I scurry up. How embarrassing! Shame! My ears are on fire from humiliation! Better yet, my eyes are burnt out! I caught myself right above his groin staring directly at it. It! Kill me now. Ugg.

There's no room for Logan and Johnny at the moment until we get him on the mega mover to haul him out of the tiny room to the stretcher. It sits four feet away, taunting. I almost ask one of the guys to trade out but decide better. That would be extremely unprofessional. It's not a life threat, having a medic in here isn't going to do him any better, so I better buckle in and deal with it.

"Okay sir, we are going to roll you on your side to get the mover under you," Garrett tells the man as I cross his ankles. What am I supposed to grab to roll him? Usually I grab belt loops, loose clothing, something. Should I grab one of his rolls? No, no! Definitely not, Kara. I'm just going to hope for enough friction and force for my hands to grip. Garrett has a brace on his neck so we can both roll, thank goodness.

"On my count. Three, two, one." With a heave, we manage to roll him over. Garrett has him braced while I work the mover under his skin. Shoving enough of it up under him so we will have something to grip from the other side.

"Three, two, one." We roll him back down. Pulling the tarp edges from the sides we find the four handles. Johnny and Logan wiggle in just enough to help slide him out the door to his ankles. Now we lift.

"Everyone ready? Three, two, one!" Garrett calls and we all lift. I have to lift extra high, so his shoulders don't dip towards me. My entire body shakes with the effort, straining to keep him up. We scuttle out the door and transfer him to the stretcher. Ahh, sweet relief. All four of us take a hand on the stretcher to wheel him to the ambulance. At least this place had no stairs. I don't even want to imagine a stair lift or anything like that.

By the time we get back to the station, we need to be up anyway. I go change into my uniform as they head to the coffee machine. With so many Kara moments this morning, the embarrassment sure woke me up. We spend the morning with some cleaning and light housework.

"Alright, before lunch, we're going to do some training," Logan informs us. My heart thumps. Training can either be fun or complete hell. "Three rounds of suicide cones, then we're going to do some donning and doffing. Seemed a little slow for the fire the other day," he continues.

Okay, I mean suicide cones suck, but three rounds aren't terrible. And donning and doffing is my game. I'm the freshest out of academy, only graduated a couple of years ago, so I've still got it. Garrett on the other hand went through academy years ago, and it's more at the three-minute mark range now I would wager.

As we gear up, I practice my donning. All my gear is strapped and secured by the time Garrett starts zipping his jacket. Yass. I am a queen! That is until we start doing the suicide cones. I will give it to the guys, they kick my butt at those. I'm sweating so bad and even though my O_2 is flowing I can't seem to get enough air, so I huff and puff. Ugg. A few seconds go by, and my breathing starts to go back to normal. Well, that wasn't terrible. Still under five minutes. A heck of a lot better than when I first started here. Really, once I catch my breath, everything is fine. I feel like I could do another set of three. I should do another set of three, maybe three hundred. Gosh darn, I need to get in better shape. Gotta' keep up with these guys.

"Alright, doff your gear and get it ready. Ninety seconds. That's the cut off. Clap three times when you're done," Logan announces. I'm sure we've all done enough drills to know to clap, but I can appreciate clear instructions.

I have a system for this drill. Everything set out in a specific place in a specific way, piece of cake. My pants sitting around my boots, hood laid on top, the coat propped up to swing over my shoulders. SCBA, Helmet, pack over my head, then gloves.

"On my count. Three, two, one!" I step into my boots and pull up the straps in one swift movement, shoving my hood on. The coat swings over and zip. SCBA on, check the seal and pull the hood up. Helmet and straps tightened. Turn the tank on, lift over my head and slide onto my shoulders. Attach respirator, stand, jump and sinch the straps. Gloves. I pound my hands together three times.

"Seventy-two seconds!" Logan announces. I always feel like Darth Vader breathing in and out with my mask on. Which I mean, he was kind of a boss dude, so I'll take the comparison. Johnny claps.

"Seventy-nine seconds." Wow. I'm impressed. He's checking over all his flaps and zippers. Technically we fail if they're not secured right. Garrett pushes still struggling to get his tank all situated.

"You've got it Garrett!" I yell. We win as a team, die as a team. They support me in everything, and even though I wanted to beat him, I don't want him to fail. He pulls on his gloves and claps.

"Ninety seconds even. I'll take that. However, now that I know you can still do it, no more half-assing it at midnight calls," Logan remarks. OOO! Burn!

I barely get my pack and coat off when someone taps me from behind.

"Tag! You're it!" I whip to find Johnny backing away. I lurch at him, and he evades by inches. Garrett stands still shrugging off his coat. I run up and tap him. Death glares are shot at me and for a second, I figure he's just going to ignore it, that is until he jumps and taps Logan. He then gets Garrett right back who starts chasing Johnny again. It's a full-on war! We're all still wearing various parts of our turnout gear, all with the pants and sweat running down our faces.

Johnny starts chasing me, a shriek escapes me. I dive under the engine and wiggle to the middle. I know he can't fit under here, or at least I don't think he can. I watch his boots stop in front of me and see his face peer underneath. He disappears and I watch as the boots run over to another pair. Did he get Logan or Garrett? He runs back over and belly flops on the floor, wedging his broad shoulders underneath. His arms stretch towards me, creeping closer and closer, inches away. I start to wiggle backwards towards the other side of the engine. A jerk grabs my legs and tugs me out.

"Aeeekkk!" I squeal. Garrett stands over me with a grin on his face. I pop up to try and run but Johnny wraps his arms around me and twirls me around.

"You're it," he whispers. I turn my head to look over my shoulder at him. He kisses me on the nose real quick and sets me down. I twist to face him and get up on my tip toes, stretching my neck up, angling for another kiss. His arms slide behind my back and pull me closer. My toes barely touch the ground as my lips meet his. A sigh escapes me, and I hear a whistle behind us. Heat rushes to my face. I forgot where we were.

I turn to face them, embarrassment coursing all through me. Slowly I raise my eyes to look at them. My eyes reach Logan's waiting to be scolded, I'm shocked when he winks at me, and a smile slowly spreads across my face.

***

Wandering the streets of Portland again. I'm not sure I would ever want to live in a big city like this, but visiting, wow, it's breathtaking. Cities are just so busy and just have this air about them. Well, besides the nasty, smoggy air. But once I overlook the people and the pollution, I guess there's a certain beauty to them. The lights, the concrete jungle. Kind of...

This time, I honestly, I took about zero care in putting my outfit together. I'm wearing jeans, flats, and a t- shirt. At least I'm not wearing boots, I thought about it, but decided, well, I am going dancing with my boyfriend. I even put on mascara.

Johnny, on the other hand, looks amazing. Well, he always looks amazing, but tonight just absolutely does it for me. He's wearing a white shirt with flamingos on it, which I find funny, but also so cute. Kind of almost a frat boy vibe, but just enough him to make it work. His glasses rimming his eyes just make him all sorts of hella' sexy. This handsome nerd is all mine. My hand twitches as I hold myself back from running my fingers through his fluffy blonde hair.

"So, Dixies? Sounds exciting. You going to save me a dance this time?" I ask Johnny with a laugh. I'm teasing really. Garrett told me Johnny was too nervous to ask me last time. He said Johnny has never really been much of a dancer. He had only danced with me at the first bar because he had enough booze to not worry about it or get all flustered. He just couldn't get the courage to do it last time. Which is fine really, but why pick a dancing bar if he isn't dancing? I'm totally okay with that, because I love to dance, but obviously I want to have fun with him too.

He gives me a shy smile and grabs my hand. We walk down to the club, our arms swinging, and my hand very sweaty. Ugg. I love it though, our fingers intertwined. He squeezes every now and then. I feel like my face wears a constant smile, I have a boyfriend and he's holding my hand. Gazing over at him, my heart dances with contentment. Finally, we reach Dixies. He releases my hand and opens the door for me.

"Thank you," I say and pat his head for old times' sake. It seems like a lifetime ago since we chased each other around the bay patting each other's heads. Inwardly I cringe at the awkwardness of that situation. How on earth hadn't I guessed he liked me? I mean deep down I believe I think I did, but I was just too scared of being wrong, of getting my feelings hurt. Unrequited love is something I've been all too familiar with over the years. Well, that and disappointment. But now, I think things have changed.

As I walk in, the bouncer checks our IDs. It feels good to be checked. I hardly ever drink so now that I'm over 21, I haven't had much use to actually flash this puppy. Boom! Ugg, yes, I am so childish. Honestly, when I had turned twenty-one it felt like the most useless thing. Why were people so excited about it? I certainly didn't get it. My birthday had been the excitement of Texas Roadhouse. I may not have drank, but I ate my body weight in those free rolls. Yum!

"Do you want anything to drink?" Johnny shouts over the music. Normally, I would always turn down the idea of someone paying for my drink. I would feel bad, guilty. But... he's my boyfriend now.

"Um, yea, could you please get me a sweet tea?" I request and look into his smiling face. He turns to go. "Wait! Uh, they don't have sweet tea out here, so plain is fine just please bring me back like four packets of Splenda?" I end in a question. Do clubs even have Splenda? Or is this considered a bar. Oh well, he's already started bumping through the crowd to get to the bar.

Some sort of pop song plays through the speakers. Not really my style. Garrett is supposed to be meeting us here with a few of his friends too.

Scanning the room, I spot him. I start to make my way towards him, but then think better of it. What if Johnny can't find me? Besides, Garrett looks way too occupied right now. His fist clasps locks of a girl's hair as she grinds into him. Sometimes, I wonder what that would be like. To have no cares at all. The alcohol lowering my thought processes, being carefree. Maybe tonight I would like to give up control just a little. Maybe I would like the alcohol to take the wheel just a bit. I feel a hand on my back and whirl around. Oh, Johnny. My face grows hot from my thoughts. The thought of me with Johnny, dancing like that, letting myself go.

"Hey Johnny? Um, I was thinking... Never mind. Thank you for the tea!" I blurt and take a big swig of it.

He wraps an arm around my shoulder and guides me over to Garrett's crowd. I recognize some of them! Well, the twins at least. They're cool guys.

They're all taking shots when we get over there. Garrett holds one out to Johnny and one to me. Johnny takes his and gulps it down. This is it. Do I take the shot? What's the harm in one little shot of I have no idea what. I shouldn't though. I don't drink. I don't believe in what it does to people. But then again, I kind of want to try it just once. Get drunk and all that jazz. I'm an adult. I'm allowed to make my choices. Does that make me a bad person? Goodness.

Before I can give it another thought, I grab the shot and tip it back. Ughhhkkkk! Coughing escapes me. I look at the little glass, ew, I still have half the liquid in the little glass. I plug my nose and tip the rest of it back. Sputtering, I hand the glass back to Garrett. Johnny pats my back laughing. He doesn't bring up the fact that I just drank alcohol, and I'm thankful for that. I'm judging myself enough without anyone else judging me. Although to the rest of the world, I suppose this is all normal.

"Yes! Another round!" Noah yells. Scott and Collin pound the table in agreement. Another one. Oh goodness. If I'm going to do this, I may as well commit, right? I grab another little glass and tip it back. My cheeks chipmunk out, how was I supposed to swallow it all in one go? I swallow bit my bit. As the last little bit goes down my throat closes and gags causing it to spurt out my nose.

"Uggghhk!" I moan out. That hurt like a lava pit in mount doom! Jeez O Pete! I blink a few times getting the tears from my eyes. Another one is pushed into my hand, and I tip it back. Then another. How many is that? My eyes are still tearing, and my throat is burning. That's enough of that! I grab Johnny's hand and pull him towards the dance floor.

"I think you owe me a dance sir!" I yell.

Party Rock Anthem comes on. It's not exactly the best song to dance to, at least not the kind of dancing I like to do. But we make do, starting off slow swinging out and to the side. He twirls me. He's a decent dancer for someone who doesn't like to dance. Maybe Garrett gave him lessons. A laugh escapes me, through my grinning face. This right here is heaven. The song is coming to an end, he spins me out again and dips me. I hit the floor with an ooomf!

"Ow," I mutter on impulse, but giggles escape me. That didn't hurt! He dropped me. That's funny!

"Can I get a drink? Like a real drink? But something that tastes good?" I ask Johnny. He laughs.

"I know just the thing." He heads to the bar, and I continue dancing. There's a group of girls nearby that I head towards. I don't really want to be alone on the dance floor inviting guys. I think I might be starting to feel something, but I certainly am not dumb. The Cupid Shuffle starts. Yes! This song totally takes me back to like junior high. Woah. The girls all scream, I guess they're just as excited as I am.

Bouncing around, scuffling my feet, my head sways. I feel like a bobble head. Someone puts a hand on my shoulder. Swivelling my head, I try to find the person. It's Johnny! He puts a glass in my hand and sways to the music with me. Hey, when did it change from the shuffle? A country song plays now. I take a sip of my drink. MMM, fruity! Swaying with my honeybee, I lean my head on his chest.

"You are so awesome! Do you know that? I really like you..." I tell him. He has a big grin on his face and his eyes appear to be laughing at me. Stretching up towards him, I press my lips to his quickly.

He pulls me closer, and the kiss deepens. Then I hear it. Blurred Lines comes on! Yasssss! This is my jam! Plus, I've always kind of wanted to try something but I've always too shy to do it. Plus, like I don't know, trampy girls do it, but I don't even care. Okay, like every girl does it, I was just always too much of a proper prude to try. I have a boyfriend now, though. So why not? I spin around.

Feeling the music, I back up so my butt presses just against Johnny. Slowly, I start swaying. My knees bend and I start to move in rhythmic circles. His hands go to my hips and pull me closer. Oh, my goodness. Wow, this is a total new sensation. I can feel pulses going on down there. Good golly. My breathing comes a little faster. I can feel his breaths against my hair. Wow, this feels amazing. I kind of want to dance a little deeper or something you know or try other things. Then the song ends, much too quickly. Disappointment clouds over me.

My brain begins fighting a little harder to focus. I tip my head lazily over my shoulder searching for him. His lips find mine, and he smiles through the kisses.

"Well, that was new. Gosh darn girl, you drive me crazy," he murmurs with his lips mere inches from mine. He pulls away but his eyes say he doesn't want to. Breaking the tension, I tip the rest of the contents of my glass into my mouth. It's like peachy orange flavored. I like it. He chuckles and takes my glass.

"Want another?" he asks arching his eyebrows. Heck yea! I just laugh and bob my head. It feels like a bobble head swinging around and floating. My hips sway to the movement of the music. I move along the dance floor till I find Garrett and his friends again.

"Someone is having fun," Garrett comments. My head swishes to look at him.

"Yea! Isn't this like the best night ever?" I proclaim as I snag a glass off a table nearby. It's like a seltzer fizzing and bubbling. I down it in just a few swigs.

"Uh, you know that wasn't yours. Or ours for that matter," Scott states. My arms swing into the air.

"Woohoo!" I cheer and swing my hips around.

"She doesn't drink. Like ever," Garrett informs them but I'm too busy dancing to hear. Johnny makes his way back over to me.

"Johnny! My favorite person. You are my person, you know. Oh, I love you. You are just so cute and hot and just the sweetest," I ramble and fling my arms around him. One of his arms holds me there for a second.

"Hey, I brought you something," he informs me laughing as he holds out the glass to me.

"Oh, my goodness. Yummy. Thank you!" I snag the glass and drink half of it.

"You should probably switch her back over to water next. She's been snagging glasses off the tables," Garrett tells Johnny. I think I see Johnny smiling, but honestly, it's too hard to focus on his face.

"Awww Garrett, don't be like that. You are too awesome to be taking the fun out of things." I slur as I wrap my arms around Garrett in a sloppy hug.

"Well since you're being the fun one tonight, someone has to play the party mom." He laughs.

See, Garrett can be pretty awesome sometimes. If he was a little more conservative with his hook-ups, I might have even had a crush on him. I mean that first fire? Come on, how hot was that? I definitely had a crush on him then. Well, before Johnny that is. I love Johnny. He's just the most handsome, caring man ever. Isn't he just perfect? I think I want to marry him. But right now, I just want to dance. My eyes swish around to him as I untangle my arms from Garrett.

"Dance with me!" I insist grabbing Johnny's hand and pulling him back out onto the dance floor. I down the rest of my glass and set it on the nearest horizontal surface. My prince charming spins me around. Actually, maybe the world is spinning around me, but I don't actually care.

Flashes here and there, only flashes. I come to as I feel Johnny lift me up into his arms. I'm barely able to tell that we are moving aside from the slight rocking in his steps. My head droops back onto his shoulder.

My mouth slowly chews something as someone shoves it bit by bit in my mouth. It takes so much effort to swallow.

"Ugg," I moan as I sit up. My head is pounding. My eyes only half open groggily look around. I'm in Johnny's bed. I have all my clothes on, except my shoes, so that's one good thing. My hands fly to my eye sockets, closing out the bright world. As I start to slide out of bed, my feet hit something.

Opening my eyes, I see Johnny sprawled on the floor with a sweatshirt under his face and a throw blanket over just his legs. His shirtless top sticks out back side up. If I didn't almost feel like I was going to hurl, I would really like to admire his body.

Oh my gosh! I drank last night. This is a hangover. Golly, what did I do? Thinking real hard it comes together in pieces, dancing, grinding, drinking, yelling, everything I'm not proud of. Luckily, besides some light making out, I don't recall anything more physical with Johnny. Thank goodness. I would have been exiling myself in shame should something had gone farther. Even still, guilt washes over my whole body. How could I have let myself get this way?

Lord, please forgive me. Ugg. Why am I such a weak Christian? I just want to be a positive influencing ray of sunshine and here I am going out and partying. What an example I am. Bad me. I can't believe I let myself go down that road. Next time I will be stronger.

Hey, on a positive side, I did get a pretty good boyfriend, didn't I? He didn't try any funny business, and even took my shoes off. I mean seriously, letting me sleep in his bed while he took the floor. How sweet is that?

CHAPTER 21

Happy Thanksgiving. It doesn't really feel like Thanksgiving not being home with my family. Usually, my mom and I watch the Macy's day parade in between cooking various dishes. We have a gigantic family gathering for lunch. My dad has six sisters, each of them has three to five kids and each of the kids has at least two of their own. So, yeah, we have a big family. We all eat three times our share of food. In my family though, it's all about the desserts. We have one table of real food and three to four tables of desserts. Carbs and calories for me, meats and sweets for the men.

Then my family plays games all afternoon, laughing and enjoying each other's company. For supper, we always head to the other side of my family. It's a much quieter, peaceful gathering where we actually have the stillness to go around and say our thanks. Without my family, it just feels like a normal day. My heart clenches, missing them.

Somehow, I've been lucky enough to have Garrett and Johnny also working with me, along with a few volunteers. I volunteered to switch shifts with Caden. He actually has family here and really wanted it off to see them. I figured since my Thanksgiving would've been spent alone in my drafty house, why not. But I'm curious about Garrett and Johnny.

"Hey, Garrett, I don't mean to pry, but I'm surprised you and Johnny came for this shift. Isn't your family having dinner today?" I can't imagine living with my cousin and not going to a holiday dinner with family, or even a little Thanksgiving for ourselves.

"We have ours on Saturday. So many of us typically have to work different shifts, with factory workers, ranchers, firemen, and such it's just easier to do it the weekend after," he explains as he continues sharpening his tool. Oh, that makes sense. Duh. I never thought about having it another day.

"Oh, that's cool," I mumble my lame response. Really, I'm stoked to spend it here with these guys, with my boyfriend. Actually quite a few members of the public brought us food. We have enough food to feed an army. But hey, I saw corn pudding and pumpkin pie, so my heart feels content. If I can't be with my family, at least I can have my favorite meals with my favorite man.

"How come you traded shifts? I mean didn't you want to go home, we just got off shift this morning." Oh, he traded so he could have this weekend off. I guess technically I do too, because Caden and I switched. I actually hadn't thought that far ahead, I figured I would come in anyway as a volunteer, who knows. Or maybe I will just have a movie marathon in my room. It's been a long while since I watched all the Harry Potter movies. I couldn't afford to go home, as much as I would have loved to. A plane ticket back east for the holidays is like seven hundred dollars, and I don't have enough vacation time to try and drive it. But Easter, hopefully then I can go home. I'm not about to tell him my sad money problems though.

"Nah, it doesn't feel all that special when I'm this far from home. May as well be productive." Wow, I don't know where that confession came from. I hate sharing my feelings. Plus, staying busy keeps my mind off things. I look around and catch Johnny's eye across the bay. He heard. Crap.

"That's it, you can come to our family gathering this weekend. I mean you and Johnny are dating after all," he proclaims as if he discovered the cure for cancer. Garrett is the sweetest. Always trying to make everything perfect. Except, that's a huge step!

"No! That's okay!" I choke out. We haven't been dating that long. This is way too much. I don't want to meet his family at a big family gathering! That would be terrible. My socially awkward nightmare! Think of all the small talk. I don't do small talk! I don't like strangers. I don't like meeting new people. No. It's a firm no.

"Yes! That would be perfect! My momma's been dying to meet you!" Johnny hollers hustling over to us. Crap. I'm dead. Is it too late to move states in two days? Just be like, welp sorry, I got a job back home. No, Kara, that's terrible. I will have to meet his family sometime, right? Besides, Oregon is my new home, so I may as well meet my new family too.

"Uh, I don't know..." I trail off not even knowing how to proceed from here.

"Yup, you're coming. Okay, so we're all working today and get off tomorrow. How about on Saturday you drive up to Portland, then you can ride with us for the gathering, and you can crash at our place again?" he proposes like it's set in stone, and I suppose it is now. Ugg, not just meeting the family, but also staying over. The memories from last time are not something I ever want to repeat again.

"Yeah, okay. Sure," I stammer and busy myself with some organizing.

If my hands keep moving it keeps my mind from moving a little too much. This is happening. This makes everything real. I'm no longer living in the fantasy; it's real life now. Wow, meeting his family. I wonder how my family would like him. I'm sure my momma would love him, my dad on the other hand... I don't really know. I've never had much experience with dating, so he never got to do the whole, scare the poor dude with the gun thing. I figure he would wish that Johnny was more of a rugged mountain man cowboy, but really, I'm sure they would just be happy for me. My brother would probably like him just fine, so really, I see the whole meeting going quite well. I should give his family a chance too then. I just hope they like me. But I am me. Gosh darn. I like him way too much; I wouldn't want to lose him over his family not liking me. Just then the tones drop.

Saved by the bell.

We jump from call to call for a while. Oven fire, skin burns, and so on. It seems like we are running from one to the next, but busy is how I like it. Until we hear the next one. Suicide.

Pulling up on scene, my whole body goes tight. My stomach clenches and the nausea hits. Suicide calls and self-harm always hit a little too close to the heart for my liking. Hesitantly I follow Johnny into the house. Garrett starts talking with a neighbor who had come over to see her. When he couldn't get a hold of her, he used the spare key and gone in, worried. Worried for a good reason.

As soon as I step into the bathroom, I know, I know it's too late. My heart drops to my stomach, breath catching. Pain, all I feel is pain for her. Her still body pale and cold. Blood coating the water surface of the bathtub where she lays. I clench my teeth tight and hold back the tears. I push myself to breathe, or at least try. Don't show anything, ever. I pull up the block, block it all out. It's just another call.

Rushing over, I help Johnny lift her from the tub to the floor. He goes through the motions of checking for a pulse, breath anything. But we both know from how stiff her body is, the lividity, she's beyond our help. We were too late to help her. The whole world was. I send up a quick prayer asking God to be with her. Help her. No one deserves this ending. Johnny heads out to help Garrett bring in the stretcher. The emptiness of the room crashes down.

Clenching my teeth harder, I quickly wrap her wrists, my lips quivering as I hold her hand. I know she's gone, but I just can't bear to send her off with the gashes running up her arms. Was it loneliness? Maybe she had no one for the holiday. Maybe she had a past trauma with Thanksgiving.

My mind goes through one thousand what ifs, my heart breaking more and more with each one. On the outside though, only calm and collected radiates from me. Years of practice hiding it all.

Riding back to the department, staring at my own scars, I can't help thinking about the girl. Her name had been Bri. Bri was only nineteen years old. Today, I'm even more thankful for the family and friends I do have. Without them, I very well could have been Bri. I almost was. A few years ago, back in high school, I had been a cutter. It had been going on for years. I even tried to take my own life once. Luckily, with God's guidance, my family and friends helped me. Thank you, Lord. My mind repeats over and over the whole ride back.

Once we get back, I doff my gear. Heading to the bathroom, I scrub down my hands, arms, and face, just as I've done a thousand times after calls. It's more about the cleansing of my mind, than my body. I'm not just scrubbing the germs, and such away, I'm scrubbing the traumas, the bad memories, letting it all flow out. So that by the time I step out this door, I'm ready for the next call, the next victim, the next meal, the next smile, whatever it may be. My skin feels a little raw today as I step out. My heart bleeding too, but I push the smile on my face. I'm ready for whatever comes.

As I walk down to the kitchens, the smell of the food wafts over to me. Oh, my sweet goodness. I had forgotten all about the food. It's Thanksgiving! Yass, I completely forgot what amazing foods were waiting for me! Yum.

Entering the kitchen, I see the table spread with donated dishes. Garrett sits already chowing down as Johnny fills his plate. You know, I'm not at all surprised about Garrett. He will probably be filling his plate at least another two times. Heaping my plate with corn pudding, some green beans, sweet potatoes, and two slices of pie, my heart swells. I do have a family here too. These guys, all of them, even the forest service dudes have made my transition out here way easier than I anticipated. I bow my head and thank the Lord for every single person he brought into my life. For all the blessings, opportunities, everything. Most of all, for letting me be alive.

CHAPTER 22

Right now, I am legit sitting in my car outside of Johnny's apartment thinking about cancelling. Forget the fact that I just drove three hours to get here, my heart rapidly flutters with anxiety over meeting new people, about meeting his family. My hands knead the steering wheel roughly. The blood still shimmers across some of my skin from where the fingernails used to be longer. Ripped, all of them long gone. My breathing rapid and shallow. How many people are in his family? My family gatherings can have over one hundred people! What if that's like his family? You've got this Kara. Game face.

Taking a deep breath, I open the car and step out. Okay Kara, you're a big girl. I can pry open a door in seconds, and chop through it in less than twenty, I've got this. Courage! I practice conserving my oxygen. If I can talk myself out of hyperventilating in a burning room, I certainly can on the doorstep of his house. I inhale deeply as the calm rushes over my pounding heart.

Quickly we're all in his car and heading to the gathering. His family lives in Gresham so unfortunately, we get there in less than twenty minutes. My heart feels ready to pound out of my chest again. I wonder if they can hear it. Working really hard to not let them hear my breath sounds, I really am like hyperventilating. Oh, my goodness. Pull yourself together! It's just his family, he's your boyfriend, it will be okay. Besides, I bet I'm about to eat some pretty darn good food. Focus on the food! Yes, the food.

Johnny reaches over and gabs my hand. His thumb working circles on the back while he drives. With each circle more and more calm washes over me. I love him, I love who I am with him, and he makes me happy. I've got this.

Garrett and Johnny walk right in the door. I hear shouts of joy coming from inside. A glimmer of hope sparks through me as I reluctantly walk in. Right away I'm pulled into a woman's arms.

"It's so good to meet ya' hon! I have heard so much about you!" She gushes as my face is smashed into her shoulder.

"Isht grooodte meet yosh to," I try to say as my face remains splattered across her shoulder. My anxiety eases though. I never thought I would be welcomed like this. It's like being pulled into my own family. The joy and love consume me, the vibe calming me. I ease out of her arms and get ushered into another pair. Luckily, it's just a quick hug, and someone pulls away. Johnny's sister. I recognize her, they legit look like twins.

"Hi, Kara, I love all of your adventure posts. And it's great that you've been getting Johnny out on some, he's such a bum sometimes." I laugh. I forgot we were friends on Instagram.

"Yea, he kinda' is. Speaking of adventures, how was Mexico?" I ask about her trip down to Mexico a few weeks ago. Her dad's from there as is much of their family. I know Johnny has a different father but grew up with him as his dad.

As I gaze around, I see three of their little brothers with rich, caramel skin. A little man stands in the corner with matching skin tones, this must be their dad. She continues gushing about her trip and I make sure to pay attention. Everything she describes sounds amazing, but I know there's hardship there.

After chatting with her for a bit, I make my way back over to Johnny. He's talking with his dad, maybe I should turn around. I'm sure he doesn't get to see him much; I should give them space. Just then his eyes catch mine and he waves me over.

"Kara, this is my dad." He gestures to the man as he wraps his arm around my shoulders.

"Hi, it's so great to meet you!" I say and really it is. Now that I'm here, it's really nice to meet his family. Still a little awkward but nice. Someday soon, I hope he gets to meet mine. I bet my dad would love him. My brother would absolutely geek out about every single nerdy thing with him. Well, and I am sure my mom would just be glad I'm bringing home a good man. No scary tattoos or piercings, a good job, and a Christian. What more could a momma want? Although, I know just how much more he truly is. He's my perfect world.

"Eits, so nice to meet you tuoo..." He continues on. I only catch a word here or there of the rest of the conversation. He's speaking English, mostly, but with a dialect I can't understand. I'm awful with accents. Everyone back home has the same accent so when I travel, I'm screwed. Shoot. I think he asked me a question. My mouth opens but nothing comes out. I don't want to ask him to repeat himself. I give a little side smile as I think of what to do.

"She moved here about what, eight months ago now? Roughly." Johnny answers for me. Thank goodness. I don't mean to be dumb, but he's speaking way too fast in too much of an accent.

"How do you like it?" His dad takes the time to pronounce the words slow for me. Thank goodness. A smile lights my face.

"Oregon has definitely stolen my heart! It's really starting to feel like home. Of course, a certain someone helps to," I admit nudging Johnny as my face heats up. When am I going to stop blushing like a teenager every time I realize he's mine?

"Food!" A shout hollers from the kitchen. Saved by the food. I am legit so stoked for this. I should have offered to help in the kitchen, shame on me. My Midwestern roots would be disappointed. I'm shocked that it's just his immediate family. Perhaps I shouldn't have come, but really, I'm too happy to bother thinking about that anyway. Who cares if it is just his siblings, Garrett, and Johnny's parents?

"Guests first!" His momma yells as she hauls me to the front and shoves a plate in my hand.

"Oh no, that's okay!" I say as I try to shuffle back. She clucks her tongue and moves me towards the dishes of food. Gingerly, I plop a little helping of some corn pudding on my plate and start to move to the next dish.

"What's this? That isn't a helping!" She cries, grabbing the spoon and in one motion slopping a heaping glob on my plate. Good golly that could be my whole meal!

"Oh, uh, thanks, but that's way too much," I say not sure what to do, can I slide some back in the dish?

"Nonsense, if you're one day to become a wife, you must have the body to become a mother. Skinny, skinny. Eat!" My whole body almost breaks out in embarrassment and sweat. Oh, my goodness. I make my way through the line, making sure to grab enough to not cause another scene, but not too much that I'll hate myself. As I reach the end of the line I start heading to the table. Caline, his sister, walks right behind me with a plate piled higher than mine.

"Don't worry, she does that to every girl in the family, me included," she informs me coming up to me. A laugh escapes me.

"Well, at least that eases the tension. I was worried she was going to go into one of those speeches about wanting grandkids right then." I chuckle. That's what my grandmother would have gotten to next. She's always talking about wanting a new baby in the family. But then again, my grandmother doesn't hide any thoughts or feelings at all.

"Oh, that will probably be the dessert conversation," she says with a laugh. As soon as we all sit down, they start joining hands. Clasping Caline's to my right and Johnny's to my left they start in prayer. It's in Spanish! I let the words flow over me. I may not understand any of it, but it feels special. I send my own silent thanks. There's just something so magical about being prayed over or praying in another language. Where I might not understand the words, but God's love connects us all. It's so powerful.

Dinner is fantastic. Honestly, I have no idea what half the food is, but it's really good. Me from a few years ago would have never tried all this food, but today, out of politeness, I did, and I'm so amazed at how freaking pretty darn decent it is. I mean yum! I do know that at least one of these things are tamales because that is all Johnny ever talks about. He's extremely proud his mamma makes the best tamales.

My heart is absolutely content today. It is so great to be with a family for Thanksgiving, even if it's not mine. Well, I guess it's kind of mine, isn't it?

***

"So, what do you want to do today?" Johnny asks.

"Well, what do you want to do?" I hedge. I don't really want to pick if it's not something that he might like.

"Nope it's your birthday, it's your day, so you get to pick!" Crap. Just my luck. I'm terrible at making these sorts of decisions where it might affect the happiness of others.

"Um, well, I was happy to just get to go somewhere for Thanksgiving yesterday, so at least give me some ideas."

I've had terrible luck with my birthday. So many years it falls on Black Friday or close to Thanksgiving, as it's the 27th of November. Heck, when I was younger, I hardly could get any of my friends to come to my birthday parties because their families went shopping or had a family dinner. Not like it got any better as the friends got older.

"What do you normally do on your birthday?" he asks. Well, I've spent birthdays at Thanksgiving dinners, out hunting with my dad in the awful terrible cold or standing for five hours in the night to be one of the first ones into Cabela's. But there is one thing.

"Well, my best friend and I usually go ice skating for my birthday. We skate all the time on my pond at home, but for my birthday we always splurge and go to the nearby rink."

I love my skating days with Elizabeth. So many good memories, and really it dawns on me, this is my first birthday without her for like over a decade! A decade and a half! Ice skating remained a tradition. But he's a guy, and they don't want to ice skate. Well not guys like him anyway. Hockey dudes sure! But he's far from one of those guys. And not like the rink was ever a big deal. It actually cost only five dollars, but our families never had money to throw around and we had a perfectly good pond in the backyard. Still there was something about that fresh, smooth ice. Gliding across it. For the second half of open ice, they would even bring out a disco ball!

His face almost scrunches for a second, but he hides it with a smile. "Okay, then ice skating it is. There's actually a small rink in the Portland mall."

My heart leaps. I'm really getting to go ice skating with a guy! My boyfriend even! Are you kidding me? I begin wiggling around with joy.

"Wow thank you!" I wish I had worn some cute clothes to go ice skating in. But honestly, I had kind of forgotten it was going to be my birthday while I was here, so not like I was expecting anything like this. I feel like I'm in a Hallmark movie anyway! Although, for me at least this is a cute outfit. It's different from my typical hoodie and sweats routine anyway. Skinny jeans and a nice sweater are my type of fancy.

Before I know it, I'm lacing up my skates. This feels like a huge serotonin boost. All the happy memories that come along with lacing up a pair of skates. Plus, at least at an indoor rink I don't have to wear my hundreds of layers of winter clothes. Ohio winters can be brutal and if you want to skate, you bundle up and put on layers. I always start sweating with the first few glides, but the layers are a must when it gets around to those negative temperatures. As I finish up tying my skates I look over at Johnny. One of his skates is loosely tied and he's trying to lace the other.

"May I help?" I prod gently; I know some people snap when asked if they need help.

"Yeah..." He sighs. "If you can't tell, it's my first time," he admits. My heart warms and my face smiles. Aww what a cutie. I love that he's letting me tie his skates.

"Oh, my goodness. I hope you like it. I would hate for you to do this if you don't! An ice-skating virgin. I am honoured" I wink. Especially since he paid. He wouldn't let me contribute a dime. Propping his skate up on my thigh, I yank on the strings, cinching them as tight as I can.

"Ow. You are kind of hulking out there Kara," he claims.

"No trust me, you want them this tight," Is all I say. I stand up and hold out a hand to him. It's good to be back on skates. Like the pleasure of wearing heels after a long time, they have their own feel to them. I've had plenty of horror stories on skates, don't get me wrong, but it still feels like home. One time, my dad tried to punt a football on ice skates and broke his leg! We lost countless hockey pucks into the void of unfrozen ice, and may have even fell in a few times ourselves, but such is the nature of the beast.

Hauling him to his feet, he's wobbly even on the ground. They have nice thick mats here which is nice on the skates, but also in case he falls. Using it as an excuse, I slip my arm around him, ready to support him if he does go down, but more importantly, just getting close to him. We hobble over to the ice.

I step on, breathing in the crispness, and glide onto the ice. Circling back, I wait for him just feet in the doorway. Supporting himself with both arms on either side of the door, he slowly puts one foot on the ice. It slicks right out from under him, yet he catches himself with his arms. Guess those pull ups pay off, well and the other foot still on the solid floor.

"You've got this. You're a fireman!" I encourage.

"Exactly, fire doesn't do ice," he mumbles under his breath. I pretend not to hear, because really, I'm just stoked he's doing this with me. Finally, with maximum effort, he gets both feet on the ice and instantly hugs the wall. Swivelling over to him, I slowly skate beside him as he pulls himself along the wall.

The good news is, he doesn't really completely fall. Bad news is, he never leaves the wall. I guess I am just glad he tried it. It's still so special. I do leave him every couple of laps to skate around.

By the time I get back to him, he has only moved fifteen feet or so, after I've done a whole lap, so I doubt he knows the difference. He puts on a brave face the whole time, trying to smile for me. That right there makes my day more than the ice skating. He is willing to try something he doesn't particularly enjoy just to make me happy.

Looking at my watch, we've been at it for an hour. Back home, we would go the full public skate time, which was about three hours, and we would spend a whole day on the river and ponds, but I'll cut him some slack.

"Hey, why don't you head over to the benches after this lap, and we can go do something else?" I suggest. I could stay out here all day, but I know he's tired of it. Relief washes over his face. But he just turns it into a smile.

"Are you sure?" he asks.

"Yeah of course, my feet aren't quite used to it anymore. I'm going to take a few more laps, then I'll head over to meet you, okay?"

"Sounds great," he agrees.

Pushing off with three big glides, I zoom into my hockey brain. I love whipping around the arena, weaving in and out of people. I do a few circles, flip backwards, and do an additional couple of laps. Ahh. So satisfying, just like home. Well except the fact that I'm in a mall. That's a new one for me. I'm so thankful for this day, for Johnny, just for the life I've been given.

Once my feet are back on solid ground, it always feels weird. Without skates, I'm a really bad duck walker, always walking with my feet leaning in. But I learned at a young age, when on skates, I had to put more weight on the outsides of my feet. So, the switch is always a new feeling, that's for sure.

We walk hand in hand through the stores. Not really looking for anything besides spending time with each other. In Bath and Body, I spray him with a perfume. We try on hats in Hot Topic and have a race to see who can jump on the first bed in Pottery Barn. It's nice to just have someone I can be myself with and act a little dumb.

"How about some food?" he asks.

"Yes, I'm legit starving," I proclaim rubbing my stomach. Anyone who looks at me can tell I'm not in fact starving but my stomach doesn't know that.

"What looks good?" He asks. Wow, that's a loaded question.

"What doesn't look good?" I say giving him a wink. "I mean I could really go for some chow mein, and maybe a piece of that cookie cake, but a pretzel also sounds good." I finish as I point to each store.

"Okay, you go get a pretzel and that will be our appetizer, we can have Chinese for lunch, I'll go order that, and a cookie for dessert?" he questions grinning and races off to the Chinese place. I stand there shocked for a second. Wow, I was like kind of joking, but honestly, that sounds like a really good plan. Cool. I feel a little bit embarrassed, but he doesn't seem to care about my weight, or obsessive eating habits.

Scurrying off to the pretzel place, I sniff in the aroma. I love food! Quickly, I order a large pretzel, we can share right? Then I hurry over to the cookie place before Johnny can get there with our food. I'm just being handed two very large cookies when I see Johnny picking a table in the court. Perfect timing.

"Best idea ever!" He declares.

"Well, I wasn't being serious, so thank you for going along with it," I reply. "My dad would have a cow at how much we are eating!" I laugh. But he seriously would.

"Everyone needs a fat kid's day every now and then," he mentions. I burst out in laughter.

"Johnny, you legit say that every shift while we eat ice cream, and who knows what else."

"Well, that's because we deserve it extra." He laughs.

Goodness, isn't this man just the best? Seriously, how did I end up with such a cool guy? Plus, like he lets me eat whatever I want, and he eats it too. Best boyfriend ever!

CHAPTER 23

Ugg. Why can people never get lost at sea during the day? Okay, I take that back. I love my job and what I do. I would never ever trade someone's life for anything. But seriously, it's three in the morning in January and I'm about to jump in the ocean. Trying to yank my dry suit on while half asleep this morning was a struggle.

Now that I am awake though, my adrenaline is flowing. I live for the rescues; water rescues are just the cherry on top. How cool is it, that I get to be a firefighter and rescue swimmer? My body shivers as I mentally do my checkoffs. Garett and I are going in the water for this one. Johnny will be on the boat and Titus came down for the call to engineer and captain it. A vessel capsized about twenty minutes ago.

By the time we got the distress call, got downstairs, out the door and in the bay, many minutes have gone by, the stakes getting higher and higher by the second. Three souls are stranded out there.

My light beam sweeps back and forth across the water as we zoom towards their last coordinates. The waves lurching us up and tossing us about, the sea raging tonight. Coast Guard is on their way, but they're coming all the way from Newport and the closest aviation is Astoria, so we are their hope right now.

"Sighted! Off the Port side!" Garrett exclaims. I strip off my headset and drag on my helmet. Gathering the gear to go over, I work my way towards Garrett. As the boat comes to a halt, I see two bodies bobbing with the waves, hollers coming across the water. That's a good sign.

"Garrett! Two sighted," I concur pointing. "We are going to work our way over to them, searching for the third as we go! Keep a steadfast eye!"

"Copy. Heading towards those two on your lead!" he shouts over the whipping wind and the roar of the waves. We reach our deployment area, as I scour one last time checking our safety.

"Left, center, right, clear! Swimmers a go?" I shout signalling to Titus.

He signals back giving the okay and I fall in. Eekkk! My mind jolts. Even with the dry suit, it takes my body a few seconds to acclimate. I give the okay signal back to the boat. In jumps Garrett. As he bobs to the surface, he gives the clear to the boat, and off we go. Paddling with everything we've got, we crest the waves. Swallowing some of the sea with every few breaths, the ocean pulls and tugs at my body. Keeping the destination in sight, I swim with everything I have.

We cut through the waters and the wreckage comes closer and closer. I scan the waters as the boat's light remains trained on our victims. Finally, we're a few feet away from the two people floating.

"We are Mid Oregon rescue swimmers here to help you!" I yell as I swim closer. Both appear conscious, wearing life vests, but I can tell they are entering stages of hypothermia just by knowing where they are and how long they have been here. The man splashes around frantically.

"Sir, I need you to calm down, so we can help you," I shout over the wind and the sea. I've been drug under way too much by victims to know better than to just rush in.

"We, we went over, the b-b-boat is gone. S-s-s—s-he won't respond anymore." The man informs us, splashing a little more towards her but becoming a little calmer.

"Okay, Sir, we are going to get you both to safety. Was there a third member of your party? Have you seen them?" I probe as I move around to her. She moves her head to look at me as I grasp her life vest from the back. But her eyes look through me, she's not all there. We need to get her warmed asap. Garrett treads by him, ready to take action.

"Ga-Gary. H-He floated somewhere."

"Copy. Garrett here is going to help you back to the boat!" I exclaim as I start swimming with her.

I hear Garrett tell him to be calm and go over what to do. With one arm holding her to me with the life vest, I stroke with the other, kicking as hard as I can. It takes too long, but it always seems to fly by, my body going through the motions. As we reach the boat, I signal up with my light. A head peers over as they lower the net.

"Have you seen anyone else? One more is confirmed out there!" I holler up.

"Negative," Johnny hollers down. I unravel the net and float her over to it. I don't know if she is cognoscente enough to understand but tell her anyway.

"Okay, ma'am, I am going to cross your legs and arms. This net is going to roll you into the boat, let them do the work, okay?" No answer, so I give the ready signal. In one swift motion, she rolls up the boat and they heave her over. Garrett is almost here with the man. The net drops back down and I ready it for him. We slide him into the net, then haul ourselves in the boat.

"Start working on them, we're going to look for the last victim," I declare, but Garrett already knows. I might be the officer for this water rescue, but when it comes to the medical part, he needs no guidance. Grabbing a search light, we sweep the ocean as we sputter through. Hours seem to go by, but only minutes pass.

"Got one!" I holler as my beam washes over one more body. He's upright and looking at us waving his arms, until a titanic-sized wave crashes over him and sweeps him under.

"Swimmers a go," I signal and I'm in the water racing over to him. I paddle, breathe, paddle.

As I reach his last location, I scout around. Where is he? *Lord, please help him. Help me find him Lord, please!*

My eyes dart around as the boat lights scan different areas around me. There! As I reach him, he's no longer responsive. Grasping his life vest to me, I swim with everything I have. We're in a race against time now.

As soon as he's in the boat, Johnny reaches down and hauls me up in one swift motion. I briefly notice Garrett has the woman in a hypo wrap and the man is clasping her hand. I make my way over to Gary.

"No pulse, no breath. Starting CPR!" I vocalize. Johnny is already readying the BVM, manual suction, everything we might need. My teeth chatter as I count. My adrenaline keeps me pretty warm, but my teeth don't know that. Round after round we go. It's so hard for a hypothermic, water victim. Johnny and I switch. We switch again.

Suddenly a sputter, we roll him into recovery position as water and anything else comes out his mouth. Johnny suctions as I hold him in position. Relief crashes over me. We saved all three. *Thank you, Lord, thank you.* That's rare for this type of rescue. *Thank you, Lord!* We steady the patients and go through more assessments as the boat zooms towards land. Lights, so many lights are waiting for us on shore.

All of the sudden, my body weighs heavily with exhaustion, my brain ready to just shut off. The adrenaline leaves and I practically collapse. Johnny readies Gary in a hypo wrap. Peering over the boat, I'm thankful we're almost back to the docks. I see the lights of two ambulances. Awesome. Titus is on the radio with the Coast Guard. They finally arrived and will meet us at the docks.

So many hands help as soon as we land. Hands tying the boat up. Hands loading the victims to the stretchers. Hands putting away gear. My mind remains in the numb after rescue phase. I think I'm cold. Hands guide me out of the engine. Did I get myself into the engine in the first place? I don't even remember the ride back.

"You need a warm shower and to get out of that suit." My head swivels to see Johnny talking to me. I nod, my head feeling like a bobblehead. Yes, that makes sense. I need to get warm. "Is it okay if I help? Not all the way, just some?" My head still bobbles. My brain slightly registering that he's pulling off my life vest, unstrapping my helmet. My hands fumble as I strip off my gloves. He unzips the back of my suit, and tugs on the sleeve as I work my arm out of it.

"I can get the rest. Thank you," I mumble numbly as I fumble up the stairs to the showers. Slipping my other arm from the suit, I squish it off my legs. As the warm water rushes over me, my brain slowly leaves the gray void. The water massages feeling back into my muscles. I could stay in here forever, but someone else might be waiting, and you never know when the next call might get dropped. As I step out of the shower, I realize I didn't bring clothes in with me. Crap!

Wrapping my bright yellow towel around me, I peek out the door. I don't see anyone. I step out and I'm greeted by a sudden whistle. My body jumps as my breath catches.

"Look at those legs!" Garrett says with a wink. "Seriously though, good job out there. You are definitely a natural leader in the water," he proclaims before brushing past me into the bathroom.

Wow. That means a lot. Definitely not the legs comment! That's way embarrassing. But the fact that I did well out there. Garrett just got his water rescue certification a few months ago. I happened to go through a swift water rescue course a few years back when I worked as a raft guide on the Gulley. Then I got an updated rescue swimming certification from the Coast Guard out here when I first moved. I just feel at home in the water. I mean, I guess I've kind of grown up around it, from my pond to the Blanchard River, to Lake Erie, to the West Virginia waters, to white water all over, it's kind of in my veins by now.

CHAPTER 24

Kara, Chief needs to see you." Garrett calls as if he's a child informing another they're being sent to the principal. Great. What did I do? I don't think I've done anything wrong on a call lately, or even here at the fire department. I mean most of the guys know Johnny and I are a thing now, maybe he wants to talk about that. Pain stabs through my heart. What if he assigns me a new shift? That would be terrible. Then it would be almost impossible to plan days with him.

I am hard core stress sweating as I step into the doorway of his office. I tap lightly on the frame, almost not wanting admittance.

"Ahh, Kara, come in. How are you?" He begins friendly enough.

"I'm good Chief. Everything is going well. How about you, Sir?" Am I talking too much, that was the right amount, I hope. Is it just me or does stress sweat smell like one hundred times worse? Definitely not just me, I picture a pig pen cloud around me as I move to sit down in front of his desk. Do you think he can smell the fear radiating off me?

"Good, good. Well, I'm going to get right to the point. You have been an amazing addition to this department. I've heard good things all around and you have definitely taken an initiative in action," he declares grinning through his mustache.

"As you know the B shift Lieutenant, Kaisley, is being promoted to a Captain next week at the banquet." He continues as I nod. Yes, I am so proud of him. Logan was being switched to another shift as they needed another crewman there.

"... and I wanted to know if you would be interested in being promoted to Lieutenant?"

Wait what? Me? A lieutenant? Woah.

"I am speechless Sir. This is an honor! Of course, I would be very happy with that, but are you sure, Chief?" Dumb. Why would I say that? Mentally kicking myself I bite my lip. That promotion would be huge for me, wow. What if he changes his mind now? Great job, Kara. Why do I always have to talk like an idiot? Goodness!

Yet, he gives a light chuckle and continues.

"Yes, the board and I have discussed it as have I with all your supervisors and officers. We all believe you would be a fantastic leader for a crew," he reveals as he stands, extending his hand to me. Mine grasps his and we shake. I can't help but smile. Gathering my composure, I straighten my face.

"Thank you, Sir, it is an honor," I proclaim as he sits back down. I follow suit.

"Now it will be officially announced at the banquet next week as well. We are a small department so most everyone already knows, but there will be many civilians and families there so we will tell the community then. Who would you like to pin your new badge on?" he questions.

Oh shoot. I forgot about all that. Who should I ask? Johnny? Goodness. Is that inappropriate? A lot of times, it is a family member. But I don't have any family out here. The thought saddens me deeply. My father pinned it on last time, as he was beaming. So proud of me. He told all his friends, and every stranger on the street about it for months. That was back home though. Um out here, my only friends are here at this fire department. I mean I had the wildland guys for a while, but most of them are seasonal so they're all back in their home states for the winter. Would it be wrong to ask Johnny to do it? I mean he's the first one who popped into my head, but I don't know if it's appropriate. Then again, I've had Captains give me my challenge coins and such before, so technically he is still my commanding officer.

"Sir, I would like to request to ask Lieutenant Kaisley to pin my badge," I inform him with the most respectful, calm face I can.

"I assumed as much. Granted. Congratulations, Lieutenant Craig." He stands to shake my hand one more time with a knowing glimmer in his eyes.

As I step out of the office, Garrett, Logan, and Johnny all stand there clapping. My heart! It swells with so much joy right now. They walk over, clapping me on my back, saying congratulations, and just showering me with love. Johnny sweeps me up in a hug and spins me around before setting me down. A giggle escapes my lips. He gives me a quick peck on the lips.

"Now Captain, I don't know if that was appropriate," I say with mock sternness with a quick smile over to Logan. Everyone laughs, but we separate anyway. We do try to keep things decently classy and professional around here. Kind of.

***

The banquet arrives all too soon. My hand brushes the top of my head in a smoothing motion. Is my hair, okay? I always completely cheat and use a hair donut to make my bun. I think it's slightly ridiculous that I have to wear a low enough bun to put my hat on, yet we never actually wear the hats. Oh well, I have too much joy for the day to care about any such things.

With my shoes shined, my pants pressed, and even a bit of makeup applied, I think I'm ready. This is a big day. Never in my dreams did I imagine I would get this honor. Luckily, it's not raining, so I do ride my bike the short trip over to the department. Had it been raining; I would have gone fancy and driven my car over. Alas, it is not raining, but I smile the whole bike ride.

I am a bit nervous. I'm not sure why, but I am. Probably more nervous than a call. At least then my brain knows what to do or can come up with a solution. Here I will just have people looking at me. I hate having people look at me when they actually see me. When I can no longer blend into the background. Nonetheless, I'm excited.

As I walk in, my eyes instantly find Johnny. Ugg. He looks so darn good in his uniform. I half wish he could grow a little facial hair. I think he would look incredibly good with it, yet, as long as he's a firefighter, he never will because the only facial hair he would be allowed to grow is a mustache so his SCBA would still fit. Let's be honest, I do not want a guy with just a mustache! Unless maybe when he's fifty, then I might allow it. I think his clean-shaven face is hella' sexy.

"Kara!" Someone calls off to my side. Turning to look, I see Caline. Goodness, that girl is just the sweetest. I stride over to greet her, and she wraps me in a huge hug. "You look awesome," she proclaims.

"Thank you. It's so good to see you!" I reply and it really is. My heart swells. I kind of have a family here. No, I do. It may not be home in Ohio, but between the fire department, and Johnny, I do have a family out here and a home. Hugs all around. I've never been much of a hugging person, but when someone I actually like initiates it, I mean how can I say no. Somehow those hugs always just hit different. Like healing hugs. Superpowers and all that.

Before long the banquet is starting and all of us take our seats. Johnny looks really nervous too. What the heck? This dude isn't scared of anything.

What does he have to be nervous about? Unless it's maybe a line dance. I laugh as I my thoughts drift to my memories of him trying to dance.

As I stand at attention, my eyes stay on the flag at the back of the bay. This is my moment, and I know if I look at Johnny or Caline or Garrett, or anyone really, I might cry, or smile. I don't really know, instead focusing on not locking my knees, on my hand gripping my wrist behind my back.

"... Lieutenant Craig." Chief calls. Shoot. That's me. Will my legs work? Then I realize they're already moving on their own. Step, step, pivot, step. I'm standing in front of the Chief, and Johnny wearing the proudest face ever. Those eyes convey so much. Working hard, I keep my face straight and void of emotion. Standing with all my composure, I keep my professionalism, staring ahead as he pins my new badge. Wow. This is real. My boyfriend, now my Captain, pins my own Lieutenant badge. Never in my wildest dreams would I have imagined this could happen to me. As he straightens back up, he winks at me. I can't help it; a smile crosses my face.

I watch proudly as he is called next, his short little dad pinning the badge. His father wears the proudest smile the entire time. Admittedly, I am wearing the proudest smile too. Look at that amazing, handsome man that I get to call mine.

After the ceremony, we all mingle talking with the public, getting congratulated a million times, and so many handshakes. At least it is better than hugs. Handshakes I can do. I peek at Johnny every now and then. He still seems a little out of sorts. Wringing his hands every so often and his eyes darting all over. But I can't watch him for long as person after person comes up to me. Ugg! I thought this was supposed to be fun.

After way too much small talk, I make my way to the refreshment table. Finally! I am so not going to miss out on a piece of cake. These pieces are so freaking small, and hey, it is kind of my party. So, I pluck two more little squares off and stack them on my plate too.

"Save some cake for the rest of us!" I turn to see Johnny with a broad grin.

"Ahh, there is plenty still there. Besides, it is your day to celebrate too, you deserve at least five pieces!" I mention.

"Yeah, actually that sounds really good. But here, I got you something first," he informs me producing a little pot from behind his back.

"A baby snake plant!" I cry in joy. Those are like my favorite house plants. And wow, I didn't expect anything. Goodness. I smile down at my new little plant. I love it! I love him. Aww, I'm full of so much happiness.

"Yea, I uh, saw a few in your house, and I know that you aren't much of a flower person because you feel so bad when they die, so I thought maybe this would be okay," he explains.

Oh, my goodness. I could cry. He noticed that? He knows me so well. I do always feel bad when people cut flowers for each other. Why should they die for a moment of our happiness? But a house plant, now that can live with me forever. He really is my person. Anytime I'm not with him, I miss his aura, his personality. It's like he completes me, like I'm missing half of myself without him.

Setting my cake on the edge of the table, he grabs my hand and pulls me to the other side of the engine. My arms fling around his neck, careful not to tip my little baby snake plant. I crush my lips to his, pouring all my joy inside out to him in that one kiss.

"I love you, Kara," he declares in a breath, giving me another quick kiss.

"I love you too, Johnny. Always." I pull back, straighten my uniform, and stand up straighter. All I want is to fling my arms around him and keep on kissing him.

I see him pause, and suck in a deep breath. He steps back a little, grabs my hand and sinks to one knee. No, no way! A gasp releases from my lips as my heart skips a beat. Is this really happening? Can I believe it? Am I awake? My right arm hugs my plant to my chest as he holds my left hand firmly in his.

"Kara, I've known since the minute you walked in that door what an incredible woman you are. You have this confidence about you, and a glow everywhere you go. You light up the world with your love and compassion. You add a spark to my life every day. I love you today and always. Would you please do me the honour of becoming my wife?"

OHMIGOSH! OHMIGOSH! This is happening!

"Yes! Yes!" I scream and launch myself at him crushing him in a huge hug, a kiss, a few tears. This just happened! He laughs and whirls me around, the little plant spilling some dirt as we go. I hear hoots and hollers.

Looking up, I see Garrett, Logan, Titus, Caden, Lily, and Caline, all up on top of the engine looking down at us clapping and yelling. For the millionth time, my face goes hot. I don't even care. He is my man.

CHAPTER 25

Half my thoughts or more are about Johnny. I still can't believe I get to be the girl with the Hallmark story. I mean seriously. My parents are super stoked for me and they're planning a visit out to see us next month! Can you believe it? We both face timed them to let them know the news. I found out Johnny actually called my dad for permission, and they are totally like best friends now.

We think we want a little fall wedding next year, so we have plenty of time to plan. I smile everywhere I go and can't help but hum as I walk. My heart is just so happy. Right now, we are on shift. It has been a perfect day, even with all the calls.

First thing this morning we had a medical call, an overdose, and later a psychotic patient who dove into the bay thinking he was a deity. Crazy day, but we got Chubby's for supper. We ate in the engine with Garrett and Titus as we all sat out on the bay watching the ocean. As the sun set, peace filled me completely. I wouldn't trade this for anything. Moving here was the best decision I've ever made.

Between finding my confidence, a job I adore, an amazing place to call home, and a fiancé, I would say this past year and a half has been very good to me. Oregon really is home. The mountains, the ocean, Johnny. This feels like my perfect fairy tale ending I have always dreamed of. I get the man! I get the awesome job! And I just get to be me.

You know, for many of my years growing up, I struggled with self-esteem. I hated myself at times. But now, now I'm perfectly content with who I am. I love myself. Without me, my personality, my body, I wouldn't have the life I do now, and really this life is more than I could have ever asked for. And Johnny, he is more than I could have ever imagined. I can't believe I get to spend the rest of my life with him out here in the beautiful Pacific Northwest.

After the sun completely sets, we drive on back to the department. I love that we got to watch the entire sunset without a call. Just sitting in the engine, listening to the roar of the waves as the colors washed the sky, it was perfection. We walk inside, all grabbing bowls of ice cream. Unfortunately, Johnny and I were featured in the paper the other week for our promotions so there's still plenty of ice cream. Since I bought it, I am certainly going to eat my fair share!

All four of us sit on the couches watching an Adam Sandler movie. I love that dude. If I ever had a movie about my life, I would want Jennifer Lawrence to play me and Adam Sandler to play Johnny. He may not look anything like Johnny, but I love his movies. Who doesn't love Adam Sandler? I mean if you don't are you human at all?

A pitch sounds and the tones drop, all of us rushing into action. Plopping our bowls aside and hurrying down the stairs, we jump into our boots and pants. Every movement engrained in our bones.

"House fire, up on Overlook Drive," Johnny calls. Oh, those are the bigger houses. My hood is scrunched, I swing my coat on and jump in. As soon as I am in, I radio dispatch.

"Dispatch, Engine 7901 enroute," I call through.

Dispatch updates us. A neighbor called, a family of five live there and are suspected to be home. Johnny is engineer tonight on shift, but he will be incident commander on scene, while I'll be taking charge of our crew.

"Titus, I'm going to need you to engineer when we arrive. Garrett, you and I will be ready for the initial search and attack. Johnny, if not already notified, contact Seal Rock and Yachats for mutual aid. The ambulance should be behind us soon."

As we arrive on scene, like a colony of bees, we all know our place. Johnny swings the engine around; Titus jumps out and sets up the hose line to the fire hydrant. I scope out the fire, as Garrett readies our tools. It has not fully consumed the house yet. Mostly first story working its way up, meaning it started lower, first level or basement. Suddenly, I see the woman running and screaming towards us.

"Help! Help! My family, my family is still in there. Help!" She rushes up to Garrett blubbering and flailing her arms about, her face streaked with tears, snot, and soot.

He probes, "How many people are still in there?"

Just then, a man covered in black, coughing sporadically, carrying a child emerges from the smoking front door. Fire whips in the background.

The ambulance pulls up on scene and starts unloading a stretcher. I hustle over to the man and child. The boy is conscious, and has a few burns, as does the man, but both should be okay. The man makes a move to run back towards the house as Garrett and I grab his arms.

"My girls are in there! I have to get them. My girls!" He cries, fighting for a second then as if every ounce of energy leaves his body, he droops.

"Sir, your other children are still in there? How many?" I ask with hushed urgency.

"Two. I couldn't get to their room. I couldn't get there. I failed my children," he wails and sinks to the ground sobbing.

My heart breaks for him. *Lord, please let us get there. Save them Lord, please. Lord, please be with them.*

The medics rush over and will care for him. I hurry over to Garrett already holding a line ready to go in. He holds out the Halligan to me and I clasp it. He is going to be lead, navigating, while I search.

"Two in there. Safety check," I say as I engage my SCBA. He looks me over, and I him. Everything's in place. My heart is rushing, but my breathing remains steady.

"Woman says the kids were in their room. Second story, north side, no accessible window," he advises over the air pointing it out.

"Copy. On your lead!" I state after his check is complete. I signal to the engine. He's ready. Johnny, a few feet away, hurries over.

"Seal Rock will be here in about three minutes, so a second team will be ready outside soon." Garrett and I nod.

"Be careful brother," he declares knocking helmets with Garrett as they do before every fire. He puts a gloved hand to the side of my face over my SCBA and hood.

"I love you, Kara, take care of yourself. I will be waiting for ya'," he says and gives a quick kiss to my face mask.

My hand brushes his cheek real quick and I turn to go. Garrett and I stand outside the door. He checks the knob, unlocked. Stroke of luck. Adrenaline courses through me, my heart ready to leap out of my chest. This is it!

"Ready?" he questions. I nod. "Three, two, one!" I shout and we crawl through the door.

I hurry and shut the door as much as the hose will allow. The outside crew will take care of it. With my left hand on his ankle, I sweep around with my Halligan. Nothing. I see nothing. Just barely my own hand, and soon it won't even be that.

We wind through the house. My hand never leaves his ankle as I sweep about. Garrett quickly locates the stairs. He sounds them as we climb. He's a good fireman, so much experience. If anyone can find these kids, I know Garrett will. *Lord, direct us, please. Lead us, Lord. Help us find those kids.* I pray over and over. How long has it been? Seconds? Minutes? All sense of time is gone. Smoke clouds over everything. I check my tank, still green. Okay, Kara, we still have time. Breathe, focus on your breathing.

"Anyone there?" I holler over and over. "You good?" I check with him every so often. "Good, you?" he hollers back.

We sweep the first room, nothing. So much smoke. Black, it's all black. My heart beats faster and faster. We need to find those kids! Focus Kara, breathe. Wall, desk, box, I name off everything I find. *Come on! Lord, lead us! Please!*

A few feet into the second room, my irons hit something not quite solid. Quickly I sprawl out, feeling. It's one of the kids! Thank you, Lord! *I praise you!* My heart leaps. Joy, that is all I feel right now. One down, one to go. Breathing coming faster, heart exploding.

"I've got one!" I inform Garrett. I pull the body over to us. I sprawl back out and sweep. Garrett extends off the wall, I extend off him. Feeling a bed, I launch to the top, scurrying I hit another.

"Victim two!" I cry and grasp the tiny body in my arms. *Thank you, Lord!*

Both children unconscious, but both breathing I think, best as I can tell with my gear on. But they won't be for long if we don't get them out of here fast. Oh gosh. We need to get them out now.

Closing my eyes, I take two deep breaths. I need to stay calm, for the girls' sake, for Garrett's sake. *Help us Lord, please!*

He radios command and each of us with a child we work our way back down the hose line. My tank is less than half, we really need to move. I see his leaning closer and closer to red. Crap!

As we reach the bottom story, I'm certain it's soon to be fully engulfed.

"We got to move! Rollover happening soon!" He yells. We crawl faster and faster moving through the rooms.

"One more hose length!" he cries. Fifty more feet! We've got this. Just then the whole world slows down. The house groans, and I'm pitched into a void. A scream rips from my throat. Falling, falling, and I fall into a black hole. Grasping the child tightly to my chest, I roll to take a landing on my back. Heat soaks every inch of my body as I land.

A cry escapes me as all my breath wooshes out from the impact. My whole head swims. The tank stabs my back, and the air is knocked from me. Broke, I am broke. Are my eyes even open? Oh my gosh. Oh my gosh, pain, so much pain.

Breathing fast and heavy, gasping for air. I've got to focus on my breathing. Slowly, steady, I get it back under control and gain my bearings.

"Mayday! Mayday! Mayday!" Comes Garrett across my radio. "One down, north wall, around one hose in through the first floor to basement..." He communicates to command. The urgency apparent, spiking my heart rate even more.

"I am okay!" I holler up to Garrett as best as I can. I can't muster enough breath to yell loud. The roar of the fire would probably cover it anyway. I can't see him, but I can faintly see the hole. I know this is not a good place to be, I need to get this kid out. *Lord, please, get her out.* Help her Lord, please. *Don't you dare let her die! That first floor is going to rollover in seconds! Save her Lord!*

My head threatens to give into the pain. I need to get her out. I don't have enough strength to get myself out, I would never be able to reach the next story and wouldn't be able to haul myself up. And I know if Garrett stays more than another minute or two, then I am killing him and the girls.

Half a sob escapes me before I clamp it back down. I've got to lock it in. These girls and Garrett are what matter now. I am stuck. I know my odds. Acceptance slowly washes over me. I might not be able to save myself, but I will save her. With everything I have, I am going to get her out!

"Garrett, I am going to hand her up, you've got to take them and get out. Send in the RIT team as soon as you can!" I radio up to him. The roar, the rush is growing louder and louder. Her skin is probably blistering by the second.

"I can't leave you!" he radios back. My heart is breaking with each second, but she's all that matters now. I haul myself up into a standing position. It's so hot, my back screams, and my body feels like it's ready to shut down. *I can't do it. Lord, please give me strength! Save her Lord!*

"It is our only choice. I will look for an escape route after you take the girl!" I scream back, knowing that my options are very slim. *Lord please just get them all to safety. Help them, Lord, please. Please Lord, help them!*

What if he won't take them? He will be sentencing us all to death.

"As your Lieutenant, I command you to get them and yourself out. First floor is about to rollover. Lower your webbing!" I scream with all the courage I have. Using every ounce of authority, I can muster.

My headlamp briefly catches sight of the webbing. With every ounce of energy, I have left, I hoist her up to my chest and wiggle the webbing around her back. It is lowered just enough I can hook it through her arms. Lord, please give me strength!

"Got her secured! On three, I am going to lift! One, two, three!" I radio to the void, screaming as I push her up with all my might. Her legs dangle for an instant then disappear into the void. Garrett has her. *Lord, please keep them safe.*

Lightheaded. I am lightheaded. Is the world tilting? I can't breathe. I suck in gasp after gasp.

"The RIT team will be here soon! Hang on! Hang on!" He calls across the radio. My world is spinning. I hear my tank faintly in the background yelling at me telling me my air is running out. I don't think I'm standing anymore. Everything slowly fades into the black world, the smoke-filled void.

"Johnny? Johnny, I love you." I radio with the last of my will. Static fills the air. The room grows warmer and warmer. Pain, pain rips across my whole being.

"Don't you give up! RIT will be there soon! Fight Kara. Fight like the girl I love. The one I first met. Use that spunk of yours! Don't you dare leave me!" The radio calls back.

Smiling as the tears stream down my face. At least I got to hear him one last time. My love, my Johnny. The void is calling, the blackness consuming me.

Through the deep water, far in the distance, I hear my radio informing me Garrett is out accompanied by two children. They have a pulse.

Heat. So much heat. They are safe. *Thank you, Lord. Thank you. Thank you.* The blistering, smoldering, hotness. My tank is screaming, alerting no one to where I am. But now, even the screaming fades to the background as the water pulls me deeper.

I am alone. No one. Only the warmth, the searing sensation all over. So much pain. I scream out with the last of my oxygen. No more air as the deep abyss swallows me. I am so scared. Is this it? What about my family? What about my grandma? What about Johnny? Johnny. So much black. Are my eyes even open? You know, I don't even feel much now. Nothing. There is nothing. Even the nothing begins fading.

A face. A beautiful face. Someone dressed in white holds me as the fire and smoke completely consumes my world. I know that face. It is Christ, my Jesus. The terror slowly fades. I am cradled. Safe. No more fear. No more pain. I am safe. Love spreads through my body, through my soul, consuming my entire being. I look up into those eyes as he smiles down at me rocking me as he holds me to his chest.

"You were never alone," he states with pure love as the world fades away one last time.

White. Blinding, beautiful white.

"Well done my child."

EPILOGUE

I can't believe my wedding day is finally here! My eyes drift to Elizabeth curling my hair, and Caline doing my makeup, while my sister-in-law, Lila paints my nails. My heart squeezes as I look around the room and the love surrounding me evident. This is my day, today I feel beautiful and special. Today is about Johnny and me. Everyone has been treating me like a breakable china flower since the incident, but today, there is no pity, no sorrowful looks and I'm grateful.

Their hands work on making every hair sit perfectly, making my eyes pop, and most of all just making my soul completely vibe. I feel like a princess as they pamper me with love and style me up. For the first time, I am getting to live that life. The life I believed only gorgeous, amazing girls get to experience. Although today I am both of those things, aren't I? Luckily, most of my scars are healing pretty decent. I will have a few, both mentally and physically that will stick with me forever, but I was saved for a reason. Someday, God is going to shed light on that reason, but I am certainly going to make the best of it. Use this to spread as much love as I can and live it up every day.

That day all those months ago, I really thought it was going to be my end. I had been ready to say goodbye and made my peace. Terrified maybe, but as much at peace as you can be in that instance. My breath catches and my body tenses as I think back. A lot of it remains a bit muddled and hazy, but sometimes, sometimes I swear I met the Lord. Well, I know I did! I remember so much white, the bright glory of it all. I remember Jesus holding me in the end, taking away my fear, my pain, my worries. God saved me, that I know for sure. The RIT team somehow managed to get through the cellar and rescue my body before the fire rolled over. I had been unconscious with no pulse, no breath, nothing. Yet here I am. I remember the pain; I'm still dealing with some of the pain to this day. But I remember Christ and his love, all my fear washing away.

I woke up in the hospital a few days later, with many burns, a few fractured bones, but most importantly, Johnny sitting right next to me asleep. I swear his snoring was probably what woke me up. Snoring to wake the dead, right? But really, it was the most heavenly sound I ever heard. Tears sprang to my eyes. I was alive. I knew I would never be alone. Christ would always be with me, and Johnny too. Johnny, my Johnny. All I can do is stare at him with absolute love.

Just then his eyes slowly blink, and he stretches rubbing his face. With a yawn, he looks over at me. As he sees me staring, the yawn catches and he bursts from the chair. Shining in his eyes is a spark, a light, so much containing pure joy. Rushing to my side, he gingerly places a hand on the side of my face, the other on top of my hair. Ever so slowly he leans down and kisses me. A tear sliding from his eyes to my face. As his lips touch mine with the softest of brushes, a heat spreads, awakening my heart, my complete soul.

"Kara, you are the most beautiful bride. I am so proud of you baby girl," proclaims my momma from behind me, pulling me out of my thoughts. My eyes meet hers in the mirror. It takes everything I have to hold back my tears. This day is finally here. My fairy-tale ending. The one I dreamt about my whole life. The one I didn't think girls like me got. Flinging my arms out, I turn around and grasp her in a hug. My body smashes as I almost tackle her to the floor. She gently rocks me as a silent conversation happens between us. Knowing her love, my worth, and joy encompasses us.

Everything is moving so fast. I step into my dress as they pull it up. Together they lace the back up, then help me step into my heels. A huffed chuckle escapes me, yes, me in heels. Luckily, they are like character shoes, so I am ready for dancing. I'm stoked I got Johnny to practice some with me. It took a little coaxing, but not much. I think right now, I could ask to give him a makeover and he would happily do it. We have hardly spent a moment apart since getting out of the hospital. But I believe it's because our souls are in sync. Two hearts totally beating as one, today, and hopefully forever. Love cascades around me from every direction. Everything passing in a blur, and suddenly I'm standing right outside the doors, waiting to hear Pachelbel's Canon start. My feet shift as I wiggle in anticipation. My face remains tight in a constant smile.

"Honey, I am so proud of you, this will be your biggest adventure yet," my dad encourages as he gives me a hug.

"Don't get all sappy on me now, Dad, you'll make me cry," I scold. But his eyes glisten with tears and I know in this moment, this is all I could ever want. As I break away, I fan my eyes. Don't cry, don't cry. I breathe in a deep breath and exhale. The first notes sound, and my dad takes my arm. For once in my life, I am not nervous at all. My breathing is normal, my heart rate steady. This is who I'm meant to be, and Johnny is who I am meant to be with. All I feel is love today and always from him.

The doors open, my dad helps me take the first step. My eyes sweep up the aisle, and then, then I see him, my chest tightens. Johnny. My Johnny with tears in his eyes and a smile on his face. His face expressing everything he can't say. As my eyes meet his, he winks.

A little giggle bursts from my mouth. I'll never get over it. This nerdy, gorgeous, kind, rad guy is all mine. And forever until the end of my days that wink will capture my whole heart. I really am the luckiest girl, aren't I?

Thank you, Lord.

The End

ABOUT THE AUTHOR

Ashton Stevenson grew up in the corn fields of Ohio. Once she graduated high school, she attended West Virginia University. There, she became a timbersports competitor and earned her BS. During her school summers and after graduation, she traveled and went on every adventure possible. Starting off working as a Wildland Firefighter for the Bridger Teton in Wyoming. She has since lived in Maine (Acadia NP), West Virginia (WVU), Oregon (Siuslaw NF), California (Mt. Shasta), Wisconsin (Fox Valley), Wyoming again (Jackson), and everywhere else in between. She has become a rescue swimmer, structure firefighter, arborist, zipline guide, park ranger, natural resource coordinator, tour guide, carriage driver, river ranger/ raft guide, EMT, and kept loving every minute of EMS and rescue work. Her adventurous spirit is calling, but her heart will always belong to the Buckeye State. Between escapades, you can find her chilling with her rad family and friends back home.

She currently resides in Ohio, where she plans to continue writing in her spare time, but only the Lord knows where the wind will blow her next.

CPSIA information can be obtained
at www.ICGtesting.com
Printed in the USA
JSHW031911101222
34646JS00004B/19

9 781639 842377